TRANQUEBAR PRESS
BYSTANDERS

Vidya Madabushi grew up in Tirupati and later attended Krishnamurti Foundations Schools in India and England. She holds a BA in Communicative English from Mount Carmel College and an MA degree in English Literature and Creative Writing from the University of Sydney. She lives and writes in Sydney.

BYSTANDERS

VIDYA MADABUSHI

TRANQUEBAR PRESS
An imprint of westland ltd

61, II Floor, Silverline Building, Alapakkam Main Road, Maduravoyal, Chennai 600095
93, I Floor, Sham Lal Road, Daryaganj, New Delhi 110002

First published in TRANQUEBAR by westland ltd 2015

10 9 8 7 6 5 4 3 2 1

ISBN: 978-93-85152-00-9

Typeset in Warnock Pro Light by SÜRYA, New Delhi

For my parents
M. Dorairaj and Sulochana Dorairaj

Hari

1

Every year since the old man in apartment 3C died of pneumonia, someone I have known has died in December. I am not a superstitious man, yet I have become wary of December days even if they come dressed in March's clothes.

It was three in the afternoon and I was sitting on a stool at Sai's tea stall across the road from my office, drinking tea and smoking a cigarette while listening to Sunil, my boss, repeat the joke about the barber and his monkey. Half the moon had shown up early. There was a breeze running through the jacaranda trees, breaking off only the yellow leaves and sending them hopping across the pavement. I watched as Madhavi, our office receptionist, came running towards me in a flimsy yellow kurta that I adored and which the sun, had it been brighter, would have loved.

'Where have you been?' she said. 'I have been trying and trying your mobile.' She placed a hand over my hand. I glanced down at her knuckles. They were dry and coated white like powdered sugar on doughnuts. December does that to skin.

'I have bad news, Hari,' she said in her husky receptionist's voice. She let her gaze taper to the ground. Her real voice is a few octaves higher and more endearing. 'Your mother called to say that your uncle Vasan is in a critical condition. I am sorry. I looked everywhere for you.'

The word 'uncle' struck me as an odd choice; that all-inclusive Indian term denoting any man older than you, and with whom you have a relationship that isn't easily qualified. I imagined that the word had come with some hesitation from my mother's mouth. Quite likely, Madhavi, in her usual manner, had wanted all the details and questioned her, and my mother had been put on the spot and forced to pick a word.

Sai, who was fishing out vadas from a frying pan, cocked his head to listen. With a quick shake of his hand, he allowed the oil to drain through the strainer before turning off the stove to join us.

Madhavi handed me a yellow office 'While You Were Out' note. She'd ticked the 'urgent' box.

To: Hari Vasan Sharma

From: Parvati Sharma

At: 2.33 p.m.

Message: Uncle Vasan is critical. Call immediately.

An electronic copy would be waiting in my inbox. She was clean and efficient, just like her small, neat handwriting. My eyes began to defocus, causing the curly black letters to change shape and blur until the writing had become illegible. I jerked my head away from the note and stared into my teacup instead. A delicate skin formed and crinkled on top of my milky tea. I peeled it off and hung it over the ledge of the cup. My ribs were tightening under my shirt. Sunil and Madhavi looked at me with collective big eyes. There was a complicity in their gaze which unsettled me.

'Can you please leave me alone?' I said as politely as I could.

They exchanged glances. Suddenly they had become conspiring parents and I had turned into their eight-year-old child.

'You are in shock,' Sunil said, squeezing my shoulder. 'We are here for you, man.'

There was something about his manner as he spoke to me then, how his chin was raised and his words came out like a tag line in an advertisement, which made me think that he had been a better friend when he was telling me the monkey joke. When they left, I glanced at Sai.

'I am not leaving,' Sai said. 'This is my stall!'

I held out my cup for a refill. 'This tea is cold.'

'I wouldn't be sitting here drinking tea if my uncle was lying in a critical condition in a hospital somewhere,' he said without looking at me.

I didn't feel like talking. I lit another cigarette. Sai waved away a customer and drew a stool next to mine. He smelt of talcum powder, smoke and frying oil. It made me queasy. Without thinking, he handed me the plate of vadas he was holding. I shook my head and fished around in my pocket for my wallet.

'Now you want to pay me?' he said. 'Three months I've been chasing you to pay your tab and today of all days you find the time to pay up?' He offered me his cell phone. It was a better model than mine. 'Come on, son,' he said, jabbing my elbow with the phone. 'You are simply wasting time.'

I didn't take the phone. Sai looked at me with a mixture of disgust and concern. His expression caused his cheeks to slide downwards alongside two deep creases on either side of his face. His mouth was partially open, revealing two large front teeth which were stained brown. The heat and the smoke from the cooking had made his face red and shiny. He picked up a vada and bit into it. I had never before seen Sai eat any of the food he had cooked himself. He was showing signs of stress.

'Five minutes,' he said finally. 'That's all my conscience will allow me. You want more tea, you go somewhere else. Five minutes and then I am throwing you out.'

I felt better as soon as I left Sai's tea stall. I avoided eye contact as I ran up the stairs to my desk to retrieve my phone. I put it in my pocket without looking at the screen, knowing that that there would be missed calls or messages from my mother. Sunil hovered about me. 'Don't forget your lunch box,' he said.

I have always enjoyed walking. I like to walk slowly and watch the college women, so often dressed like twins, strolling in pairs, or look into a shop window and catch someone in the midst of a haircut, or peek into the deserted ice cream store to see if the bored sales girl is resting her head on the counter. Sometimes we smile at each other awkwardly and smile to ourselves at the awkwardness later.

As I entered 80 Feet Road, I collided with a man holding the hand of a very pregnant woman. She was so pretty that I knew she would have dimples even before she smiled. 'Look where you are going, brother,' the man said. He did not sound irritated at all, which surprised me. The woman smiled at me. Dimples.

I made my way back to my apartment. I live in a small one-bedroom apartment in the southern end of the city. It isn't one of the many new apartments that are cropping up everywhere with giant billboards promising more amenities than one could possibly need. This is a house-conversion and designed haphazardly, with stairs running from both the back and front, and walls where one might expect doors and vice versa. All in all, there are four floors and nine apartments. I like it because it is unabashedly ugly. It's garish and multi-coloured, and my apartment itself is larger than one might expect for the rent I pay. It's close to a Sagar where I eat my idli-vada-sambhar on my way to the office, a general store where I buy my provisions, and there's an auto-rickshaw stand right round the corner where there's always a driver sleeping in an auto who doesn't mind being woken up, so long as the price is right.

At the time that I moved in, I was told that my flat had been lying vacant for over a month. Because of its proximity to the cemetery, the going rate for the flats in this building is generally low. People come through word of mouth, as I had done through Sunil, although he moved out as soon as he got promoted to being my boss, or acquired his girlfriend, I cannot remember which. There are no advertisements for this place in the *Deccan Herald* and no amenities are offered. Hence this building is only popular with students and bachelors, and loners. Sometimes a young family will be lured in by the low rent, but noticing soon the abundance of the male youth who inhabit the building, the father will seek to hide his girls, and make a hasty exit as soon as the next opportunity presents itself.

When you first enter this apartment, it feels as though it is a few hours ahead in time than everywhere else because the one small window lets in little light and darkens the room prematurely. The window was jammed when I moved in and I have not yet bothered to fix it. The few women I have brought back home have all remarked upon it as though they were making an acute observation about me. Now I think that they were probably right.

On the vertiginous climb up the back stairs, I bumped into Mrs Joshi, my landlady, carrying a plastic bag full of rubbish. Her hair was straggly and appeared to have been newly coloured. Some of the jet-black hair dye had run onto her forehead and stained it. In contrast, her teeth appeared abnormally white.

'Not one of you has any respect for the rules of this building,' she said without preamble, positioning herself in my way. 'Nobody pays any attention to my notices. How many times must I request you all not to throw cigarette butts into the backyard?'

She held up the bin bag for me to see. I could make out little thumbs of cigarettes wedged between juice and cigarette cartons, empty chips packets, banana peels, and one blackened whole banana.

'Mrs Joshi,' I said, putting an arm around her. 'I should be at work but I am home at three-thirty in the afternoon because I have an important matter to attend to. Can we discuss this problem later?'

She dropped the grim expression. Now she was kindly and inquisitive.

'Oh, is anything the matter?' she said, clearly hoping that there was.

I came close to telling her that my Appa was in hospital. I felt that simply to utter the word 'Appa' would help set right my mother's use of the word 'uncle'. It would have felt good to say it aloud, even to someone who had no idea about my life except that I occasionally discarded cigarette butts out of my half-open window, a small and insignificant acknowledgment that, for a time, I'd had another father. But even such a gesture wasn't possible, for Mrs Joshi is well acquainted with my parents, and the word Appa would have caused Mrs Joshi to assume wrongly that it was my father Ram that was ill, and her solicitousness would have proved unbearable. So I left her there in the hallway with her face wrinkled into a question mark.

2

When I was six years old, Vasan told me that my mother had died of tuberculosis. He was my father and I believed him.

By then I was already familiar with all the killer diseases: tuberculosis, typhoid, malaria, diphtheria, whooping cough (which only killed babies), and the stealthiest of them all— cholera. This was 1971. Neighbours counted the people who had died that year while drawing water from the well, fathers warned their children of which streets to avoid when there was an outbreak of jaundice, and in the summer, when the mosquitoes clung together and scratched at the white gauzy mosquito nets, mothers kept a fierce gaze on their babies.

If I had to place a finger on that spot in time where it all began, it would have to be the day I became Sorry Hari. Whenever I reach into the scrabble bag of my memories, this is invariably the piece I pick up. On this yellow day in my memory, I am sitting on the warm bench in my classroom with the sun blasting through the big iron windows. Beside me is Michael Pinto, the boy who sat very straight and was two long inches taller than me, with a green toffee wrapper sticking out of his breast pocket, bright and fluorescent against his white cotton shirt. Michael Pinto's socks were always at equal lengths on his shins. He was from Madras, and although we all wore identical uniforms, it was clear to everyone that he was a city boy. Only city boys sat that straight on their benches.

I reached into his pocket to grab the toffee. Michael caught my hand with his teeth in the way I had once seen an Alsatian grab a kitten's neck, clamping my hand firmly in his jaws and shaking it until my hand went limp and I had dropped the toffee on top of the desk. There was just enough blood to mix with his saliva and turn it a frothy pink on my hand. I screamed. Michael began to cry when he saw what he had done. Only city boys cried inside classrooms.

There were over one hundred children in the classroom, so until the boys started to gather around us and take sides, Miss Prema, our class teacher, did not notice our altercation. She was a short, prim woman with plump, chalky fingers. She wore platform heels to elevate her height, and was constantly getting her sari caught underneath them. It caught then, as she approached us, her hand still clutching the duster, and she steadied herself against one of the desks. We began to speak simultaneously as she made her way to my desk, Suresh talking the loudest, 'He would not let Hari's arm go, Miss. I never saw so much blood.' Some of the rowdier girls began giggling in the aisles. Miss Prema rapped the duster twice against my desk and the room fell silent as a cloud of chalk powder rose up and then settled. She took me by the arm and led me to the school infirmary, while Jaydeep, the older of the Gopalan twins and our new class prefect, stationed himself at the door without intimation. The classroom plunged into chaos behind us.

The old nurse was the only one in the school infirmary who still wore her white uniform and cap. It was a minor victory for the other nurses that they were able to replace their tight-fitting uniforms with the more comfortable sari, but Miss Bose liked routine and old habits.

She stuck her tongue out at me as she bandaged up my hand. Mine was not the first limb she had seen bitten by a fellow student. Miss Prema disappeared behind a curtain and emerged with a folded note to give to my father. 'Hari, be sure to hand this to him, okay?' she said, flicking a thumb over my cheek. I nodded and she seemed satisfied.

She caught sight of herself in a mirror and ran her tongue over her lips. 'Well,' she said to Miss Bose. 'Some term this is turning out to be.' Then, taking me by the hand, she said. 'I am going to have the school bus drop you home. But before that, the class has something to say to you.'

We returned to the classroom where Jaydeep was making unnecessary adjustments to the timetable scribbled on one corner of the blackboard, appearing not to notice us when we walked back in. Miss Prema patted him on his back and sent him to his desk (in the front row). She then ordered Michael Pinto to stand atop our bench for the rest of the hour. Several of us noticed then that his shoes were still glistening with polish and had not acquired the sheen of dust which on our own shoes made Miss Malli, the music teacher, wince and instantly cover her nose with a handkerchief when we entered the music room. Miss Prema handed me the toffee with a smile which she abandoned when she heard a murmuring amongst the girls. She rapped the duster again.

'Hari is a poor motherless boy,' she announced to the class. 'He doesn't have what you all have. From now onwards, I want everyone to be kind to Hari. Everyone say, '"Sorry, Hari".'

Everyone said, 'Sorry Hari.'

Some of them laughed.

Is it possible that looking at her thin-lipped face I felt the same dog-like urge to bite? I remember being filled with rage. In various imagined versions of this event over the years, I picture myself biting her plump forearm, her screaming, and the boys urging me on to bite harder. In any case, it had seemed unfair to me then that I had been singled out that day for my motherlessness. I certainly wasn't the only one in my class without a mother. Anand Mohan's mother had set herself on fire only a few months earlier, and more than once, I had caught sight of Lata Raj sniffling in school corners because her mother had only recently been killed in a bus accident returning from her cousin's engagement ceremony which Lata herself had nearly attended.

My father had remarked on Lata's mother's death when he had seen her obituary in the *Rayalaseema Times*. 'Isn't this the mother of the girl with the three pigtails?' he asked. That had probably been her mother's touch and it disappeared as soon as she died. There were others too like us, without one or the other parent. I knew this, though I had never spoken to them; ours was a big school. I never learnt their names, although we recognized each other out in the playground, or by the school bus, as though we had been marked with a highlighter pen, and could easily be identified. It wasn't that we were different, but that talk of our dead mothers or fathers preceded and succeeded us wherever we went. We knew this, and we hated it and we manipulated it as best as we could.

Miss Prema was often prone to paying excessive attention to me. This was as clear to me as it was to most of the boys in class. I was often asked to read aloud passages from textbooks, and she made a point of saying, 'Good, Hari!' when I finished. She even handed me her handkerchief once when I sneezed and I heard no end of it from the Gopalan twins for a whole month. Miss Prema's attention was not directed at me, so much as it was at my father, for whom she had a quiet passion. This was of course why Miss Prema often requested the presence of my father at the school to talk about my 'disturbing behaviour', although she never once chided me at school. Suddenly, at these encounters, bright pink lipstick appeared on her lips and a visible coyness as she smoothed down her starched white sari and jingled the bangles on her wrist.

Miss Prema led to me to the parking lot. The bus driver was dozing underneath a tamarind tree and she awoke him in a shrill, irritated voice. He was a substitute driver. I did not recognize him. He roused himself quickly. 'Sorry, Madam,' he mumbled, wiping the sweat off his face with the edge of his scarf.

That day, sitting in the school bus on the ride home, looking out at the hills where I could make out a thin ant-line of cars climbing, I was possessed for the first time with a curiosity about my mother. I was on my own except for the bus driver who, annoyed at having to make an extra trip, was honking even when there was no one blocking the road, and cursed loudly when the railway gate came down at the crossing. Vasan never mentioned my mother to me. I was only reminded of her when people repeatedly asked, the way they did when you were a child:

'What is your name?'

'My name is Hari,' I said, with my arms folded across my

chest, standing upright in the same manner as when I was asked to recite a poem in class, answering each question by rote.

'How old are you?'

'I am six years old.'

'What is your father's name?'

'My father's name is Vasan.'

'What does your father do?'

'My father is an accountant.'

'What is your mother's name?'

'My mother's name is Devaki.'

'What does your mother do?'

'My mother is dead.'

Then their jaw would drop a little and they would feed me butter biscuits and a glass of Horlicks and send me off to play with my toys.

I had gained knowledge of my mother's death in the same manner that I had learnt of God; without knowing how, or who first spoke of them to me. It was the sort of knowledge that hung about you, and seeped in surreptitiously. It didn't matter about God until Vasan changed religions, and it had not mattered about my mother until the day I became Sorry Hari.

'Death toll rises in Madhya Pradesh to thirty-five,' my father said, without looking up at me, reading aloud from the *Rayalaseema Times* as soon I entered the house. He was sitting on the red rexine sofa in the hall. A packet of unopened glucose biscuits lay beside him. 'Poorly maintained sewage systems and lack of sanitation has caused the killer disease to thrive.' I dropped my school bag on the floor. 'Let's see if you can guess which disease this is.' He rolled up the newspaper and whacked my bottom with it lightly as I went past him.

He noticed the bandage on my arm. 'What is this?' he said.

I handed him Miss Prema's note. I had read it in the bus and felt it safe to deliver. It was not written on office stationary, as usual, but on a slightly crumpled sheet from one of Dr Reddy's prescription pads.

The note read:

Dear Mr S. Vasan,

Due to a very unfortunate incident in the classroom, your son's hand was hurt. He has been given first aid and we are assured that he needs no other medical attention. Hari may take leave till Thursday if you so desire. Please do not hesitate to call me on my neighbour Mona's telephone (***) if you wish.

Yours sincerely,

Prema Pankaj

Class Teacher, UKG Children of Tomorrow School

PS: If Mona's mother-in-law answers the phone, please speak loudly into the receiver as she is hard of hearing and may not understand you.

'What incident?' My father quizzed me as soon as he caught the word 'incident', before he had even finished reading the entire letter. He flapped the paper in front of my face and flung it on top of the chest of drawers.

'What did you *do*?' he said. He ripped open my bandage to investigate for himself.

Although I had known that seizing another boy's toffee from his pocket would normally be considered an offence, I had become confused because Miss Prema had meted out no punishment to me, and had in fact rewarded me with the toffee. Unthinkingly, I told him the truth. He gave me one of his medium slaps on my cheek.

Before he became a Christian, my father had three different slaps for me depending on the occasion: soft, medium, and strong. Any behaviour above the slap scale warranted the use of the cane. I preferred the cane in general because he usually caned me on my bottom and although I put on a good show and screamed and yelped, it hardly hurt at all.

'Never take anything that is not yours!' he said. He slumped into his armchair and began rubbing his forehead with his fingers.

'Jayamma,' he shouted in the direction of the kitchen. Jayamma was the third occupant of our house. She was 'a maid with the personality of a mother-in-law', my father liked to joke.

'I have lived in this house since before it was built,' Jayamma was used to saying. She was doting and domineering at once. She came slowly, hobbling.

'Coffee! Jayamma, it's four-thirty! What's wrong with you?' my father said.

Whenever my father rubbed his forehead and asked for coffee, it was a cue that I should leave him alone. I had come home with a mouth full of questions about my mother, but sensing his mood darken, all I wanted to do was to slip away. Jayamma caught hold of me as I turned to leave.

'It's only three-fifteen. The boy is home early. There is nothing wrong with me. There is something wrong with your head.'

'What have you done, my boy?' she said, stroking the flesh

around the bandage. 'Who did this to you? Tell Jayamma. Jayamma will put a curse on him.'

My father had recently established a new coffee routine at home. He suffered from chronic headaches; coffee helped soothe his headaches, although if he drank too many cups, the headaches became far worse. As a result, he had created strict coffee timings: 6:00 a.m. (just after he woke up), 9:00 a.m. (just before he left for work), and 4:30 p.m. (just after he returned from work). However, he did not have correspondingly strict office timings, and the coffee schedule would often be disrupted as a result.

My father owned a small accounting practice in Sripuri and his office was located only a street away from our home which was on the west side at 12 Coramandel Street. We lived in a big white brick house in the centre of a large plot circumscribed by an irregular compound wall that was overrun with jasmine and bougainvillea. Beside the house stood a solitary mango tree that craned above the house and continuously shed its monkey-bitten fruit and leaves onto the roof. Any time there was a client visit, it only took a minute for the current office boy (none stayed very long) to run over to our house to inform my father. Then he would rush about from room to room, gathering papers, looking for a business card or a pen, yelling at us, working himself up into an agitated state before calming himself down in front of the hallway mirror and then setting off purposefully down the road. In general, he preferred to work from his study, which he referred to grandly as his 'home office', although it was not large enough to contain more than two clients, and I never did see more than one client at any point during my time with him.

My father ran his practice with little interest. In those days, Sripuri was a slatternly little town, not the bustling mini-city it is now. Those harbouring higher aspirations may have found their fires smothered quickly, for there was always someone hurrying out of town as soon as they finished high school to Bangalore or to Madras to universities with better reputations and then it was a hop skip and a jump from there to some unheard of institution in Arizona or Utah or Indiana. They bemoaned Sripuri's poor infrastructure and its open drainage systems, the lack of civic sense amongst its people, their uncouth speech, and the dearth of good hospitals and educational institutions. In contrast, those who stayed behind extolled the town's virtues. They spoke highly of the quiet life of contentment it offered its citizens, where one could still sleep with the doors open, fish in the open river and take siestas in the afternoons when the sun became intolerable. My father belonged to neither category of people. Whatever career ambitions he may have had were already extinguished by then. And my father was anything but content.

My father's headaches were something of a mystery to Dr Samuel Jolly, our family doctor. A short, balding, and energetic man, Dr Jolly liked to refer to ailments as though they were living beings. 'We will not let this pest go undetected. We will find him and throw him out of your life forever,' he said to my father time after time, thumping his prescription pad with his fist. 'I am going to have to do some new tests. It will cost you, but the best treatment doesn't come cheap, you know.'

'Leave your worries to the best doctor in town,' Dr Jolly told his patients after every consultation, and so, eventually, he had acquired the label of being the best doctor in Sripuri.

One day, when I had accompanied my father to the doctor's house (Dr Jolly had converted his hall into his evening clinic by lining up a row of white plastic chairs against the wall and putting up posters of babies and medical products like Vaseline and Iodex), Mrs Jolly pulled my father aside. 'You need a woman, Vasan,' she said. 'Your head trouble is nothing but heart trouble. But don't tell my husband I said that.'

Sometimes, my father's headaches would be so terrible he would implore me to press his forehead with the heel of my foot because my hands did not yet have strength enough. He would lie down on the rug in the living room and, using the arm of the red rexine sofa as support, I would stand with one foot on the ground and grind the heel of the other foot into his forehead. Often, I would return from playing in the park to find my father reclining on the big planter's chair in the veranda with a scarf tightly wound around his head, which would give him the appearance of a farmer or a fighter.

When one treatment did not work, my father adopted another. He tried medicinal teas procured on recommendation from one of his clients, sharp-scented homeopathic pills which he took one too many at a time and then cursed for being tiny, and at other times, on Jayamma's recommendation, he smeared his forehead with a paste of ginger which turned yellow as it dried, causing him to resemble an overzealous priest.

Some evenings, my father would settle himself in his chair with the hardbound copy of the *Modern Family Health Guide*, searching through its pages for any medical conditions which matched his symptoms. Often, he simply flipped open to a random page and read aloud a passage or two about a particular disease as he would in later days flip open his Bible looking for some hidden meaning within its pages. As much as my father approached those pages with dread, a furrow forming between his brows as his eyes darted to and fro, it seemed to me that he wanted to find something in there—anything that he could hold accountable for the perpetual state of pain in which he lived.

My father liked educating us about all the killer diseases. He translated pertinent sections for Jayamma into Telugu and occasionally even acted out the symptoms for comedic value if he was in the mood for it. My father was a handsome man with a warm expressive face, one that seemed to be constantly shifting and realigning itself under its skin. A smile when it came, settled as much in the arches of the eyebrows as it did on his lips. It was a face which people trusted although he himself trusted few in return.

I retrieved Miss Prema's letter from the top of the chest of drawers and ducked into the kitchen where Jayamma was putting ground coffee into the copper filter. I copied Miss Prema's signature over and over again below where she had signed on the letter.

Jayamma said, 'Your father's headache is my biggest headache.'

The next morning, I was allowed to stay home from school. My hand had swollen up and the skin had turned a delicate pink. It felt soft, sinking like a pillow at the touch of my fingers. It was a deeper red where Michael's teeth had torn off the skin and it was tantalizingly itchy. I drew deep blue circles around the wound with a ball-point pen.

Jayamma made a turmeric paste and smeared my wound with it. She redid my bandage and slapped me lightly a few times for fiddling with the wound. She kissed me and said, 'Boys like that need to be bitten back.'

I asked Jayamma whether she had known my mother. 'No,' Jayamma said too swiftly, and began sweeping the kitchen floor. 'Now get out of here and stop spreading the dust all over.'

I hung around in my father's study, scribbling on his carbon paper, getting ink on my hands, rolling letterheads with 'S. Srinivasan, Chartered Accountant' into the typewriter and leaning back and forth in my father's red leather chair. My father came in from work and found me rummaging through his desk.

He yanked me off the chair and deposited me onto the floor. 'Peace of mind!' he yelled. 'All I want here is a little peace of mind.' My father's face became swollen with anger and his eyes seemed to bulge out of their sockets and turn a lighter shade of black. He slammed his fist on the table.

I realized that I would have to wait for him to be in a better mood before I could ask him about my mother. Although Jayamma could slap me almost as hard as my father did, I was never afraid of her. Whenever I mentioned my mother to Jayamma, she picked up a broom and began sweeping the floor. I took this action to mean that she didn't know anything about my mother because Jayamma always reached for the broom when she was asked a question to which she didn't know the answer. She swept briskly, lifting things, and dusting corners with the dust cloth she always had tucked in at her waist. Jayamma was always moving, even though her bow legs and fat calves conspired to challenge her and I had to chase her around the room in the haphazard sideways fashion in which her broom moved. If I pressed her with my questions, she would point to her mouth and move her jaw up and down to indicate to me that chewing tobacco was all her mouth was capable of doing at the moment.

I had expected that I would be something of a hero when I went back to school. But in the toilets, behind the school compound walls, and at the little shop on stilts where we bought red syrupy sweets stacked in bottles, and in the places where the talk happened away from the school teachers, I was long forgotten. Instead I heard kids talking about Kavita, the 'tallest girl in class' as she was commonly referred to, who had been sent to the principal's office for stealing Miss Prema's purse and who had returned with purple knuckles.

My hand was still puffed up, but the tear was practically invisible and it was no surprise that being unaccompanied by pus, it failed to arouse interest in anyone except Michael Pinto. I made a big show of displaying my wound to my friends Saleem and Suresh, peeling off the bandage with great precision, and squeezing my eyes together dramatically. Saleem made a face of disgust and Suresh said, 'Very nice,' but they gave it only a perfunctory glance.

Michael Pinto, looking nervous, informed me that Miss Prema had also written a letter to his parents and, as a result, his mother had beaten him with a ladle and had sent me an entire packet of toffees as retribution. His face crumpled when he admitted that he had eaten them all because he had not seen me at school. When I asked him what kind they were, he said, 'The ones with the green wrappers,' and his face acquired a funny look as though he may have been lying or thought that he ought to have been.

'My mother told Miss Prema about the packet of toffees.' His eyes were pleading. 'Please don't tell Miss that I ate them.'

He placed his new pencil box on the desk. It was a red plastic case with a smooth wide back and had the words 'Mowgli and Friends' written in large letters. Around the letters were pictures of Baloo, Sher Khan, Bagheera, and Kaa. Inside, it had separate compartments for pencils, a sharpener, and an eraser. It was a beauty. I gave him back his pencils and put the pencil case in my bag, thus settling the matter peacefully between ourselves.

In the canteen, I thought I heard one of the Gopalan twins standing behind me in the queue call me Sorry Hari, but when I turned around, my hand already balled into a fist, both boys appeared to be examining their new spin tops.

I found Jayamma in the kitchen pounding rice in the grinding stone. When I asked her where my father had gone, she said, 'Does he tell me where he comes and goes?'

It was an unusual answer. My father was a predictable man. He rarely ventured out of his office or home. He resisted all shopping, and he disdained crowds. Besides, he never went anywhere without indicating the exact time of his arrival to Jayamma.

'He is a strange one, your Appa,' she said, pausing to looking at me. "Don't you grow up strange like him.'

My father arrived after sundown without an explanation. Jayamma and I were playing a game of five stones on the floor of the living room. Jayamma ignored him and told me to do the same.

'What's that game you've got going?' he said, putting his bag down on the sofa.

'Not there,' Jayamma said.

He hastily retrieved the bag and hung it from its hook on the wall.

By then, his interest in the game was lost. He retreated to his study. He had a Do Not Disturb sign which he had saved from a trip to Delhi that he hung over his door knob whenever he wished to show his displeasure with Jayamma or me. He hung this sign now, deliberately, and shut the door behind him.

Jayamma abandoned the game as soon as the door closed, told me to put the stones away in their little basket and rose with some difficulty. She entered his study without knocking. Jayamma would not let the matter rest until she had learnt where he had been.

A breeze blew past the row of neem trees lining the drive to the school gate, tousling their leaves, momentarily bestowing on them the same animated look we had on our faces as we queued up to get on the school bus.

Saleem threw a pebble which stung me on my shoulder. I threw two back and missed both times.

'Ready?' he asked.

'Ready,' I said. We had plans.

School was over and we were making our way to the school bus which was already jostling with kids scrambling to sit close to friends. Some of the girls had squeezed into the same seat so they could talk on the way. Saleem and I hugged our bags close to us and made our way to the back of the bus. This was the time of day when our textbooks got stolen and the bigger kids demanded our water bottles and we handed them over subserviently with little frightened smiles.

Saleem and I attempted to get off the bus at Bazaar Street, but Mohan, the bus driver, stopped us. He knew where each of us got off, and judging from the look on his face he also knew what Saleem and I were planning to do. He wouldn't have cared if Saleem's father wasn't in the army. He told Saleem, 'No thanks, I am not having that military man coming after me again.'

So, we got off at our usual stop, the Lakshmi temple, and walked all the way back to Bazaar Street. Diwali was coming up and all the new firecrackers of the season were being displayed in boxes in the shop windows. Saleem and I had been given a budget of fifty rupees each to spend on fireworks even though he didn't celebrate Diwali in the same way that we did. We had made completely different lists so we could get a good range between us and had handed them to our fathers, although having seen my father drop my list on top of a pile of papers on the chest of drawers, I was doubtful he would make the right purchases.

The shops were full of other kids like us fingering boxes of the firecrackers they wanted the most. We could almost taste the sweet metallic odour of the firecrackers. We argued about the merits of the Atom Bomb versus the Nitrogen Bomb. Some of the kids had older brothers or sisters who were allowed to fire up the big bombs. Most of the kids our age had to settle for the tame firecrackers such as the sparklers, cap-guns, snakes, and butterbombs, but we were already adept at surreptitiously stealing the big bombs from the older children.

'Hari,' I heard a voice behind me call out. It was Sandeep, the younger of the Gopalan twins. His shorts were sagging, revealing his sharp pelvic blades. He had cankers in the corners of his mouth that made all the 'a' sounds come out with an 'o'.

'This year my father is going to buy crackers for two hundred rupees,' I said, before he could open his mouth again.

'My father is going to buy for five hundred rupees!' he said.

'I bet he is not!'

He smirked. 'I bet your father is not going to spend more than twenty. He is right behind you, so I can go and ask him.'

Saleem and I turned around and at the same time tried to crouch behind the big crates of firecrackers in the store. We spotted my father on the other side of the street entering a narrow alley that ran between two identical looking costume jewellery shops.

What was my father doing in this part of town? We tried to search for a reasonable explanation. We knew that it was in this same alley that our English and PT teacher, Chalapathi Sir, lived in an upstairs flat. We had often sighted him on his balcony on Sundays, working out with weights and flexing his muscles to the beat of women walking on the road. On Tuesdays, if we forgot to wear our white uniforms, Chalapathi Sir made us walk on our knees from one end of the field to the other. We searched our minds for what I could have done that necessitated my father's presence at Chalapathi Sir's house when he should have been at work. I had stolen a cricket ball from the PT room, but I was sure that when it had happened, Chalapathi Sir had been on the field, his red whistle hanging from his neck, forcing an exhausted football team to run laps around the ground as punishment for their poor performance. Saleem and I looked at each other. It was clear what we were going to do.

At the door, the shop assistant grabbed us by our collars and checked our pockets to see if we had stolen anything. Then he gave us a big smile and released us. Our schoolbags felt heavy on our shoulders as we ran across the street. An old woman with dreadlocks was sitting on a gunny sack on the pavement with her legs stretched out onto the road, swearing rapidly beneath her breath. Saleem thought she was cursing us and that it was not a good omen. As we reached the gully, I began to have second thoughts. We had already lost sight of my father and I was beginning to panic. Before Saleem got his braces, he was the bolder of the two of us.

Saleem said, 'You fool. If your father is talking to Chalapathi Sir, don't you want to know what all he is saying about you?'

I let Saleem lead, following him a few paces behind. This was the older section of town where the houses were built leaning against each other. They were long and narrow, creating tunnels between two parallel streets; the front entrance opening onto one street and the back entrance onto another. Sometimes, two adjoining houses shared a door, so it was easy to have a chat, or to drop off a child onto a neighbour's lap when one wanted to take an oil bath, or borrow some rice or jaggery. Often, people left their doors open and we always took the shortcuts through other people's homes to go from one street to another. But we all knew to avoid Mrs Perumal's house. You would never emerge on the other side because she liked to talk about her granddaughter in 'The States'. 'My granddaughter could sing before she could speak. She is going to a special school,' she told us in a wobbly voice. Even though she always bribed us with coconut barfi, some of us had eaten her barfi too many times for it to taste sweet any longer.

Saleem entered the house that he thought would give us the best view of Chalapathi Sir's balcony without our being seen. Then he gestured for me to come over. The house had a small pyol out in the front with built in red-oxide benches, so we were able to climb on top of one of them and look out.

An old woman emerged from within the house.

'What are you doing?' she asked, placing an unsteady hand on my shoulder.

'Our grandmother told us to wait here, she is at the vegetable shop,' Saleem said.

The old woman said, 'Why don't you boys sit down? Benches are made for sitting.'

Saleem gazed at the sky. 'I can see the kites from here, grandma,' he said, although kite-flying season would not begin for a few months yet.

She was not interested in kites. She went back into the house and returned with two glasses of cold salted buttermilk. We drank greedily. She sat down on the other bench and waved at passersby.

Outside, on the street, a few old men were beginning to drag tables and chairs out from their houses, setting the stage for a game of cards. With a deft shuffling of the pack, they seemed to announce that the day had ended and the evening had begun. I felt frightened. I told Saleem that we had better be getting back because his father, Khan Uncle, was quite strict about punctuality. Saleem grinned and said, 'My father isn't in town.'

We heard a child wailing from within the house and, begrudgingly, the old woman got up and left to tend to it.

Suddenly, there was my father. He was two doors from Chalapathi Sir's house. He was leaning over to take off his shoes before entering into a dark doorway.

The old woman came out just as we were skipping over the steps to leave. 'Where's your grandmother?' she called after us.

'That's her,' I said, pointing in the distance at an indistinct group of women who had gathered around a vegetable vendor.

Saleem laughed and said, 'Very good.'

We broke into a run and I was relieved when I caught sight of Chalapathi Sir coming out of his house escorting an old hunchback woman down the front steps. Their noses, rising at first and descending sharply, were identical. She wore the same stern expression on her face as he did, and for a moment, I imagined her making Chalapathi Sir walk on his knees across the balcony of his house while pointing at him with a ruler. He caught my eye, but when I waved to him, he didn't seem to recognize me at all.

Saleem slowed down in front of the large brick house that my father had entered. There was a big poster stuck to the door with words in Sanskrit around a symbol of the sun. There was a window to one side of the door which was covered with an iron grill. Saleem and I peered in through the bars and found that my father was sitting amongst a circle of men, in the lotus position, bare-chested, and chanting in Sanskrit. All the men had their eyes closed except for one older man whose belly hung over the waistband of his white cotton pyjamas. He was watching the others and chanting the loudest, and we assumed he was the leader. The light from the oil lamps combined awkwardly with the light from the setting sun, partially illuminating their faces and throwing ghosts of shadows on the walls. I had often seen people meditate, especially in temple hallways. I had even seen the beggars lining the paved walkway to the temple from time to time close their eyes and chant a shloka or two. Nothing about this scene struck me as particularly unusual. Generally, there were other things that caught my eye, like the temple elephant or the one-legged barber, and now I felt almost disappointed that our trail had led us to nothing more exciting. However, Saleem seemed to have a different reaction. He crammed his fingers into his mouth in an effort to stifle his laughter. I was old enough then to recognize that my allegiance lay with my father. I did not say anything, but Saleem caught the look on my face and his laughter stopped instantly. 'I was laughing at the fat man,' he said. 'Did you see his stomach?'

As soon as he returned home from the meditation, my father asked Jayamma for a cup of coffee. She reminded him that it was his third cup of the day, and he yelled at her.

'I asked only for coffee, not for any of your thoughts,' he said.

Then, when there was no sign of either Jayamma or the coffee, he was forced to seek her out in the kitchen and apologize to her.

'I have a lot of things on my mind, Jayamma,' I heard him say. 'Don't think badly of me, Jayamma. You know how I get without coffee—could you not make it a little easier for me?'

'What things have you got on your mind?' she asked, incredulous. 'Seems to me that your head is as large and as empty as our rice drum at the moment. And why must it always be me that makes it easier for you? I am twice as old as you.'

I stayed out of his way until dinner when he patted me on the knee and attempted a joke as Jayamma served us the food.

'Be careful, Hari,' he said, with an impish expression, looking up at Jayamma. 'Jayamma is in her Kali avatar. You and I are in danger of being beheaded.'

Jayamma ignored him.

He took three deep breaths. 'I think the meditation is helping me, Jayamma. See, you are angry with me and I am not returning your anger,' he said.

He finished eating the remnants on his plate with satisfaction and licked his fingers.

"I can feel the effects of the meditation,' he said pleasantly.

3

It took me two weeks to muster up enough courage to ask my father about my dead mother. Somehow, I had known that any questions I posed about her would not be well-received. Just as I had known, standing at the edge of the school grounds, which were deserted even by the night watchman, that to jump over the iron railing and pick guavas from the tree was not permitted; instinctively I had felt that I was trespassing and that it would not be tolerated.

The following Thursday, when my father returned from his meditation, I noticed at once that he was in a good mood. I was on the porch playing with Julie, the mongrel dog that had grown accustomed to the curd rice Jayamma fed her in an aluminium plate and usually fell asleep in the sprawling shade of the mango tree. When my father was not home, Jayamma sometimes brought Julie into the house, having extracted a silent promise from me that I was to keep this information from him.

My father came in through the gate humming an old Hindi song. He stopped when he saw me and announced, 'I am going to teach you chess.' He brought out the carved wooden box containing his old chess board which had been locked away in the almirah and gave it to Jayamma to dust and polish. He moved the chairs in our living room so we could sit on the rug. 'If a man can play chess well, there are few things in life that will baffle him,' he said, while we were waiting.

When Jayamma brought back the board, he complained that she had gotten the dust off but covered all the pieces with flour.

I did not take to chess as well as my father hoped. I liked the horses best (knights, he corrected me time and again), so I tended to move them at every opportunity I got. He explained to me what a strategy was and how important it was to plan, anticipate and manoeuvre mentally before moving to reach one's ultimate goal.

By the end of the first game, I knew I preferred playing carom. Yet, because my father had never taught me any game before, and the afternoon light swelled in the hall, and the smell of the potato bajjis came wafting from the kitchen, I was filled with unexpected warmth. We played three games, but with each game it became more challenging for my father to avoid taking my pieces.

Finally, he said, 'We will keep trying. You didn't do too badly.' When he reached across to pat my shoulder, the pieces seemed to hold their places on the board with a will of their own.

And right then, without knowing what I was about to do, I asked him.

'What happened to my mother?'

I remember my father sweeping the pieces across the board with his hand, and how the knights, the rooks, the queens and the kings, which had stood proudly a moment earlier, all crashed to their sides before he cast them callously into the purple velvet pouch. He folded up the board and replaced it in its box. He leaned back against the legs of the sofa.

It later occurred to me that my father had learnt those lines by heart for just such a time when I should surprise him with this question. He spoke with a calmness that was unnatural for him.

'Your mother died of tuberculosis when you were three years old. She was a beautiful woman and a wonderful mother. I miss her every day. She loved you very much. One of these days, I will bring out a photo for you to see.'

I asked to see the photos immediately, but he told me that the few photographs he possessed were all locked up in trunks in the garage and that he would fish them out for me someday. He began rubbing his forehead with his fingers and I realized that the effects of the meditation had begun to wear off.

Soon after he began his meditation sessions, Jayamma and I began to observe strange differences in my father's behaviour. One welcome result was that his headaches appeared to have become less painful. In the evenings, when there was a soft light pushing through the curtains in the hall, he took to playing one of his favourite records, usually Musiri Subramanya Iyer or Ariyakudi Ramanuja Iyengar; and with his eyes closed, he would keep the beat to the music by rapping his knuckles against the great sloping arm of the planter's chair. A transitory calmness would appear on his face, but as quickly as the light faded, a sudden excitement stemming from the music or some melody within himself would rouse him and he would gesture animatedly for me to sit alongside him. Before long, I began to know the songs and even now, though I rarely listen to classical music anymore, a refrain will come back to me, but only on a day that seems to have come back from that time, with the same gentle light. Sometimes it makes me wonder whether the music etched itself into me or into that sky.

Next came the early morning chanting from the scratched tape recorder in his room, a rendition of the Upanishads by a man whose voice seemed to be split up into two different voices, one higher and more nervous than the other. Unlike the music which he shared with us, the chanting tape was reserved for him alone. He always listened with the door closed. Peeping through the keyhole one morning revealed that he had brought the meditation home.

One evening, striding straight into the kitchen from work, without even pausing to hang up his shoulder bag, my father forbade Jayamma from using peanuts or onions in her cooking.

'I don't want those filthy foods anymore. They are poisons, Jayamma, killing us slowly,' he said, and proceeded to look in the kitchen cupboard for signs of the offending items. He rattled the tins in the cupboard one by one. We heard the swoosh of the peanuts as they crashed against the ends of the tin. He flipped the lid open in triumph. He marched to the backyard and scattered the nuts across the ground, beckoning to birds in the sky as he did so.

'He doesn't want peanuts in the house but he is about to grow them in his own backyard,' Jayamma muttered, but my father, if he heard her, ignored her comment. He began looking for onions under the kitchen counter. Jayamma said something about her uncle in the village who lived to a hundred and two years on a diet of just onions, pickle and rice.

'Please,' my father implored, showing more patience than he was accustomed to with Jayamma. 'Can you please, please just listen to me for once?'

Later, when I asked her what pickle her uncle had chosen for his unique diet, Jayamma said, 'You mustn't believe everything I tell your father.'

But the most disturbing of my father's behaviours was that he had started to watch me. Whether I was in the front yard playing with Julie, or doing my homework on the kitchen floor beside Jayamma, I would feel his eyes travel towards me through lowered reading glasses.

He also began to insist that we sit together at the table during dinner. Jayamma had always fed me in the kitchen, telling me the same stories that I loved over and over again. Even as I ate, he would watch me intently, and if I dared to meet his gaze, he would mutter something like, 'At least try to not spill the rice grains all around your plate,' or, 'Jayamma does not know how to brush a boy's hair properly.' However, he ate his dinners quickly and left before I had even gotten to the curd rice on my plate. It was Jayamma's theory that someone had warned him that not eating at the dinner table was killing us slowly, just like the peanuts and the onions, and that however difficult it was for all concerned, it just had to be endured.

I did not mention my mother again, but I began to keep track of my father's mood patterns so that when the time was right, I could strike him with my request for the trunks to be opened and my mother's photographs to be revealed. That would be my strategy.

It began to rain two days before Diwali and a week after my school closed for vacation.

'It always rains at Diwali,' Jayamma said, when she found me in the veranda watching the sky sweep up the clouds together in our direction. It would be difficult to set the firecrackers alight; they would merely whimper in the wet weather.

'The good news is that your grandfather is coming to visit. The bad news is that it may be the last time you will see him,' she said matter-of-factly. 'He is not well, your grandfather.'

If I had met my grandfather before, I had no recollection of it. He had already cancelled his visits on two occasions that very month, after days of eager anticipation on my part.

'Once again, my stomach has been giving me some trouble,' he had said over the phone to Jayamma both times.

'He is already on the train. He will arrive by nightfall. Too late to change his mind now,' Jayamma said, reading my mind.

She told me that I would have to move to the upstairs room because my grandfather was weak and would not be able to climb up and down the staircase.

'What is wrong with him?' I asked.

'His stomach is eating itself,' she said.

Jayamma gazed at me a long time as I sat on the kitchen counter swinging my legs. She squeezed me into a tight hug. 'Hari, my boy,' she kept murmuring in my ear.

My grandfather had the biggest moustache I had ever seen. It was thick and silver and fanned out in perfect symmetry on either side of his face before curving downwards, much to his despair. When I saw him enter the house with his ivory-capped cane in one hand and a portable transistor radio in the other, dressed in a navy blue suit, I suddenly became aware of my father's worn appearance, his creased shirts with yellow stains at the arms and the trouser cuffs that stopped well above his ankles.

'You are a fine looking boy,' my grandfather said, depositing his cane and transistor radio on the sofa.

Nobody had called me a fine looking boy before. I warmed to him instantly. Jayamma, who was always able to hear things that were not said to her, suddenly appeared. She had tears in her eyes.

'How are you, Jayamma?'

'Life goes on, you know,' she said, hiding her pleasure at seeing him with a swift movement of her hands as she retrieved the radio and the cane from the sofa.

My grandfather was a professor of English at St. Vincent's College in Delhi. For many years, until the death of my grandmother Malati, he was the Head of the English Faculty at Vivekananda College, in Sripuri. The love between my grandparents was rumoured to have been legendary. My grandfather had taken my grandmother's death hard and chosen voluntary retirement immediately after her passing. He had left for Delhi at the insistence of his old friend Sadanand Sharma, initially to recuperate and then to find a new life. When his colleagues asked him why he did not choose to return to Vivekananda College, he told them that there was no point in trying to teach English in a town where the only English one heard was in a dark cinema hall when a Bruce Lee movie was playing.

'You haven't seen Diwali unless you have seen it in Delhi,' my grandfather told me during dinner. It was the first time in days that my father had taken his gaze off me. Now, he was watching his father with the same intensity.

In Delhi, my grandfather said, the firecrackers were bigger and brighter than anywhere else in India. The streets were full of vendors brewing tea with elaichi or frying jalebis, heaping them like jewels onto brass plates. In Delhi, the women glittered in gold and the cars were so shiny that the moon, when reflected in them, was at least twice its actual size.

'I hope you will see it someday,' he said, casting a glance at my father, who quickly averted his eyes and appeared to be playing with the curry leaves on his plate.

'You can't call yourself an Indian until you have been to Delhi.'

My chest swelled. No one in my class had ever travelled as far north as Delhi.

My grandfather had what Jayamma liked to refer to as, 'the largeness only short men have'. He had a wide face that could not only accommodate his moustache, but also a large smile that displayed a set of even white teeth. His hair was thinning and he combed it back unabashedly, revealing a polished oblong forehead. When he spoke, it was as though he had beaten words to submission; they would arrive from his mouth like a row of soldiers during a procession march, lifting up their arms or turning around just as he commanded them.

My father remained silent during the meal, listening to his father with almost the same rapt attention as I, and although he had finished eating long before we had, my father stayed at the table until my grandfather rose. I noticed, as my grandfather walked towards his room, that he looked taller than he had appeared when he had first entered the house.

Even Jayamma's fervent prayers (the clothes were refusing to dry) could not stop the onslaught of the rain. The clouds stuck together in clumps so that it was impossible to make out where one ended and the other began. Occasionally, an Atom Bomb would go off in the distance and we wondered where in the town there was a sky that was not falling down.

On Diwali day, Saleem arrived at my house early, clutching his portion of the firecrackers that he had to share with three brothers. He had wrapped them in a sturdy plastic bag which he held close to his body underneath his yellow raincoat to protect them from getting wet. From where I stood, it appeared as though he had no arms because the sleeves of his raincoat were flailing limply by his sides as he came running towards me.

I had been waiting for him on the veranda, leaning over the metal latticework fence, already bored with the sparklers. The fumes had whetted my appetite. I loved the way the residue from the pyrotechnic composition coated the inside of your hands with a shiny silver dust and how your hands felt slippery when you rubbed them together.

We arranged all of our fireworks together under the stairs in the hall, examining the pictures on each box, conjuring up a vision of how the rocket would soar towards the sky and probably land next door in Mr Narayan's front yard. My father had been burning incense in the puja room, reading the Vishnu Sahasranama since before sun break. The house was filling up with the scent of sandalwood where there should have been the far sweeter scent of gunpowder. It was strange that when everything else conspired to give my father a headache, the cloying fragrance of the incense had somehow managed to spare him. My grandfather usually remained in his room until he had finished the daily crossword. Jayamma had learnt in only two days how to recognize a crossword, to fold the paper so that the puzzle faced upwards, and to hand it to my grandfather on a tray with his morning tea.

'If one has to drink coffee, the other has to drink tea!' she would complain. Nevertheless, it was with pride that she carried the silver tray that had never been used before or since, with her hands steady and held high to prevent the tea from tipping over the edge and staining the porcelain.

Generally, after his breakfast, my grandfather set out into the town. He had lunch with his old colleagues, meetings with his lawyer and his accountant. He visited the Lakshmi temple on his way back, though he was not known to be religious, and fed bananas to the monkeys within its compound walls. On this day, he emerged from his room, smiling, but not as jubilant as he had seemed the previous two mornings. He caught sight of the two of us huddling in the alcove underneath the stairs. Unlike me, Saleem had not gotten any new clothes for Diwali: although Saleem's family joined in the celebrations, their enthusiasm didn't extend that far. My grandfather took in Saleem's old khaki shorts and his washed, but still dirty, white t-shirt. He looked at Saleem with a mixture of pity and contempt.

'So, you have a partner in crime,' he said. 'What is your name?'

'Saleem Imran Khan.'

'Ah,' my grandfather said, as though he had been given an explanation.

Saleem was unable to take his eyes off my grandfather's moustache. His own father boasted a very fine moustache, but on my grandfather's upper lip was a truly spectacular sight.

'Well, the rain may be no good when it comes to firecrackers, but it is certainly a good thing when it comes to storytelling,' my grandfather said.

And it was. My grandfather's stories were strange tales that began and ended suddenly, but always took you by surprise. They were of gods entering men's bodies, travelling from heaven to earth with the mere blink of an eye, of women who fell in love with horses, mothers and daughters who exchanged souls, men who drowned in one land and woke up as women in another. We kept pleading, 'Just one more, Tata,' and the next story would begin riding on the tail of the previous one. We felt the hours pass by like galloping waves carrying us back and forth to places from which we never wanted to return.

Finally, he rose from the armchair. 'The old cannot keep up with the young,' he said. 'We need our rest.

'You are a fine looking boy, Saleem Imran Khan,' my grandfather declared, before retiring to his room. I felt a little cheated hearing those words again, addressed this time not to me, but to Saleem.

It was Saleem who pointed out to me that my grandfather and my father were not on speaking terms. This was a revelation to me, one that I felt I ought to have discovered myself. So I asserted that this was not the case, and that my father and grandfather spoke to each other all the time, just not in his presence.

We had just finished eating lunch after Jayamma had threatened to give away all of the rice to Julie if we did not 'eat lunch at once'.

Saleem was a year older than me and his voice was full of authority. He insisted he could identify when two people were not talking to each other; it was the same way with his father and his uncle, he explained. They would simply know when to pass the rice to the other without ever saying a word or looking up from their plates.

Since the rain was still beating down, fogging up windows, lifting up litter from the ground (the single slippers, the plastic bags, the cigarette butts) and dragging it through the streets, making it impossible to set foot outside, Saleem and I were forced to amuse ourselves indoors.

'I bet you a 5 Star bar,' he said, 'that we will not hear your father and grandfather speak a single sentence to each other all of today.'

All day, we loitered downstairs, waiting for my father and grandfather to be in the same space together while Jayamma chased us from room to room with a mop, wiping up our muddy footprints. My father seemed preoccupied at lunch. Saleem noticed that he did not enquire about his parents as he usually did, but soon settled into a reclining position on the sofa with his scarf tied around his head and an upturned copy of *The Divine Way* on his face.

By mid-afternoon, we were exhausted from waiting. We stole a wad of office stationery from my father's study and made paper boats out of it. We sent a whole fleet on their way and watched the boats drift rapidly in the current along the street till they crashed into a cement dustbin and capsized. It seemed that the monsoon had permeated even our house, infusing it with the same grey of the sky, seeping into the Cuddapah tiles, causing patches of dampness on the ceilings, and making us so drowsy that we went up to my room and fell into a deep sleep.

We were both awakened at the same time by voices coming from downstairs. The grey had thickened to black, and I felt that peculiar disconcerting sensation I have always experienced when falling asleep in light and waking up to the dark.

We could make out their voices now, identify the deep baritone of my grandfather, the slightly higher nasal voice of my father, but the words did not travel well, tripping over the stairs and reaching our ears disjointed.

Neither of us was thinking about the bet then. We could sense the heat generated from their tones—the friction caused not by raising one's voice, but by holding it back. Crouching at the stairs, we listened with great attention, as you do in the final scene of a movie; that scene when the audience falls silent without any prompting and every word reveals the solution to a previously unanswered puzzle.

'I will not set foot in this house again,' my grandfather said, his voice suddenly loud and clear, before both voices abruptly ceased. We imagined that one of them had left the room.

Suddenly, we heard the honking of Khan uncle's jeep. Even though Saleem lived just around the corner on Small Coramandel Street, his father had sent the driver because of the rain.

When I went downstairs, I felt my grandfather's absence. I ran into the kitchen to find Jayamma. I wanted to know if my grandfather was really gone—but again I was arrested by a conversation between Jayamma and my father.

'It's your father, isn't it?' I heard her saying.

While both Jayamma and the house had been happier when my grandfather was around, she was now quick to blame him for my father's unpleasant mood. 'Please can you keep your thoughts to yourself, Jayamma? Can you do that? I have far too many of my own.'

'That man can come in with all his Delhi ideas. They won't sell for ten paisa here,' Jayamma said. Now that Jayamma had identified the cause for my father's dispiritedness, she was no longer charitable towards my grandfather. 'What does he think? Let him try living here. He'll know then how far away he went when he moved to Delhi.'

'He's not coming back,' my father said, morosely. 'You heard him. He is never setting foot in this house again.'

I knew I would get the 5 Star bar; Saleem always honoured his bets. Yet, I did not feel as though I had won. Something heavy had fallen over my house. I wondered if it would ever stop raining.

I ran upstairs to my room and I lay on my bed. Something had settled inside me like a tablet dissolving in a glass of water, spreading a cloudy bitterness over me. It was the first time that I had heard a disagreement in my house. It was not unusual for Jayamma and my father to fling words at each other over whether the coffee beans had been brewed too long or who left the balcony door open for the monkeys. Invariably, these conversations ended with my father accusing Jayamma of a failing memory and senility, and Jayamma retorting that she wasn't the one with the need to bandage her head with a scarf every evening before the sun came down.

I did not go downstairs even when Jayamma called out my name three times. I had planned to tell her that I had a stomach ache. When she finally came up to my room to check on me, Jayamma said: 'My God, boy, are you going to vomit?' She touched my face and wiped the sweat from my forehead with her sari. A whiff of sour buttermilk clung to her. I shook my head. She appeared relieved even though she didn't seem to believe me entirely.

Jayamma must have understood the cause of my 'illness', because she said, 'Why do you think your grandfather has come here? He has travelled all the way to argue. If he was not a teacher, he would be a lawyer.'

Jayamma often made fun of situations that other people took seriously. When the head priest of the Lakshmi temple knocked himself dead with the heavy brass bell that hung from the ceiling, Jayamma said, 'That bell is going straight to heaven.' When the milkman returned to work three days after his daughter had run away with a truck driver from a neighbouring town, his face pulled down with shame, Jayamma remarked to him that his daughter was better off living in a town where they could tell cows from buffaloes and did not pass off one's milk for the other's.

The first time I saw Jayamma anguished, I, like her, had mistaken pain for a fever. Her eyes had turned a pale yellow and the cataract which had been forming in her left eye appeared thicker and greyer. Julie had not been seen for three days. At the end of each day of waiting, Jayamma threw out the uneaten rice on an aluminium plate crusted with so many ants that when she lifted it up, the ants would crawl in sudden confusion up onto her wrists and arms. She would then rinse off the plate under the tap in the backyard and, the following morning, place fresh food under the mango tree. The only signs of Jayamma's distress were her silence, which stopped conversation in our house altogether, and the fact that when she ladled sambhar onto our plates, I could see a swollen vein in her wrist that throbbed as if a ladybug were trapped inside her arm.

On the third afternoon, she put out the kerosene stove in the midst of making chapatis for dinner and told me that we were going to look for Julie. Together we searched for her from ditch to ditch along each of the streets in our neighbourhood, going as far as the temple tank. When old Mr Senthil, owner of The Coramandel King bicycle repair shop saw us on our knees peering into a drainage canal, he laughed and said, 'Going back to where you came from, Jayamma?'

Jayamma did not lash out at him in her usual way. She did not appear to have even heard his words. She had just caught sight of the white flash of Julie's tail, and she clapped her hands with delight before berating her, her words so tightly squeezed together that only Julie could have understood them. A few Sundays later, when Jayamma remembered Mr Senthil's remark, she marched up to the bicycle shop, where his son Raja was dousing a rubber tube in a drum of water, and said to him in a calm voice, 'Tell your father that people may forget what happens to them in their houses, but they never forget what happens to them in the ditches. And that washerwomen talk while they are washing clothes.'

Raja's mother often disciplined him with threats of, 'If you don't finish what's on your plate, I am giving you away to

Jayamma.' The sight of Jayamma that day, he said, had loosened his bowels and made the inside of his hands wrinkled even though he had only had them in water for a few minutes. Mr Senthil never made another comment, made self-conscious by Jayamma's knowledge of his incontinence. Whenever Jayamma went past his shop, he asked after her health cheerfully.

I was allowed to stay in my room for the rest of the evening. Jayamma brought up some rasam-rice on a plate and watched me while I ate it.

'You cannot go around vomiting every time they fight; I have enough things to do in this house already without having to mop up your vomit as well,' Jayamma said.

She felt my forehead to check if I had a fever. Satisfied, she took the empty plate from me and as she was leaving, said, 'That makes three of you, eating alone in your rooms tonight.'

'Is Tata back?' I asked jubilantly.

Jayamma grinned, pinched both my cheeks and left the room without a word.

Sometime later, when I heard the shuffle of footsteps, I knew somehow that it was my grandfather. I heard a knock on my door. It was confirmed. Neither Jayamma nor my father ever knocked.

I sat upright in my bed.

'Asleep already?' he asked, entering the room.

'No, Tata. I am wide awake,' I said, anticipating a story.

'The time for stories has passed,' he said, settling himself at the end of my bed.

'Jayamma said you are too sick to climb the stairs,' I said.

He laughed. 'She'd have it that way if she could. I plan on breaking all her rules.'

'Why aren't you reading?" he said, looking around the room in search of books.

'I don't like books,' I said, wishing immediately that I hadn't when I saw how his nostrils had begun to flare.

'Don't like books?' He was aghast. He sat at the edge of my bed. 'Do you know that when I was your age, we didn't have any light bulbs?' He paused. 'That's right! We had only oil lamps, and my mother always blew out my lantern at precisely nine every evening because oil was a costly commodity in those days. Each night, I would listen carefully for the clicking of the latch on her door, and quick as lightning, I would have the lamp going again with matches I stole once a month from the kitchen. I would have to strike the match with great care, looking upon the wind as a thief, because if I stole the matches too often, my mother would be sure to notice. Then I would read till the oil dipped to a level that would make my mother curl her lip questioningly, but would never give her the certainty with which she could accuse me of stealing her oil. Do you know why I would read every night?'

I shook my head.

'Curiosity,' he said. 'Do you know what that is?'

'No, Tata.'

'Curiosity is the desire to learn about things you don't even know exist.'

He considered the blank expression on my face and said with renewed effort, 'Now, have you seen that milk boils over?'

'Yes.'

'Well, do you know why milk boils over but water never does?'

I was shaking my head a lot.

'Aren't you curious to know why?'

I said, 'Yes', by which I meant that I understood the meaning of the word.

'You have to ask a lot of questions. Now if my mother had ever found evidence of my using up her precious oil, the ladle would have gone into the coals, and there would be a big ugly mark on my bottom. But it would not have stopped me. I was a very good thief,' he said, laughing. He stroked my hand. 'Will you remember to be curious?'

'I will, Tata,' I promised.

In the light, he looked tired. I saw that he was fading, and I did not want him to leave.

'Did you know my mother?' I said.

'I met her once,' he said truthfully, taking my hand in his. 'She was a lovely woman.'

'Appa has a photograph of her in the garage. He says he will show it to me.'

'Don't let him forget to do so,' my grandfather said. 'Remember. Be curious.'

'Don't go, Tata,' I said to him. 'Stay here.'

'If I tell you why I need to go back, will you keep it a secret?' he asked. I nodded.

'I have someone waiting for me there. A lady, a smart and intelligent woman who wants to stay by my side till I shake off this old mortal coil, as they say.'

'Bring her here too,' I said.

'She wouldn't like it here,' he said. 'This is a small town, that's a big city. And moreover, I am afraid no one here would like her.'

'Why not?'

'I wish there was a simple answer to that. Your grandmother was much loved here. I don't think I could bring anyone in her place. Let's just say that you cannot plant a mango tree in the shade of a banyan tree.'

'When will you die, Tata?"

'Soon,' he said. 'When I've put everything in order here.'

The difference in the house after my grandfather's departure was the difference one felt after leaving the cinema to re-enter the streets. You left one kind of commotion for another and even after the curtain had come down and you had walked through the door with the sign 'EXIT' shining in green above it, you heard the music for days and everything appeared in a different cinematic golden light.

'That man knew how to appreciate me,' Jayamma would say, ostensibly to me, as she folded the clothes into a basket, or brought my father his coffee. She had changed sides again, having grown accustomed to my grandfather's easy manner. He had also told her that she didn't look a day over sixty, and encouraged by his compliment, Jayamma had begun to powder her face every evening and apply a fresh red bindi on a forehead so wrinkled that the bindi rippled when she laughed.

Only my father seemed relieved. As abruptly as they had begun, the meditations ended. The tape recorder went silent and the man with the two voices was never heard again.

Soon, he even recanted his ban on peanuts and onions, and

Jayamma found innumerable innovative recipes that included both (the onion-peanut chutney had been a triumph). After the third day, he reinstated the ban citing a digestive problem, but by then, having been nauseated with the smell of peanuts frying, neither Jayamma nor I complained.

At the railway station, I had made my grandfather promise me just as he was about to enter his coach, that he would make all the necessary arrangements to have me visit him during one summer vacation.

He shook my hand and told me that he never imagined that he would have 'such a fine grandson'. To Jayamma he said, 'I hope I live long enough, Jayamma, so that I may have the pleasure of seeing you again.'

'You are lucky you have your mother's nose,' he said to me after he had boarded the train. During this entire time, my father remained subdued. However, just as the train began to depart and my grandfather's face was receding behind the window bars, my father suddenly shouted, 'Telephone me when you have reached.' Now that my grandfather was safely receding, my father was finding his voice again.

My grandfather's mention of my mother had startled me. Now, when I recall his words, how deftly he had uttered them just before the train pulled away, but loud and clear for our ears, I find myself smiling. He must have thought about those words carefully, and known how only the most casual utterances sometimes have the profoundest effects.

Then, however, on that still day except for the dull sky lowering steadily over us, as we drove back from the station, the fact that my nose resembled my mother's had seemed incomprehensible to me. She had never had a nose or even a face in my mind. She had simply been that word—Mother.

4

Not long after our conversation in my room, I received a postcard from my grandfather. It was of India Gate. The Gandhi stamp on the postcard had been stuck upside down. The postman handed it to me himself.

'Big enough to get mail now, are you?' he said, with a smile. I ran into the kitchen holding the postcard and screaming.

'Jayamma, post for me!' I exclaimed, running inside to find her.

My father, who had been in the hall giving instructions to one of the office boys, a young man with long arms and a perpetually puzzled look, shouted after me, 'What post is that? Bring that to me, Hari.'

He quickly scanned the writing while I waited and the young man, who didn't know what to do with his long arms, slapped his thigh in nervousness.

'It's from your grandfather,' my father said, finally, handing me the letter. 'He wants to give you his books. He hopes you are going to be a professor like him. Professor Hari Srinivasan!' he said, laughing.

The letter was written in English:

My dearest grandson,

I hope you haven't forgotten my words urging you to read more and to keep your eyes wide open. There is a very special reason for my request. I have, over the years, acquired a number of books, and there is no one to whom I would rather hand them over than to you, my dear child.

Your efforts will be rewarded in more ways than you can imagine.

Your loving grandfather,

Sarangan

My grandfather had overestimated my reading abilities, and if he had counted on my father offering to read it aloud to me, or in my asking him to do so, he had been wrong. Had Jayamma been literate, I might have asked her. Under the circumstances, the best I could do was to simply read a few of the words out loud, but I did not read them in any order, and the meaning that threaded them eluded me entirely. My father had mentioned the books to me, but books did not interest me. I sat in a pleasant daze on the steps of the kitchen, excited simply to hold a postcard that had once been in Delhi and was now resting in my hands; a postcard that had come especially for me, and I did not care too much that I didn't understand what my grandfather said. I spent the afternoon clutching the postcard and thinking about him. I remembered the remark he had made to me at the station about my nose resembling my mother's, and on an impulse I decided to look for the photographs my father had mentioned, to find out if what he had said was true.

The garage was attached to one side of the house and had housed a black 1952 Fiat at the time that my grandfather lived in Sripuri. My father had never learnt to drive nor had he needed to, rarely travelling farther than to the office or to Dr Jolly's clinic. In the absence of a vehicle, it had become a storage space for discarded furniture, household items in need of repair, tools, and other articles that had ceased to have relevance in my father's life. Jayamma had arranged the things one on top of the other, or pushed them tightly against each other, as though we could be expecting company anytime, for which we would have to make ample room. The garage shutter was usually left half open so that Jayamma could have easy access to it; it was too heavy for Jayamma to pull up and down, and my father always opened and closed it begrudgingly when he was required to do so. Jayamma maintained that no thief would dare steal from a house in which she resided, while my father reasoned that it would not be an altogether bad thing if someone disposed of all the junk that Jayamma insisted on storing.

Like everything under Jayamma's care, the garage had a look of orderliness that was forced upon it against its natural will. In the corners of the ceiling, indomitable spiders were renewing their efforts. Underneath the tin oil drums, behind the abandoned cane sofa or the disused standing fan, I imagined that there were large spotted lizards lurking. As soon as you entered the garage, you became enclosed by its darkness. You felt that the stillness concealed underneath it a sinister turbulence, and that it might spring upon you anytime. You prepared yourself to be startled, and you jumped when you felt your own shoelace against your ankle. It was as though having been abandoned, all these things had spawned a new life together. It was uncanny that although you could not see the dust, it still burned your nose with its thick ancient odour.

It was a bright Saturday morning. My father had gone to the temple, carrying with him a garland of jasmine that Jayamma had strung together with flowers from the creeper rambling all over our front gate. Jayamma was in the kitchen, sitting on the floor with her legs stretched out in front of her, patiently sifting batches of rice grains from a gunnysack and then pouring them into the big brass drum where the rice was stored.

I found the two red metal trunks easily. They were sitting one on top of the other and were wedged between a ramshackle cupboard and an unsteady three-legged chair. Each trunk was printed with the words 'Property of Srinivasan' in large white letters.

The trunks had been secured with two small identical gold locks. However, the hinge on the top trunk was breaking off, and it occurred to me that it would be easy to pry it apart using a stone. I looked about in the yard but I couldn't find anything that would suit my purpose. I went out onto the road where I noticed a small block of granite jammed under the front wheel of a scooter that had been parked on the side of the road. I used the stone to pound the hinge. The red paint flaked off immediately, and the metal too, began to crumble. Just then, I heard the wailing of the gate. Thinking that my father may have already returned from the temple, I ran to the entrance of the garage and, hiding behind a mirror, peered out into the yard.

It turned out to be Mrs Narayan, carrying a tray with a coconut and betel leaves, having come to invite us to some puja at the house. I ran out of the garage and hid behind the mango tree. Julie, who had been curled up in her usual spot, lifted her head, wagged her tail twice, and then rolled over onto her back. Her exposed stomach was covered in soft skin that folded at the slightest touch of my hand. I loved the slightly stale vapour that rose from her, a sticky smell that I grew to love because I had learnt to recognize it. I put my nose in her belly and inhaled her warmth.

With my head still resting on Julie, I watched Mrs Narayan kick aside her footwear at the entrance to our house and re-adjust the pleats of her heavy silk sari with her free hand. I sat up when I saw Jayamma appear at the front door. Mrs Narayan stepped back a little. She may have said that she would come back at a later time when my father was at home, because she left almost immediately, still clutching the tray to her large bosom.

Jayamma's eyes were experienced at spotting me.

'What are you doing there?' she said, casting a glance at the garage and then back at me. 'Come in and help me shell the peanuts.'

Later that night, Jayamma, who was never invited to any of the gatherings except when another hand was needed to help with the preparations or to sweep the yard, said to my father, 'She stepped back so fast, it is a pity she didn't trip over the steps.'

Mrs Narayan's unannounced arrival had forced me to abandon my project in a hurry and it only occurred to me that night after I was already under the covers, that I had forgotten the stone bearing the chipped marks of my efforts in the garage. When I went back to retrieve it the next day, I found the garage secured with a gleaming new brass lock. When I told Saleem, he said he could have broken any lock with his mere fist and had done so many times in the past.

All week, the weight of what I had done lodged somewhere

between my throat and my chest. At dinner each evening, I found the saliva in my mouth drying up, and the rice grains sticking to my palate. My father seemed to be considering the course of action he would take with me. I wanted to apologize, but I had never done so of my own accord before, and I didn't know how to begin. My father's eyes, which had been following my face all through these months, now rested firmly on the food on his plate. Their startling new indifference unsettled me, in much the same way that people who have lived all their lives by a railway station find themselves turning in their beds when away on holiday, longing for the whining of a train. The loss of my father's gaze, although it had been disconcerting while it had lasted, left me with an inexplicable urge to lift it from his plate, and place it back upon my face.

I was surprised when later that night I caught sight of him as I sat crouched on the floor-mat in my room, playing with the 'velvet bug' I had found, and which I had settled onto a bed of grass in a matchbox case. My father simply stood there, half-hidden, his hair standing upright and casting shadows like finger puppet men on the yellow curtain. Even when I looked up, he waited a moment before he entered my room. I stood up and almost bent over voluntarily, ready for my punishment, but I noticed that there was no cane in his hand.

He held a photograph in his hand. He raised it towards me and in a barely audible voice, said, 'Your mother.' He then placed it at the edge of my bed.

Once he had dropped the photograph, my father seemed embarrassed; his lips were twitching, trapping his words and dragging them back towards his mouth even before they had formed. Finally, he said, 'There is the photo you wanted.'

By the time I turned to look at the photograph, had run my fingers over the grainy paper and brought it so close to my face that I could smell the years under which it had laid in the trunk, my father had disappeared, and the velvet bug, too, had made its escape.

The photograph is not of my mother, Parvati.

It is of a young woman sitting on a bench. She is wearing a purple sari, and her hair is in a long plait and hangs over her right shoulder, although some strands appear to be lifted off her face as though caught in the path of a breeze. You think the photograph might have been taken on a cold day because of the manner in which she sits with her shoulders huddled together and her hands clasped tightly in her lap. She is almost, but not quite, looking at the camera, and the photographer seems to have caught her at a moment on her way to striking a pose; her eyes on their way to the lens, her lips on their way to forming a smile. In the background, there are shapes of two couples sprawled on the lawn.

On the back of the photograph, written in a hand that I did not recognize, were the words:

Vasan,

Thinking of you on a cold Christmas morning,

Devaki

I scrutinized her nose. At once, it struck me that it was nothing like my own nose. Hers was small and upturned, unlike mine, which was large and pointed. However, the more I looked at the photograph, the more it seemed to me that my grandfather had been right. That evening, as I stood in front of the mirror in the bathroom and gazed at my reflection, my nose, always long and pointed, became for that time just as small and just as upturned as hers.

When Jayamma found the photo by my bedside the following day, she smiled an enormous smile. 'Now, you have any questions about your mother, you can ask her directly, and stop bothering your father,' she said.

'Go, get a clip from the home office,' she ordered me. She then clipped the photograph to the hardback cover of one of my old Mathematics textbooks, and parting the pages in the middle, set it upright on the table in my room.

And that is how her photo still remains, in its makeshift photo frame, one of the few possessions that I have from my childhood.

Without realizing it, I memorized that photograph. I know, for instance, even though I haven't seen it for some time, that her left little finger sticks out unexpectedly from her clasped hands and that you can only see one of her feet, which is bare. For a long time, whenever someone mentioned their own mother, it was her face and not my mother Parvati's that would be summoned up, complete with the wrinkle in the middle of her forehead, which a crease in the photograph had bestowed on her. In the same manner that the word 'volcano' still brings up the image of the green crumbling volcano model that used to sit in the staff room of my school in Sripuri, the word 'moustache' will forever invoke my grandfather's, and the word 'dog' will always bring up a picture of Julie lying beneath the mango tree. Her face had been the missing illustration beside the word 'Mother' in my English textbook.

Having the photograph was like being given a wedge of wet chocolate cake when I had merely hoped for a toffee. It left me feeling full, and with no room to want anything else. I had nothing more to ask my father about her.

Slowly, my mother seemed to step out from the photograph and into my life. At school get-togethers and birthday parties, when I was asked why my mother had not come to pick me up like the others, I told them that my mother had guests at home, and I could almost see my mother, serving tea to Mrs Narayan from the silver pot that Jayamma rarely used, modelling her mannerisms on Zakira, Saleem's mother. When Mr Chalapati asked us to write a passage titled, 'What I did this Sunday', I wrote about my trip to the Sunday market, replacing Jayamma with my mother, both in my words and in my memory.

I am not sure whether it was the impact of the photograph or the sudden cessation of the rain that washed out the greyness and finally ushered into our house the blue light that had been filling the streets but evading us until then.

5

December came early, blowing its crisp cool breath. When the rain finally cleared, people came streaming into the streets in its place. Hawkers and vegetable vendors once again set up their carts along the pavements, those among them without carts squatting on the ground with their baskets of lemons or cucumbers in front of them. They told customers who complained of their steep prices that the rain had ruined their livelihood, that dampness still clung to the walls of their houses and while they bargained, they kept an eye on their children who were attempting to wander away from the roads and their gazes. The younger men sat on the compound walls lining the edges of colleges, swinging their legs within their bell bottomed trousers, running a comb through their hair and cooing at the women passing by. The women arrived in groups, oozing a collective lustre; like the tomatoes that sat atop the carts in pyramids, each giving and receiving from the other a share of the luminescence, creating an effect a single tomato or woman would never be able to achieve individually.

In contrast, my father became more withdrawn and spent longer hours at the office. As soon as he caught me waiting by the door for him, clutching the Class Reader in which I had

located a map of India and circled the red dot that was Delhi
with a pencil, he said, 'Don't mention the word "Delhi" to me
once more or I will go mad.'

It had become a habit with me to inquire after my grandfather
each day. I wanted to know how many days he had left to live,
how much of his stomach remained left to be eaten, and most
importantly, whether we could go to Delhi to visit him.

From what I learnt from Jayamma, there was little news
from my grandfather. Like me, she was keen to hear about his
health and rushed to the telephone whenever it rang thinking it
might be him. All she could confirm was that my grandfather
was very much alive, and who knew, if anyone was going to rise
from the dead, it would be him.

Each day, my father came home later and later, often arriving
only in time for dinner. During the meal itself, we ate silently
and when his eyes rested on mine, I thought he was not looking
at me at all, but at someone else far away; his hand at times
stopping on his way to his mouth, clutching a ball of rice so
tightly that the rice grains squeezed through his fingers and
scattered onto the table. He rarely raised his voice at me then.
In fact, he seldom spoke. He ate little, and often Jayamma had
to clear his plate, still heavy with a mound of uneaten food.

One day, as she was serving his food, Jayamma said, 'You
should have married a nice girl. You could have married Devaki.'

My father seemed to freeze in his seat at this remark. He
raised his eyebrows, indicating that she was not to speak in my
presence.

'He is just a child. What does he care?' she said,
underestimating my interest in this conversation. 'If you had
someone to love you, someone else to feed you, you would be

sitting here enjoying your rasam, instead of becoming an old man ten years before your time.'

'You don't know what you are saying, Jayamma,' he said.

'It's not too late,' Jayamma went on. 'The whole world knows that his Prema teacher is waiting around without getting married in the hope that you will ask her. And apart from her short legs, and a spotty complexion, there isn't anything wrong with her.'

'Mind your tongue. You don't know a damn thing about love.'

'Why don't I know? You think because I grew up in the gutter that there is no smell of jasmine there?'

'This has nothing to do with the gutter or jasmine.'

'Yes it does. This home is becoming a gutter—for you, for me and for this little boy.'

My father got up, poured some water from his drinking glass on his eating hand over his still unfinished plate and left the room.

Jayamma's words seemed to push my father further into a dark corner. He became moody and irritable and avoided our company. Yet, when he sat on the veranda, lost in the same page of *The Divine Way* for hours on end without reading it, Jayamma began to worry.

Jayamma was prone to paying little attention to my father's maladies. In private, she often laughed at his complaints. 'Don't talk so loudly. Don't you know your father has a headache?' she would begin when I was being troublesome, and midway through berating me, would burst out laughing.

His headaches were back. He banged his temples with closed fists. He reeked of the distinctive smell of Amrutanjan which he applied over and over again till his forehead was glossy with the ointment. He moaned. He turned clients away.

Feeling remorseful for pushing my father further into gloom, Jayamma attempted to treat him as though he was a convalescent, softly urging him to eat, occasionally chiding him when he declined.

'You should go see Dr Jolly,' she said. 'This time, I think my remedies are not going to cure your illness. You really are an ill man,' Jayamma told my father one night when he was doing particularly poorly. He had not touched his food at all, pushing away the plate of upma that had been laid in front of him to the far corner of the table, and asking instead for a glass of cold water.

Jayamma's earnest remark incensed my father. It was both a reminder to him that she had not taken him seriously on those previous occasions, and that on this particular occasion, there was indeed cause for concern.

'Keep quiet!' he told her, emphatically.

All evening, he paced between the hall and the veranda, unable to decide on a place in which to settle. In the hall he felt suffocated, even when, at his urging, Jayamma threw the windows wide open and a light wind rushed in and out of them laced with the scent of roses that it had plucked from the shrubs in Mr Narayan's yard. On the veranda, the mosquitoes mauled him, and sitting cross-legged on the rug in the hall with my Telugu textbook open in front of us, Jayamma and I winced when we heard the sound of his hand slapping his thigh or arm in frustration.

'Dr Jolly cannot help me, Jayamma,' he said, finally, before deciding to retire to his room. 'It's only eight o'clock; even the boy is not ready for bed yet,' Jayamma shouted after him, but his back was already turned. This change in my father's attitude towards Dr Jolly's treatment was unexpected and took Jayamma by surprise. Each night, she took to bringing him a tumbler of hot sweetened turmeric milk, and as she did with me, waiting by his side till he drank it. Then, as he reclined in his chair, she would gently massage his forehead with coconut oil that had been heated up in an iron ladle which she reserved for this purpose. The house would fall so quiet that the sound of the crickets outside would seem to reverberate within the walls of our living room. Even though a radio would be turned on next door, or people on the road were talking, these sounds would invariably get caught in some invisible mesh, barring their levity from entering our house. On nights when I woke up to go to the toilet, or because I had wetted my bed, I would find the light in my father's room still burning, and a cloud of incense smoke hovering beside his door. If I listened, I'd hear him groaning, the creaking of the bed as he sat up in it, and a moment later, the thud, when having changed his mind, he would drop back onto it. I, like Jayamma, thought my father was an ill man.

Jayamma always said that there was no better sound to wake up to than the voice of the man who sang the morning prayers at the mosque. It sailed over the flat white rooftops every morning to reach us through our windows.

By the time the prayer had finished, she would have bathed, swept the yard, and painted a kolam on the front steps of the house with a wet block of chalk. Then, she readied the kitchen. First, she boiled the milk which, if the milkman had arrived on time, would be sitting in an aluminium pail on the doorstep. She packed the coffee powder into the filter, pouring boiling water into it only after she had heard the shuffling of my father's footsteps in the corridor, so that the slender brown coffee would not seep through too soon, and would remain fresh for my father's six-o'clock-coffee. Next, she set about making breakfast, grating coconut for the chutney, checking on the batter for the idli or dosa that had been left overnight to ferment in a pot covered with muslin, and cutting the vegetables for the sambhar. By the time my father had finished bathing, the house would be heavy with the smell of frying dosas and sambhar bubbling in its pot.

Then, I would need to be readied for school, my lunch packed, and after we had left, there were other things to do: rooms to be dusted and swept before being mopped with Jayamma's homemade disinfectant that left the house smelling of overripe roses, clothes to be washed and rations to be bought. In the afternoons, when she finished the morning's chores and had fed Julie, she unrolled a bamboo mat onto the kitchen floor and took a nap during what she called her 'intermission'. Before my father's four-thirty-coffee, she would have to wrest herself free from the cocoon of warm sleep, and begin again the cycle of cooking and cleaning. While her duties fluctuated in their timings according to my father's behavioural rhythms, the duties themselves never varied. It is possible that it suddenly occurred to Jayamma that no one had ever massaged her head or brought her a cup of coffee, or she had simply grown tired of my father's behaviour. Or perhaps thirty years in the household had worn and cracked her nerves, as well as the soles of her feet.

One night, when my father had become quite accustomed to the head massages and the hot cup of milk, she simply stopped providing them. Agitated, my father yelled, 'My head, Jayamma, the pain is terrible. Bring the coconut oil, and this time, make it really hot.'

Jayamma said, 'There is only so much I can do for you.'

For the next week or so, my father did not eat at home.

'I've already eaten something. No need to worry yourself for me,' he would say markedly, before disappearing into his study.

I learnt to tiptoe around him. I often waited for him to leave the room before dashing across the hall to enter the kitchen or to run into to my room. Jayamma disregarded him for much of the day, too, but towards the evening her resolve would soften, and she would place a glass of hot milk on the table, just in case he should desire it later.

A few days later, when I had already been fed, the dishes washed up, the kitchen floor swept and wiped, my father had still not returned home. Jayamma remained calm while she performed her daily rituals, absentmindedly singing the same refrain of a song over and over again. But once she had finished the last of her chores, and there was nothing else to occupy her mind, she began to wring her hands in panic.

Jayamma led me to the front yard, holding me by the hand as though she was fearful of being left alone. Outside, it had grown dark. Just beyond our gate, a crowd had gathered on the street. In the lamplight, their heads appeared large and looming.

We found that the cause for the commotion was a long and

slender rat snake. Someone had crushed its head with a stone, and now a man was dangling it from the end of a stick and deciding where to dispose of it. The sight of the snake only intensified Jayamma's anxieties.

'First, your father doesn't show up, and then a snake lands up dead at our doorstep!' she said, as though the two events were connected.

She thought she should telephone someone, but she could not think of whom to call. Besides, never having needed to dial a telephone, and only on rare occasions required to answer it, Jayamma wasn't sure how to use the instrument.

Finally, she decided that we should look for him in his office.

'He's probably fallen asleep at his desk,' she said, aloud to herself.

Hand in hand, we walked to my father's office, hoping to find him there. We found the door bolted, and a middle-aged man living in the house adjacent to the office peering at us through his window.

'They closed for the day a long time ago,' he yelled to us in a voice that had only half broken. 'Nobody ever does any work in that office.'

When we arrived back at the house, Jayamma squatted on the floor outside the puja room and began to pray. I was sleepy, but Jayamma made me lie down beside her and rest my head on her lap. From time to time she stroked my face, a habit which seemed to provide her with more comfort than it did me. The funereal voice of a woman singing to her lover came streaming in from the Narayans' radio, but was abruptly cut off by an advertisement jingle for tube lights sung by a man in falsetto. Soon, I drifted off into sleep.

I awoke suddenly, with the familiar sound of Julie's barking. We heard the sound of a car door being slammed, and then the tell-tale creaking of the gate. We rushed to the parapet on the veranda. Two men, one on either side of my father, were helping him up the steps to the front entrance. Even in the anaemic glow of the zero watt bulb, I could distinguish the tall frame, the broad shoulders, and the large conical head of Khan uncle. The other man turned out to be the driver of the jeep.

'Jayamma, you had better put him to bed immediately,' Khan uncle said when he saw us. He had about him the look of a man called upon to act in an emergency. His sleeves were rolled up, and in contrast to the look of agitation on my father's face, Khan uncle's expression was calm and purposeful.

When Khan uncle addressed most people they responded to him with obedience. Jayamma was not one of them.

'What happened? Is he sick?' she questioned him, her tone suggesting that she held him accountable for the condition my father was in.

'Now, Jayamma,' Khan uncle said, with strained patience in his voice. 'You know exactly what is wrong with him.'

She turned to my father. 'But where were you all this time? I've been worried sick.'

'All in good time, Jayamma,' Khan uncle intervened.

My father appeared to have been crying. At the time, of course, I had not understood that he was drunk. His eyes were a dull pink, the colour of watered down milky tea, his upper eyelids swollen, and from one corner of his left eye, a broken capillary had caused a bright red streak to radiate towards his pupil.

When Jayamma searched his face for clues, it seemed to

shrink into itself, reminding me of the expression I had once seen on a mongrel dog's face at school, after one of the canteen workers had broken its leg with a length of bamboo as punishment for urinating near the wash basin. My father did not look at Jayamma. He turned instead to me, but I seemed to cause him more pain, for he collapsed onto the floor, covered his face with his hands, and convulsed into sobs.

'Go inside, Hari! Go to your room and stay there,' Khan uncle commanded me.

Disregarding his orders, though careful not to be seen, I went into the hall, climbed on top of the sofa, and watched them from behind the iron grills that ran across the window.

'Come on, Vasan,' Khan uncle was urging my father. To Jayamma he said, 'Water and a towel.' A light went on in the Narayans' house.

'We had better get him inside,' Khan uncle said to the driver of the jeep.

Together, with Khan uncle telling my father firmly, 'At the count of three, Vasan, one . . . two . . . three,' they helped him to his feet. The driver, who was a young man with long, curly hair and a bristly moustache, had a look of amusement on his face. Reading his mind, Khan uncle said, 'Not a word about this to anyone. One word from you, and you can forget about driving again in this town. Do you understand?'

'Yes, Sir,' his voice was respectfully low.

Fearful of being spotted, I ran into my grandfather's room, which had become his room in my mind ever since he had occupied it, and hid behind the curtain. I pulled it open just wide enough to observe Khan uncle prop up my father against the bolsters on the sofa. Jayamma was pressing a tumbler of water to my father's lips but much of it ran down his neck,

which she wiped persistently with the end of her sari. My
father, who in all this time had not spoken, suddenly clasped
Khan uncle's hand.

'Thank you, Raheem.'

Khan uncle nodded to the driver, who understood the
meaning of the gesture and immediately left the room.

'Go inside,' he told Jayamma. 'I want to talk to Vasan.'

'Why should I go inside? What has he gone and done? I have
a right to know.'

Khan uncle laughed. 'Very well, Jayamma. You're right. I
don't think anything could shock you in any case. You know
where your ayya has been today?'

He sank into a chair, shook his head from side to side and
then crossed one leg over the other, as if he was getting ready to
tell the story well.

'I still cannot believe it. When that boy came in and told me,
I was certain it was some other Vasan he was talking about. I
said to myself, "It has to be some other fellow".'

'Please Raheem,' my father pleaded in a weak voice, but
Khan uncle went on as though he had not heard him. Jayamma
sat down on the floor beside Khan uncle.

'Anyway, there I was locking up the front door, when I hear
this little boy shouting out to me from the gate, "Khan Sahib,
Khan Sahib, your friend Vasan is lying like a dead man, and you
had better come and get him or the fellows are going to dump
him into a rickshaw or onto the steps of some shop." They send
this little boy to come and tell me this—he wouldn't have come
up to my waist, seven or eight years old, at the most. I tell you,
Jayamma, it was a shock to hear those big words coming from
the lips of such a young boy. Too afraid to come and tell me
themselves, the bastards!'

My father slumped onto his side, away from the two of them, and buried his face into the sofa's arm rest.

Khan uncle paused just long enough for Jayamma to comprehend what he had said. 'Anyway,' he continued, 'he is lying on the floor, and they don't know what to do with him. Time is running along, and in such places, they don't have patience for people taking up room like a wretched old cow sprawled on a street. There is more traffic there than there is on Bazaar Street. So they start to ask a few questions, and you know this town, it doesn't take long for them to figure out who their eminent guest is. It's a good thing they sent the boy to my house. Imagine my surprise, Jayamma! Luckily, the driver was around and so I managed to sort things out quite quickly. Or else, who knows?'

'Don't!' Jayamma said.

'Don't what?' Khan uncle was not used to being interrupted.

'Don't humiliate him,' she said.

Surprised, Khan uncle slapped the arm of the chair he was sitting in.

'Well,' he said. 'You never cease to surprise me.'

'It's okay,' Jayamma said. 'You should know. It's nothing that unusual in this town.'

He turned quiet. 'This is what I like about you the most, Jayamma,' Khan uncle said. 'Your fierce loyalty.'

Jayamma's words seemed to have had a calming effect on him. He walked over to my father, who attempted to sit up on the sofa, but slid back against one of the bolsters.

'Any woman would be lucky to marry you,' he said to my father. 'It is time.'

'No, please don't mention that word to me!' my father said, sounding afraid.

'Marriage? '

'Never mention that word to me. It is my penance that there will never be any other woman in my life.'

'I don't know whether to laugh or to be angry with you,' Khan uncle said, with unexpected gentleness in his voice. 'I was happy I was there to help you. But it could have been a different story had I not. This is a mean, unforgiving town. People's stories are told over and over again for years. I don't want that to happen to you. Be careful. You don't want your son hearing them.'

After Khan uncle left, Jayamma stayed with my father, swathing his forehead with a wet towel, and stroking his hair tenderly.

'Where is Hari?' my father asked suddenly.

'He is asleep.'

'I want to see him, Jayamma. Bring him to me.'

There was a feverish edge in his voice that made me want to go to him, but also made me apprehensive. I felt a sense of pride that my father had remembered me even in the state that he was in.

Jayamma cut him short. 'Nonsense, you've done enough for one day.'

I lay awake a long time, even after Jayamma herself had dozed off on the mat by the sofa, and broke the night rhythmically with her heavy breathing. By the time I had awoken the following morning, my father had left the house.

In the morning, the phone rang.

There was no one to pick it up. I lifted the receiver and held it to my ear.

The voice of my grandfather came booming.

'Happy birthday!' he said.

'Tata! You are alive!'

'Yes, of course I am,' he said. 'How else was I going to wish you a happy birthday?'

'Is it my birthday in Delhi also?'

He laughed.

'Where is your father?' he asked.

'He has gone out, Tata.'

'It's quite all right. I wanted to talk to you anyway. How are things at school?'

'Okay,' I said. 'There is a girl in my class who is taller than me.'

'So? All the girls I've known have been taller than me. Height has nothing to do with stature. Tell me, have you been reading?'

'Yes, Tata,' I lied.

'My grandson,' he said. 'It's okay if you lie to me. I don't mind being made a fool of. Just don't lie to yourself. Okay?'

I felt chastised and close to tears. 'Will you come to Sripuri again?'

'I won't have time to come again,' he said. 'I think about you often, and all the things I could have done differently.'

Jayamma spotted me and grabbed the receiver from my hand. She patted me to indicate that I should run along. She had forgotten about my birthday. I found Julie in the veranda and let her lick my palm.

Around midday, my father returned bearing a box of red glass bangles for Jayamma, and a skipping rope for me.

'Is this for my birthday?'

He had forgotten it was my birthday as well. He yelled to Jayamma that she should make some payasam to celebrate. She came running with Julie jogging behind her. She tried to pick me up and failed. She bent to kiss me. 'Forget payasam. I am going to make appams, his favourite sweet.'

'Don't forget to put sugar in it like you did last time,' my father said.

His face had altered overnight. Now, his eyes were bright, his hair oiled and smoothed across his head. There hung about him the scent of Mysore Sandalwood soap, and when he suggested that we bring out the firecrackers that we had packed away in the chest of drawers, there was levity in his voice. One by one, we sent the rockets flying into the Narayans' yard.

Mr Narayan, his patience worn thin when one of the rockets landed amidst his rose bushes, said rather loudly to his gardener, 'Wretched boys! Throwing rockets into someone else's garden!'

His daughter, Sita, was a year younger than me but taller by a head, and she smiled and winked at me over the compound wall.

Despite the turbulence in the household, outside the day seemed to be lifting off from the horizon with the wind. When I went to the yard in search of Julie, I felt the delicate touch of a breeze lift my hair from the back of my neck, and the sky was filling up with kites winding and unwinding around buildings and clouds.

Later that afternoon, I was surprised to catch sight of my father hurriedly entering the gate clutching a large brown paper bag in his hand. I hadn't noticed he was gone.

'What a surprise,' my father said, rushing to meet me. He shook my hand.

'I have some serious business with you,' he told me jokingly. 'Would it be all right if I came in?'

Speechless, I watched as he entered the house.

'Good morning, Madam,' he said to Jayamma, hovering by the chest of drawers. 'May I come in?'

'Say Madam again,' Jayamma said, giggling.

'Good morning, Madam,' my father repeated, pleased to make Jayamma happy.

'Well, Sir,' he said addressing me. 'As I was saying, I have come on some important business.'

'Is the bag for me?' I asked, my eyes already having taken note of it, and trying to decipher its contents from its unusual shape.

'Indeed. Very perceptive of you, Sir. I think what I have here might interest you.' We made our way into the living room.

One by one, he emptied the contents of the bag onto the rug in the living room with great deliberation, as though he were a door-to-door salesman. First, he took out a bottle of Fevicol, then a pair of scissors. Out came a spool of white thread and other small items I was unfamiliar with. So far, none of these articles interested me. Finally, he brought out a large roll of bright orange paper.

'We are going to make a kite!' I exclaimed.

'As soon as Jayamma brings out the strongest and leanest stick from her broom.'

'Say Madam,' Jayamma insisted.

Jayamma brought out her coconut broom and let my father pick his own stick. Her curiosity was aroused, and she lingered to watch.

'This is for the spine,' he said, bending the stick he had chosen to test its tensile strength. Satisfied, he placed it carefully beside the other items.

As my father proceeded to sketch the outline of the kite on the paper, he ordered Jayamma to bring him the iron ruler from his office desk, then registering the look on her face, decided to fetch it himself. Placated, Jayamma offered to hold the paper straight.

'Are your hands dry, Jayamma?' my father said. In response, Jayamma smoothed the paper emphatically with the flat of her palm.

'No harm checking.'

My father offered me the pair of scissors.

'Careful,' Jayamma yelled.

I insisted I would be the one to glue the broomstick to the paper. I relished the wet white Fevicol on my fingers, and further still when the glue dried half-heartedly and left my thumb and forefinger sticking to each other.

'Let's see if we've built her with a heart,' my father said when our kite had dried out under the full throttle of the ceiling fan. Though a little uneven on the sides, it had turned out well, the orange already turning golden when we held it against a light bulb.

When we took it to the rooftop and I thrust the kite into the air it tugged at once, like a dog on a leash, checking how far it could go and struggling to break free of my grip.

I had never seen Jayamma so excited, telling me all the time that I was doing it wrong. I was holding the string incorrectly. I had let go of it too soon. I was not a natural kite flyer.

Soon, they were both laughing, their hands on my back, patting me gently and urging me on. The kite, just like a dog, was out of wind, and flopped down no farther than the Narayans' backyard.

6

At home, I was surprised to find that we had a guest. My father had few friends throughout his life. He avoided people; politely excusing himself from weddings, turning down Mrs Narayan's frequent invitations to pujas, pretending to be asleep on buses rather than having to endure a conversation with an enthusiastic travel companion. As a result, we had few visitors to our house other than the office boys, and one or two satisfied clients who dropped by occasionally with well wishes and a parcel of sweets.

A tall, slender man, a little older than my father, sitting stern and upright on the sofa beside him, turned to look at me. He had short grey hair on his head, but at the sides, the hair had grown inexplicably long and hung over his ears, giving him an incongruous boyish look at odds with his frame and demeanour. He wore slim, silver-rimmed glasses and clutched a small, navy-coloured, hardbound book in his large hands.

'My son, Hari,' my father said when I walked in.

'Hello, Junior Vasan,' the man said, with a laugh that transformed his face in degrees. A moment earlier, he may have been Jacob Esau, the headmaster of our school, and now he was smiling at me with the tenderness of my grandfather.

'A replica of you,' he proclaimed to my father.

'Oh you think so?' my father asked, genuinely pleased.

'Carbon copy,' he affirmed.

'Hari, come and say hello to Mr Selvaraj.'

Mr Selvaraj put an arm around me while I stood beside him.

'So Hari, did you learn anything important at school today?' he asked.

I shook my head. He laughed.

'See, Mr Vasan, children are so innocent! They always say what's on their mind.'

'So, when you are not at school, what do you like doing best?'

'I like flying kites.'

'Wonderful. That's what I like to hear. These are the simple pleasures of childhood, Mr Vasan. So easy to enjoy as a child, so difficult to do so as an adult—flying a kite and watching it soar higher than the tallest building; riding a bicycle downhill with your legs stretched out, fearing you'll come crashing down, but almost wishing that you would; running in the rain; playing in the mud . . .'

At that moment, Jayamma, who had been listening from behind the kitchen door, came into the living room.

'You look filthy,' she told me. 'What have you been doing, rolling in mud?'

'He is only a child, Jayamma,' my father argued, getting carried away by Mr Selvaraj's nostalgic tone. 'That is what children do.'

'I'll remind you of that the next time you shout at me when he goes around leaving his dirty paw prints on one of your files.'

However, Jayamma was in no hurry to get me cleaned up. She led me into the kitchen and made me a cup of Horlicks. She was in one of her foul tempers. What was left of her hair had come undone from the plait in which she normally wore it. She twisted it back into a knot with considerable irritation. The milk had boiled over from the pot and had formed a sticky layer on the kitchen counter.

'Your father is making all sorts of unusual friends these days,' she said, scrubbing the counter surface vigorously with a ball of coir.

She made me wait in the kitchen while she took them their coffees.

'Jayamma, you forgot the sugar!' we heard my father's voice calling out as soon as she had returned.

Pretending not to have heard him, Jayamma said, 'You really do look dirty. Let's go get your hands and feet washed, and get you out of that uniform.'

'Jayamma!' he called again, this time sounding impatient. With a sigh, Jayamma picked up the bowl of sugar.

'He's a Christian,' Jayamma informed me in my room. 'Your father's new friend is a Christian.'

Mr Selvaraj, we were soon to discover, was the minister at the local Anglican church. St. Thomas's Church was located at the eastern end of the town, where the last of the brick houses gave way to the squatters' settlements and then to the sprawling slums just past the green sign that read, 'You are now leaving Sripuri. Thank you for visiting'. The sign was peculiar, because our town wasn't the sort of town that people visited. Everyone had laughed when it had first been erected. It had been an idea stolen from another town, or another city, brought in by an eager municipality bureaucrat on a transfer assignment. He had not stayed, but the sign had.

On Sundays, Jayamma would sometimes take me with her to the weekly market set up in the vacant lot by the church. On our way, we would pass by the families on their way to church for the Sunday service; the women wearing their shiny polyester saris, even though it was so hot that the folds stuck to the inside of their thighs; the men holding the hands of children bribed with promises of lollipops and toffee cigarettes from the market.

Often, someone would recognize Jayamma, and if they were unable to hide behind a tree or turn away from her gaze in time, they would inquire after her health politely, and tell her that she was looking well.

'Going off to see your new and better God?' she would ask, unforgiving. Fearing Jayamma's sharp tongue, they would hold their own, smiling, staring down at their feet, and wondering why this old woman, and a common maid at that, was able to unsettle their stomachs simply with a look.

The market itself was a maze. In the midst of the rows and rows of vegetables piled up in mounds, here a woman would be selling tops, making it spin on her thumb in demonstration of its superior qualities; there a man would be carving the flesh of mangoes into the shape of flowers. There were birds, their feathers dyed pink and blue and yellow, fluttering in confusion from one side to another in their cages. There was a dark scent of cloves in one corner that died down when I turned another, giving way to the thick ripe smell of jackfruit or banana. With my attention caught here and there, beneath my feet I would occasionally feel the pleasant squelch of a discarded vegetable as it ground down to pulp.

My father found the market filthy and rarely accompanied us. He complained about the rotting vegetables, the shrieking voices, and the multitude of children. He abhorred the sight of the caged birds. He found the whole process of bargaining exhausting, and yet could not help feeling annoyed if anyone tried to take advantage of him.

The organ music would come blaring from the speakers attached to the gulmohar trees within the church compound. A little while later the singing would commence, the voices in unison, but some louder, more distinctive, and more off-key than the others. A few of the vendors, having heard the same music week after week, would absentmindedly hum along.

'This is how they get you, Hari,' Jayamma said during one visit. 'Mind what goes inside that head of yours.' She shook her head slowly as though a heavy thought was travelling from one side of her mind to another.

Several of Jayamma's friends from the washerwomen's settlement had converted to Christianity since she had left it to work for my grandfather in 1935, the year she was widowed.

In the beginning, she had not been allowed in the kitchen and into certain areas of the house. My grandfather had a small outhouse built for her to reside in, but all that had changed with my grandmother's illness, and her ensuing death. Jayamma became a permanent fixture in the house, and the outhouse was demolished to make room for the garage.

At first, Jayamma had often found excuses to return to the washerwomen's settlement: a wedding, a funeral, a festival. Over time, however, she became alienated from the women who had once gone with her to temples, poured milk down anthills to feed the snakes on Nagapanchami, prayed with her when her husband was sick, and had lit lamps alongside her on Diwali. She held Jesus Christ responsible for her misfortune and treated all Christians with a mixture of resentment and envy. In my room, as Jayamma was peeling me out of my clothes, I told her about a kite I had seen. She shushed me and stopped midway whilst buttoning my shirt so that she could listen to the conversation between my father and Mr Selvaraj.

'I must advise you to think over the matter carefully, Mr Vasan,' Mr Selvaraj was saying. 'These decisions are not to be made lightly.'

'I understand, Mr Selvaraj. Should I call you "Father"?'

'No, that is not necessary.'

'You see Father—I think I prefer "Father" if you don't mind?'

'It doesn't matter what you call me. I am still the same person.'

'You see, Mr Selvaraj, perhaps I shall stick to Mr Selvaraj for the moment—'

'Yes that's fine,'

'I resisted this for a long time,' my father said. I have spent a long time reading up on religions. But I made a very foolish mistake. I thought that I could learn about religions from books. And sometimes, these books were so badly written that I either got a headache or I fell asleep while reading them. I thought I had learnt a lot. In fact, I considered myself quite knowledgeable on every religion from Judaism to Hinduism. But how wrong I was! When I came to your church last week, I realized for the first time how I have lived in an illusion all this time.'

'That is the first step, Mr Vasan. Our knowledge is always limited. And the sooner we see this limitation, the closer we are to improving our understanding of the world.'

'Exactly. Father, I mean, Mr Selvaraj, when I came to your

church, I came there on an impulse. My heart felt heavy, and I wanted to go someplace quiet and sacred. I thought of going to the temple first but that is the last place you can find quiet these days. Senseless fellows—so noisy—shouting as though God is going to confuse their wishes with someone else's. If you don't mind my saying, the church was not much better. Most of the people singing were out of tune and it was horrible to hear, but despite the din, my heart was serene. And that is the important thing, isn't it?'

'Being in a church is a powerful experience, Mr Vasan. You were in a house of God. It does not necessarily mean that you are ready for the Christian faith.'

'But Father, I felt more like myself in the church than I have in the last five years. I felt calm, as though I really could leave my worries to someone else. I felt like a child.'

'There is a little of the child in every one of us.'

'But it was as though I had finally found a way towards peace. You tell me, then? Why should I, who ought to have gone to the temple, find that my feet, as if on their own accord, are marching to the church? Why should I find myself crying when I heard your sermon? When you said, "The kingdom of heaven is within you", I could feel that kingdom within me. If God is directing me to his abode, is it right that I should forsake his will?'

'If that is indeed the Lord's will, Mr Vasan, neither you nor I have any say in the matter. Acknowledging Him as God is the first step. But living a Christian life is no simple matter. You must understand the implications of the faith before you enter it. As a servant of the Lord, I am here to guide you. I urge you to look inside yourself—'

Jayamma had heard enough.

'He is harder to look after than you,' she told me.

My father had made up his mind. This was how my father behaved. His convictions succeeded his decisions. A week or so before the actual conversion took place, my father began to prepare himself and the house for a Christian life. First, he piled up all the books that he had accumulated over the years on the living room floor. Among them, books on meditation, three volumes of essays by Swami Mahimananda, numerous slim magazines of *The Divine Way* that had arrived monthly from Madras, a biography on the Jain prophet Mahaveera, and two hardbound copies of the *Bhagavad Gita*, one of which I had been awarded when I won a poetry recitation competition at school. He ran his fingers over them tenderly before he laid them face down in a cardboard box. Next, he rifled through his desk drawers and pulled from them pamphlets on yoga, and one titled 'Spirituality and Diet', as well as the tape of the man with the two voices chanting.

When he was taking down the framed picture of Lord Srinivasa, which had hung from a nail over the entrance to our house, Mr Narayan, who was in his yard, casually berating his servant boy for not sweeping properly, ambled over to him. He saw my father prop up a stool against the frame of the door, and then climb onto it so he could reach the photo.

Jayamma had forbidden me from any involvement with my father's recent activities. My father did not protest, perhaps knowing that if he conceded to a few of her lesser demands,

Jayamma would be more inclined to accept the major change he had inflicted on us. However, since his acquaintanceship with Mr Selvaraj and his decision, my father had become more agreeable. As a result, I found myself less afraid of him, and more fascinated with the new changes taking place in my household. Despite Jayamma's warning, I stood in position by the stool, so that when he took down the photo, he could hand it to me.

'Anything happening?' Mr Narayan asked, sticking his head over the compound wall. 'Can I help?'

An active member of the Coramandel's Residents Association, Mr Narayan had become successful at guising his curiosity as civic duty.

'I am taking down the picture,' my father offered as explanation, concentrating on prying the frame loose from the nail to which it clung, and without turning around to look at Mr Narayan's face.

'Aaah. Time for a change, I see. Are you going to a hang a new one? They are selling some very fine pictures these days.'

'I am undecided.'

'What's that, you are what?'

'I don't know as yet,' my father said, bending down to hand me the picture. He smiled at me.

'Give it to Jayamma. She will be happy.'

As I ran inside, I heard Mr Narayan say, 'What's that you said? You're going to hang what there?'

I don't know whether my father told him or the blank wall was explanation enough. I do know, however, that from then until the day Mr Narayan fell down in the bathroom and broke his hip at a time when Mrs Narayan was away at the sari shop, which forced him to send Sita running to our house for help, the two men did not exchange a word.

My father had some difficulty removing the large brass idol of Ganesha in the hall. When he finally shifted it with considerable effort, it revealed a lighter patch on the floor that shone like a bald spot on a head.

'I am taking this,' Jayamma said of every article he removed, although she had nowhere to take it except to another corner of the house. Jayamma was tormented by my father's decision to convert religions, and it seemed to propel her further toward her own. She cleared a corner in her room, and all the discarded gods who, in the complacency of their status in the house had accumulated dust and grown dull, glistened anew with Jayamma's renewed interest. By the time he turned his attention to the puja room, the two of them were barely on speaking terms. Jayamma retreated into the kitchen and refused to help.

My father refrained from being drawn into discussions with her, ignoring her pleas to rethink his 'madness', and proceeded to strip the house of any item that denoted his older faith.

'You will not understand, Jayamma,' he said, standing in the kitchen beside her, nudging her elbow with the tips of his fingers affectionately. 'I am a better man.'

'You are not making a single adjustment to yourself. How is that making you a better man? All the adjustments you are making are to the house. And I am the one who looks after it.'

He seemed to consider this. 'I don't want to carry this burden for six lifetimes or more. I want to be forgiven in this lifetime.'

'And this other one will?'

'Yes, He will.'

'And how does that change anything?'

'It will give me peace of mind, Jayamma.'

'Your peace of mind is worth only ten paisa to me if it's going to steal mine.'

He fiddled with the lid of the coffee filter.

'Your coffee's coming. Go and sit in your chair and don't bother me. You had better not take anything away from my kitchen,' she warned him. 'If my Krishna leaves,' she said, referring to the idol that sat on top of the kitchen shelf, in front of a bottle of Horlicks, 'I am leaving with him.'

On the day that my father officially became a member of the church, there was an unexpected storm. A branch broke off the mango tree and fell onto the electric pole on the street cutting off the power supply for two days.

'We have our own mini Kali Yuga on Coramandel Street,' Mr Narayan said. 'What else do you expect with the things that are happening around here?'

We lived in a predominantly Hindu neighbourhood. On our street most of the families were distantly related to one another. These relationships were unearthed only during weddings and funerals, when people laughed and wept like brothers and sisters, and expected the honours reserved for kin. At other times, when there was a dispute about the well water, or the encroachment of a compound wall, these familial ties were buried by mutual consent. Small Coramandel Street, which ran from Coramandel Street and turned like an elbow of an arm towards the mosque, was occupied by a few of the town's most prominent Muslim families.

Thrown together thus, the Muslims and the Hindus had established a reasonable harmony between themselves. Only on rare occasions, during Ramadan for instance, would you find Mr Jayaram, who occupied the house at the corner of the two streets, complaining about the goats that were tied to the front gates and the ensuing blood on the roads after they had been slain.

Michael Pinto, Mr Jacob Esau and Mr Selvaraj all resided in the less cramped, newer suburbs that had just begun to crop up on the other side of the river, causing me to assume then that only Christians were allowed to reside in that area of town.

Mr Narayan's canards brought a spate of inquisitive guests to our house. They carried with them tales of people they had known who had changed religions on their deathbeds or at other convenient times.

They quoted songs. 'By whichever name you call him, Ram, Raheem, or Jesu, he is still the same bhagwan.' Unaccustomed to this attention, my father ordered Jayamma about, making her bring endless cups of tea and samosas, so that in the confusion of teacups rattling, and crumbs being spilt on the sofa, the conversation itself would occupy a minimal place.

Their faces seemed familiar to me. I had glimpsed them in a queue at the cinema hall, at the market, on a bus, or on the street, and yet hiding behind their eyes they seemed to be alien presences. They'd come to watch my father's descent. Their tone was cajoling, but their intentions seemed more devious, and though my father himself was not fully aware of them, Jayamma and I knew that he had become their entertainment.

Whether it was the impact of his newfound religion, or Mr Selvaraj himself whose calm demeanour my father may have decided to emulate, my father never turned a guest away at the door. Yet, I remember the look on his face when there was a knock on the door just after he had sat down to eat dinner. Jayamma's temper was inflating the atmosphere in the house like a balloon, and it was always on the brink of bursting when she was summoned in the midst of putting out the washing or cooking dinner, and told to drop whatever she was doing to attend to the guests. My father had not yet rationalised the emotions that had spurred him on to a change of faith. He found their questions daunting. He fumbled for answers and after they had left he wished aloud that he had Mr Selvaraj by his side to do the speaking for him. My father had until then enjoyed a measure of anonymity in our neighbourhood. He was not prepared for the fame his conversion was to thrust upon him. On his way to the office, strangers smiled at him, recognizing him as the man who had suddenly decided to hang a cross over his doorway. They asked him questions that suggested that they knew more about his life than he willingly shared with them. If one day, he complained to the manager at the Malabar Tiffin Room that the coconut chutney had gone bad to the extent that it had made him nauseous, then the next morning, someone on the road asked him how his stomach was and confided in him that they too had suffered consequences of the poor cooking at the Malabar Tiffin Room.

They knew if our water pump had broken down and how often Mr Selvaraj visited our house. Their interest was coated with mild amusement. The phone, once an inconspicuous presence in our house, now rang persistently, its voice tinny and shining and with a power to come chasing after us in whatever corner of the house we were. My father had forbidden Jayamma and me from answering it. After one phone conversation during which my father said nothing but, 'Only the Lord understands me,' he unplugged the telephone and had Jayamma store it in the chest of drawers.

'Take it out of my sight. I don't want to hear it. I don't want to see it,' he told her.

'What about your father?' she said. He set about reconnecting it without saying a word.

Mr Selvaraj dropped by every three or four days, usually on his late afternoon walk across the river and back, often staying just long enough for a cup of coffee. During these visits, he listened patiently while my father told him over and over again how peaceful he felt in his heart despite the fact that the entire town was 'going crazy' around him.

'Don't worry,' Mr Selvaraj said, placating him. 'Soon something else will come along and they will forget all about you.'

'Are you well, Jayamma?' Mr Selvaraj would always ask her, even though Jayamma invariably pretended to be out of earshot. Once, however, when he offered to carry a pot of water up the stairs for her when the pump had broken down, and my father protested that it was her job, Jayamma said to Mr Selvaraj, 'I was wrong about you.'

She never again forgot to put two heaped spoons of sugar in his coffee.

About two weeks after the conversion took place, I received a parcel in the mail from my grandfather. When he cut open the package and removed from it *The Illustrated Mahabharata,* my father shook his head and smiled.

'Your grandfather may be on his deathbed, but his sense of humour is still alive and kicking,' he told me as he handed me the book. 'He seems to have heard from one of his professor friends about me. He is afraid I am going to make a Christian out of you.'

'Am I going to become a Christian?' I asked him.

'No. As much as I want the Lord's forgiveness, I fear your grandfather's wrath more,' he said mysteriously.

When I flipped open the pages of the book, bursting with the antics of mythological Hindu heroes, a sheet of folded paper fell to the floor.

My father read through it before handing it to me.

The letter read:

My dear grandson,

I know that you will love this book. I looked all over Delhi for it when I remembered how much you enjoyed the stories I told you on my visit. You will learn from these stories that people are not always who they seem.

Your loving grandfather,

Sarangan

'You know what, Hari? I just remembered that I have to get a costume ready for you!' my father said. I had been cast as Dushyasana in the school play. 'Your Prema Miss has been dogging me with letters and phone calls as though I don't have enough to think about already.'

'I have only one line in the whole play,' I said.

'That's not the point,' he said. 'But why is it that you never get any good roles?'

I retreated to my room and lay on the bed with the picture book. My grandfather had underlined the title of the story of Karna twice with a green pen. It was the story of the sixth Pandava, son of Kunti—he had grown up as a charioteer's son, and when the time came for war, he had sided with the Kauravas instead.

My father came in unannounced as usual, clutching two shawls in his hand. 'The green one will make you stand out in the crowd. But black is a better colour for Dushyasana. What do you think?' He draped a shawl over each shoulder and grabbed my cricket bat and struck a pose as though he was wielding a mace.

'Black,' I said.

'No, green is better. I just noticed that the black one is a little moth-eaten. I'll give this one to Jayamma.'

He draped the shawl around my waist, and over my shoulder.

'I don't want to wear a sari,' I said.

His newfound faith in Christianity had no diminishing effect in the interest he began to take in my school play, a re-enactment of selected scenes from the *Mahabharata*. On the day of the play, I spotted my father in the front row, signalling to anyone who arrived within five seats either side of him that the chairs were taken, that he had reserved them for his own family as well as for Khan uncle and Saleem. He sat upright, his head tilted upwards, his arms positioned territorially on the armrests. During the performance itself, he laughed the loudest, clapped the hardest, and turned to this side and that to indicate to everyone that they should do the same.

Looking at the intensity on my father's face, you would
think that the actors on stage playing the role of Krishna or
Arjuna were not mere children, but seasoned professionals,
and at moments, the gods and the heroes that they were
portraying. He held his breath when someone forgot a line,
sighed when they remembered it at the last minute. If a child
tripped over his ill-fitting costume, or their moustache was
precariously dangling from their upper lip, he would not share
in the united amusement of the audience. Instead, he became
irritated, shushing the offenders without much authority in his
voice and receiving no one's attention or obedience except
mine.

After the show, he pulled me aside and said, 'Hari, next year,
I hope you will play the role of Arjuna. That boy did a very
shoddy job. Did you see how he kept looking at Krishna to
prompt him? Why are you not in the dramatic society? Why
don't they give you any roles in the plays? Am I not paying them
extra for these things only?'

My response to these questions invariably ended in silence.
I had learnt early on that the easiest route to peace, something
that, in coveting it as much as he did, he had unconsciously
passed on to me as a virtue, was silence. We resolved any
problems in the household through silence. He depended on
my silence as much as I did.

Gradually, our house came to be referred to as the 'Ex-
Srinivasa House'. It wasn't unusual for people giving directions
to say, 'Take a right after you've passed the Ex-Srinivasa House.'
My father took to wearing a sling bag over his shoulder, a habit
that stayed with him for the rest of his life. It was made of jute,
and contained the navy blue, bound bible that Mr Selvaraj had

presented him with, a rosary made of sandalwood, and a plastic bottle of water. For some reason, the addition of the bag altered his appearance, slowing down his gait and conferring on him a look of wisdom that he himself remained unaware of. But Mr Selvaraj had been right. While the name stayed, peoples' attention did not linger long.

By mid-May, the summer had raised its hood, hissing incessantly, leaving cracks on fields, wilting leaves on trees, melting tar on the roads, drying up the wells and our throats. The sun rose in the sky, bleaching it of colour and turning it white.

Summer had arrived, and with it, a new set of problems.

7

I was caught stealing a cap from Michael Pinto's desk.

I had seen it, liked it and decided to take it. It was black and nondescript, and when I tried it on, it fit me perfectly. Michael Pinto's mother took up the matter with Mr Esau directly, not trusting Miss Prema (rightly) to handle the issue fairly. I was beckoned to his office in the middle of our history lesson and Miss Prema, taken by surprise, asked the peon twice if he was sure it was me that the headmaster wanted. She followed me into Mr Esau's office, stopping to berate a boy who was attempting to sneak out of another classroom. I had the sense to lie spontaneously that the cap was mine, but I'd not envisaged the lengths to which Mrs Pinto, with her wise Madras ways, would go to preserve Michael's property. On the inside of the cap was a hand-stitched label with the letters M.P. sewn into it.

'He doesn't have a mother,' I heard Miss Prema explain. 'You know how it is with these kids?'

'What happened to his mother?' Mrs Pinto asked. Her presence made Mr Esau's office seem small and dirty. She was brightly dressed in a green sari which crackled when she put her one leg over the other. She took one sip of the Campa Cola that had been especially ordered in for her, and pushed it to the far corner of the table.

'Died in childbirth,' Miss Prema said.

'Oh dear lord Jesus,' Mrs Pinto said, making the sign of the cross over her large bosom.

'That's no excuse for thievery!' Mr Esau said, glowering at Miss Prema. 'If every criminal used his childhood as an excuse, can you imagine how many crooks we'd be living amongst? Guess what? I'd be one of them!' He laughed. He had a girlish laugh, incongruous with his manner.

'Apologize to Mrs Pinto, Hari,' Miss Prema urged me. 'I had better be getting back to my classroom.'

'Sorry,' I said.

'Say it like you mean it,' Mr Esau said, prodding my back with his headmaster-sized cane. 'Sorry is just a word to them. Give them a beating or two and the emotion will come along pretty quickly.'

'No!' Mrs Pinto said, rising from the chair she was sitting in by pressing down on both armrests. 'Please.' A faint smell of mint emanated from her. 'Don't beat him. It's just a cap. I feel bad for the poor boy.'

'I am not poor!' I said. The cane came down then with force and struck my bottom and sent a shock up my spine. I yelped because I'd no time to prepare for it.

Back in the classroom, Miss Prema wasted no time in tearing out a leaf from her new notepad. I noticed the tallest girl in the class, Kavita, sitting in one of the front seats, making a paper boat from a sheet torn from a notebook that almost certainly belonged to the girl sitting next to her. She caught my eye and turned away as though she was bored with me. Miss Prema had acquired a stamp pad and a stamp as well since her promotion, and she used them now, the stamp crisp and clean on the note below the writing requesting my father's presence in school.

Dear Mr Vasan,

Could you kindly come to the school tomorrow to discuss Hari's recent behaviour at school. I will be available during the lunch break from 12.30 to 1.30 pm and after school (until 5 p.m. only—as you know, I have an aged mother at home).

'Another letter?' my father said, waving the sheet of paper so close to my face that its edge grazed my eyelids. 'Does your Miss Prema have no other business than to write letters to me?'

I winced. He was about to strike me, but in the final moment, he withdrew his hand. Instead, he slapped his own forehead with the base of his palm in exasperation.

'What am I going to do with you? What is it you have done now?'

I had learnt my lesson. 'Nothing!' I said emphatically.

Sounding weary, my father said, 'I suppose I will find out tomorrow.'

There were no other teachers in the staffroom other than Miss Prema. It was a large room with long green metal tables lining three sides of the wall on top of which files, textbooks and papers were heaped in various piles. On one or two tables stood photo frames from which babies smiled through gums. A model of a volcano was perched perilously on a window sill. There were lunchboxes and handbags everywhere. A faint smell of onions floated in the air.

Miss Prema sat at one of the tables in the far end of the room. When she saw us, she stood up and smiled. As she adjusted her sari, the red glass bangles on her wrist jingled.

'Please sit down, Mr Vasan,' she said, drawing a chair for him. Noticing grains of rice sticking to its seat, she hurriedly wiped the surface with her handkerchief. I stood by my father's side, immediately crossing my arms in the tell-tale pose of penitence.

'Thank you, Prema,' my father said. 'All is well with Shankar?'

Miss Prema's brother, Shankar, had for a short while been my father's partner at his firm. Though their mother had died at the ripe old age of eighty-seven, Shankar, the youngest of seven siblings, was particularly attached to her and so affected by her death that he had resigned from his job. Shankar's wife, Lalita, who was well known for her homemade pickles, now sold them in bottles from a stall in the market to support her family. She told her customers dolefully how fate had handed her a 'good-for-nothing husband'.

'He's fine, you know, the same,' Miss Prema said. She was embarrassed at this reference to her brother and wished to exit the subject quickly.

'What a fine fellow, he was! Such a good career ahead of him . . .' my father said, not letting it go.

'Yes, it is a terrible blow to my sister-in-law. With two small children and all . . .'

'Yes, of course. Very nice children, too. So obedient and well-behaved.'

This statement inadvertently drew attention to me. They both fell silent.

'So, what is this matter, then?' My father broached the topic of my behaviour tentatively. 'Anything to worry about?'

'Oh, nothing at all to worry about. You know, just the usual thing with children.'

'Miss Prema, you must not feel shy to tell me what he has done.'

'I am not feeling shy, Mr Vasan,' Miss Prema said, too quickly.

My father was lost for words.

'You see Mr Vasan, Hari is usually such an excellent boy,' she began. I was pleased to hear this and gave her a smile. My pleasure was short-lived for her next sentence began with a 'but'.

'But lately, he has not seemed himself. Something seems to have come over him. He is very restless, and as is often the case with children who are restless, he appears to have fallen into the company of some of the rowdier boys.'

'Just come out and tell me what he has done,' my father said, growing impatient. He examined the paperweight on the table and shook it until the little snowflakes scattered within the globe. 'Made in Switzerland!' he exclaimed. 'Impressive.'

'Thank you, Mr Vasan.' She waited until he put the paperweight back down. 'Everyone in this school believes that discipline at this age is the most important thing for children,' she said.

'Definitely, I couldn't agree more. Discipline is paramount. I am very strict at home. Ask Hari himself.'

'As for me,' she said slowly, 'I think discipline is secondary to . . .'

My father was all ears now.

'To?'

'All I am saying, is that the good work we do is routinely undone by a few wayward children—the troublemakers. We must strive to protect the good ones from the bad ones.'

'I am in complete agreement with you, Miss Prema.'

'That is why I wanted to speak with you. I am of the opinion Mr Vasan, that in Hari's case, the absence of a mother's love may have something to do with this.'

My father's anger was barely restrained in his voice.

'Nonsense. No such thing!' he began, rising from his chair, but surprised by the weight of his own voice, he allowed the words to subside and sank back into the seat.

At that moment, one of other senior school teachers, an older woman with a nose that leaned flirtatiously towards her lips, walked in, raised her eyebrows, settled herself into a chair, and buried her face in a magazine.

Miss Prema lowered her voice. 'All I am saying, and you must not mistake me, Mr Vasan,' she said. 'It is only in the best interest of your son that I am talking to you.'

'Of course, even so!'

'For a boy this age . . . not having a mother . . . it must be difficult. All I am saying is that you must not underestimate the influence of a woman in the household.'

'Is that *all* you are saying?' my father said.

'I am well aware that you are an exemplary father, Mr Vasan,' Miss Prema said, unsettled by my father's rising temper.

Temporarily appeased, my father said, 'Thank you, I am doing my best. What can we do, Miss Prema? Did your sister-in-law ever expect to find herself selling pickles in the bazaar?'

Miss Prema seemed mortified by the mention of her sister-in-law in front of the teacher. She turned in her direction quickly to see if she had heard my father's words.

The other teacher grinned.

Miss Prema clenched a pencil that was lying on the table.

'These things happen in our lives,' my father said. 'I wish Hari had a mother. But can I go buy one in the bazaar, like I can go buy lime or mango pickle?'

'Please understand, I did not mean to insult you,' Miss Prema said. 'I would be very disappointed if Hari grows up to be one of those hooligans.'

'I understand, Miss Prema. When I see the faces of these boys, I know immediately which one is going to engineering school, which one is going to be hand-fed by his ayah for the rest of his life, and which will be loitering in tea shops and asking passersby for small change to buy cigarettes. Even their mothers for all their love know it. Hari's grandfather is a great professor. We come from a good family. He may not have a full family, but I can see on my boy's face that he is not going to become one of those hooligans!'

Neither of them knew how to end this conversation. Miss Prema, a little flustered, examined the ends of her sari. Taking the opportunity, my father rose.

Miss Prema stood up as well. She had taken off her platform shoes, and in bare feet, she seemed younger.

'Please give my regards to Shankar and his family. I will make sure Hari gets into no more trouble.'

'Thanks for coming, Mr Vasan,' Miss Prema said. Her lips parted again, as though she was about to say something else, but she closed them firmly. She seemed sad, and for a moment, she didn't seem to be the same person as my class teacher. When we stepped out, the sun blinded us. I saw sea horse-shaped squiggles in the light which moved when my eye moved.

Although my father had vehemently extolled my virtues to Miss Prema, outside of her office, he seemed less sure of them.

'I won't slap you,' he said. 'Tell me, what is the matter with you? What did you do?'

I remained silent.

'I told you I won't slap you. Now, what did you do? She never mentioned what you did.'

'I didn't do anything!'

He let his hand reach for mine awkwardly. We walked past the classrooms one by one, until we reached the canteen.

'Would you like a samosa?' he asked, searching his pocket for change.

'He can have one for free,' the canteen attendant said, handing one to me in a paper cone, quickly staining with the oil from the samosa. My father looked surprised. 'Why?' my father asked. The canteen attendant shrugged and left the counter, feeling embarrassed.

My father appeared lost and shaken, as though he had stumbled onto some fresh piece of evidence that provided him a new insight into my life, which changed the way he saw me. I could feel the intensity of his gaze as I ate my samosa. Again, he took my hand in his, more firmly this time, and leading me out of the canteen, held it all the way home.

While my father remained ignorant of my theft, news broke out amongst the classrooms. The girls began to avoid me, while the boys, Saleem, the first among them, flocked to my side. They wanted to know what else I had stolen, whether I had been reported to Mr Jacob Esau, what punishment I had received, how many times I'd been whipped (three times, I lied) and why I had not included them in my activities.

8

The phone rang early one morning. It rang only once, piercingly, and then stopped. It was still dark outside, but the sounds of the night—the humming and chiming of crickets, of leaves crackling and twigs snapping—were beginning to fade. A light went on in my father's room. I heard him shuffle downstairs and I rose out of bed immediately, making my way to the landing on the stairs where I perched myself on the top step of the staircase. The phone rang again, bringing Jayamma out of her room, her gray hair wiry and rising away from her head like steam.

'I know it's your father,' she said. 'I just know it's him.' When the phone rang again, and my father's face confirmed the news, Jayamma folded onto the floor in a sweeping motion, like an emptied gunny sack, and began sobbing, while my father, still holding the receiver in one hand, said, 'He's gone.'

Jayamma spotted me. 'Come here!'

'I am going to Delhi,' my father said, blankly.

'Can I come?' I asked him. His face had been devoid of any discernible emotion, so that when he pushed me against the wall and slapped me on the face, I was taken aback and started to cry.

'Don't come near me,' he cautioned me, leaving Jayamma and me to console each other.

'It's okay,' Jayamma said. She threw the pallu of her sari around me and wiped my tears with it. 'He is not angry with you. His father is dead, and right now, inside his room, he is just as small as you. It's best to leave him alone.' Moments ago, she was sobbing but now she was calm.

'Do I have to go to school?' I said, sensing an opportunity.

'No,' Jayamma said. 'You don't have to go.'

'My mother died in childbirth not pneumonia,' I blurted out.

'Who told you that?' She held me by the shoulders and pushed me and pulled me, then fixed me in one spot, her eyes having trouble focusing on me.

'Miss Prema said it the other day in Mr Esau's office.'

'Why were you in the headmaster's office?'

'I was cleaning his blackboard for him.'

'That Miss Prema will say anything,' Jayamma said, releasing me. 'She will do anything to win your father. I feel sorry for her.'

I fled from the room before she could ask me any more questions about my trip to the headmaster's office.

I saw little of my father the rest of the day, with each of us steering clear of the other. Mr Selvaraj arrived sometime after lunch which my father skipped, and suggested that they go for a walk. Gently, he reminded my father that his forehead was smeared with dried ginger paste. 'Is your headache any better?' I heard him ask as my father rushed to the sink to wash his face. Mr Selvaraj always seemed to have a pacifying effect on my father, so when he returned, my father was quiet, and set about organizing things for his trip. He made telephone calls speaking in an uncharacteristically hushed voice. He dispatched the office boy to the railway station to obtain his ticket, and began throwing things together in his red VIP suitcase that he lay open in the middle of the sofa in the living room.

I was awakened early the next morning when I heard him bang against the almirah on the upstairs landing, causing the lotus-shaped earthen money pot to crash heavily to the floor, and the sound of coins clattering broke the stillness of the house. He swore and yelled for Jayamma. Jayamma didn't surface. He left the coins on the floor (I pocketed some later that day) and made his way to my room. I pretended to be asleep. 'Hari!' he called to me from the door. 'I will see you in ten days or so,' he said, as if he knew I was awake. 'I've asked for a ticket for the thirteenth but it's not confirmed yet. So, I will see you on the fifteenth, or else sometime after that . . .'

I turned in my bed.

'Okay, then,' he said. 'I will see you later. Be a good boy and don't get into any more trouble.'

I waited until his footsteps died down. I rushed to the window just as Khan uncle's jeep came in through the gate, the headlights illuminating Julie under the mango tree. Julie whined, stretched, wagged her tail and then curled back in her spot. It was not quite morning yet; even the namaaz from the mosque had not begun. Khan uncle had promised a driver, but had arrived himself. Though it was warm, my father had worn the coat that he wore on every journey. He rushed to greet Khan uncle, hauling his suitcase with him, though small, seemingly heavy. Khan uncle heaved the suitcase into the boot, and then retrieved the flask of tea he always carried with him, and poured some into a glass for my father. My father drank it, though I'd never known him to drink tea, standing beside Khan uncle, holding the glass with both his hands. Then they got into the jeep and drove off.

The house felt desolate after my grandfather's death, as though he had been living in the room downstairs occupying my old room all along, and had only just left. I checked to see that the letter he'd sent from Delhi was still within the pages of my old Class Reader where I'd saved it. I turned on the transistor radio that he had left behind. A radio play came on and as I was about to turn the tuner, Jayamma stopped me. She was already drawn into the drama. She grabbed a bagful of peanuts and squatted on the floor and closed her eyes to listen.

'People tend to die in groups,' Jayamma told me one afternoon, a few days later when I returned from school with Saleem. She was sitting on the balcony fanning herself with a rolled up church pamphlet. 'Babies are born all together and old people all die together. There'll be some other deaths soon.'

Saleem and I wondered who else would die. We considered the most likely candidates on our streets. We made a list on the last page of Saleem's notebook. The shoemaker at the end of the street was the oldest man I could think of. He had no teeth, his cheeks were entirely sunken and each time he rose or sat down, he let out an agonizing cry. The one-legged barber was also old. He no longer served any customers himself, and let his two sons take turns, though he never left the shop. He sat on a stool in the far end of the room and smoked beedi after beedi and let out thunderous coughs that startled customers who hadn't even noticed his stooped frame in the corner. And then, there was the leper by the temple who sat motionless all day, and seemed dead already.

I peered into the shoemaker's shed each day as I returned from school, eager to see if he was still alive. I imagined that I would be the one to find him there, dead and hunched over his pile of shoes. I had become so preoccupied with this thought that I failed to notice that Jayamma herself was showing signs of slowing down.

My father returned from Delhi late one evening nearly three weeks later. I had stopped expecting him. I heard the gate open. I knew it was my father straightaway because Julie had a distinctive whine for each of us and I recognized her greeting for him. I was about to rush outside to meet him, having forgotten all about the slap I had received from him, when Jayamma reminded me of it by restraining me at the door with a firm arm around my waist.

'Want another slap?' she said.

Mr Narayan had accosted my father at the gate with his questions, and we watched while my father attempted to extricate himself with a closed mouth and sweeping hand movements. He entered the house bringing with him a strong scent of the train. His head was shaven, and his eyes were bleary. A film of hair had grown over my father's upper lip, giving him a comical appearance.

'What is this?' Jayamma asked. 'You go as a Christian and return as a Brahmin?'

My father ignored her. He motioned to the young driver following him to place the large cardboard box he was carrying in the hall. Three more boxes arrived from the car and were put in the hall.

'What's all this?' Jayamma asked.

My father put a finger to his lips and shook his head from side to side meaningfully. 'What am I supposed to understand by that?' Jayamma said. 'You are not speaking?'

He nodded.

My father had taken a vow of silence.

Jayamma and I began rummaging through the boxes, which were full of books. My father left us to take a bath, and emerged freshly shaven and dressed in a crisp white veshti and a banian. I was leafing through a book titled *Tiger on the Mountain* by an author named Shirley L. Arora.

He sat down on the planter's chair. I replaced the book in the box, shut its lid and sat on top of it as soon as I saw him. My father gave me a long appraising look.

He waved his hand in a 'come here' gesture. I went towards him and sat down on the armrest of his chair. He patted my cheek and crossed his arms diagonally across his chest, and held his earlobes with his fingers. It was a gesture of his contrition.

Jayamma laughed.

'What happened to Appa's hair?' I asked her later.

'Your grandfather has to go to heaven, no? So the crow has come and taken all the hair he can get, so your grandfather will be able to fly to heaven.'

My father shook his head vociferously. Jayamma laughed. 'That's right,' she said. 'You are going to pay the price. I can say whatever I want now, and you won't be able to shut me up.'

I told Saleem on the school bus the next morning what had happened to my father's hair. He informed me that Jayamma was feeding me with nonsense. He said that in order for the crow to take away the hair, one had to first shave it off one's head in a single sweeping motion. The hair had to peel off, he said, as a whole mop, or else the crow would not be able to hold on to it.

That same evening, I found my father's razor in the bathroom and made an attempt to shave the hair off my head, starting near my forehead. Almost as soon as I began, I cut myself. As soon as I cut myself, Jayamma was beside me. She hauled me under the tap and ran cold water over my head. She was yelling at me and kissing me alternately. She wound a cotton towel around my head and dragged me by the hand to where my father was sitting in his study.

'See this?' she said, unwinding the towel by spinning me around. 'See what you are doing to this boy?'

My father arched his thumb. He was not breaking his vow. 'What?' his thumb asked.

'Look at this cut. Where are you when things are happening around you?'

My father approached me and examined my forehead. He looked into my eyes and shook his head.

'You must not do that again,' his eyes said.

'If he carries on like this, I am going to have to do something,' Jayamma hinted to me when two days passed and my father still had not spoken a word to either of us.

Apprehensive of leaving me unattended, Jayamma instructed me to trail her wherever she went in the house. To amuse myself, I began to imitate the way she walked, bending my knees like her, and dragging myself on my heels in the way that she did. I yawned when she did. I caught her cold.

One afternoon, Jayamma did not wake up from her afternoon

nap. Eventually, my father, tired of waiting for his coffee, was forced to come looking for her. Alarmed to find her lying on the mat, he got down on his knees and shook her awake vehemently.

She sat up without a warning and started laughing.

'Don't scare me like that,' he admonished her, breaking his silence when she opened her eyes. Jayamma laughed for the rest of the day.

There was no laughter the following day. It was a Sunday morning and I had rushed to the gate after hearing the distinctive drumming sounds of a funeral procession that was passing by. Sita was already standing at her gate.

'Who is it?' I asked. 'Is it the shoemaker?'

'No, it's the one-legged barber,' she said. 'When is your father going to talk? My father says he will not talk anymore.'

'He is talking now. He has broken his vow of silence.'

'My father said that your father is not allowed to shave his head or take the vow of silence because he is a Christian.'

'Hari!' we heard my father yell out to me just then.

'I'll tell my father your father is talking now,' Sita said, scampering indoors. I made my way to the veranda where he was waiting for me.

'Go wash your hands and feet,' he said, pulling me by the scruff of my collar into the living room.

I did as I was told. I emerged from the bathroom to find my father kneeling on the rug. 'Come and sit beside me,' he said.

He gave me an appraising look and I watched as his eyes stopped on an ink stain on my shirt.

'It won't come off,' I said. 'I won't put the pen in my pocket again.'

He took my hand in his and placed it against his cheek. His cheek was cold. 'Don't be scared of me,' he said. 'I never meant to scare you.'

'Shall I tell you about your grandfather?' he asked.

'Okay.'

'Your grandfather was very sick when he came to visit you.'

It was a strange thing for him to say to me, as though I had not been aware of my grandfather's condition. He had been so occupied in his world that he had either not noted how often I had asked after my grandfather, or he had simply forgotten.

'But he did not want to go away without seeing his grandson. He liked you that much. I liked your grandfather too. I don't want you to think we did not like each other. About some things, we disagreed, but we agreed about many other things, like what a good child you are. Do you understand?'

'Yes, Appa,' I said. I thought he was about to say something more, but he stopped. I was glad. The intensity of his gaze was unsettling. When he smiled, I joined him.

'I need to go to the post-office. I promised to post something for someone a long time ago. Do you want to come with me?'

He rose and retrieved an aerogramme from the chest of drawers. The envelope was heavy.

The letter was addressed to Ram Sharma, an entirely unfamiliar name then, in a place called Wisconsin, U.S.A.

Like his father, he had stuck the stamps upside down.

'For good luck!' he said.

9

At school, the halls were abuzz with talk of our imminent trip to the town's dairy farm. It was the first outing our school had ever organized. That our class had been given this special privilege made the older boys envious enough to block our passage in the hallways and hide our lunch boxes, but for once we didn't care.

When I mentioned it at home, Jayamma said, 'If they are taking all the trouble of arranging a bus and everything, why don't they take you some place nice, like a temple?'

'Why would they need to organize a bus to go to the temple, Jayamma? Don't be a fool. There are temples in every street corner,' my father said, looking up from the book that he was reading. It was *The Secret Garden*, one of the books that my grandfather had left me, and he appeared to be riveted by it. Jayamma glared at him.

'But they need a bus to go see pigs and donkeys? Like this town isn't already brimming with them,' Jayamma said.

'I like this Chalapati fellow. He seems to have his head on his shoulders. Jayamma, why not get the boy some new clothes for the trip? He is growing tall, is he not?'

The school trip had been Chalapathi Sir's idea. Chalapati Sir taught English, mostly in Telugu. He wore floral shirts though it was against our school policy, with the first three buttons opened (also against school policy). He stretched the collar ends apart to reveal a bed of black hair in which a heavy gold chain nestled. He wore his flamboyant, curly hair long, a lock of which he arranged carefully on his forehead. With his manner of releasing his sentences through a membrane of saliva, Chalapati Sir inspired in us both awe and fear. Sometimes, on the days that he was in a good mood, the days on which he wore his green cap with the letter MCC printed in gold we'd come to learn, Chalapati Sir would teach in English.

Whenever he spoke in English, most of us, not including Michael Pinto, bent our heads, never lifting our gaze from our books, fearing that we would become the target of his impulsive questions that tested our comprehension of the language. He was a wily man who would interject what had then seemed like big words such as 'exhilarating' and 'majestic' into the middle of a sentence and then after an unstipulated period of time, ask one of us what the word meant. If we were unable to provide an adequate explanation, which was often the case, his face would acquire an expression of annoyed satisfaction, and whoever it was that had been the unfortunate victim would be forced to endure ten raps on their knuckles which Chalapati Sir dispensed with the duster in ascending order of emphasis.

The inspiration for the trip came during one of our classes in which one of the girls has asked him what the English word 'duck' meant.

'This is a useless class!' Chalapathi Sir had exclaimed then. 'Utterly useless! I refuse to waste a single more sentence on you.'

There was silence.

He shook his head in disgust. As he stormed off, grabbing the English Reader from the table with a sweeping motion of his hand, he dropped the yellow duster on the floor. No one dared to move. I was suddenly itchy.

'How many legs does a duck have?' someone asked, when he left. Although some of us had been quite sure of our definitions of a duck, the sudden scrutiny to which we now held the bird threw us in such a maelstrom of confusion that we saw in our minds four-legged ducks and chickens with duck faces.

Leaving the class with a plan already baking in his head, Chalapati Sir proceeded to the headmaster's office. Mr Esau was appreciative of all initiatives, and effusive about them, though he sanctioned only a select few. On this occasion, however, not only did he give his approval enthusiastically, he also decided that a photographer should accompany us to the farm.

On the day of the trip, we gathered together on the mangy lawn in the school quadrangle enclosed on all four sides by classrooms, where we assembled for prayers in the morning, practiced for school plays, and on Tuesdays, performed our PT drill. We had been told to arrive there at eight o'clock sharp, but in our eagerness most of us had arrived as early as seven, looking scrubbed, with tamed hair, shirts that were whiter than they had been before, and shoes that were greasy with fresh polish. Khan uncle had arrived in his jeep at half past six to pick me up. Both Jayamma and my father had forgotten about their decision to buy me a new outfit for the trip, and each blamed the other when I protested that my shorts were too tight, and that I couldn't button them up properly.

Like us, the photographer had arrived early. His camera was slung around his neck and he was plucking leaves from a shrub impatiently and throwing them about his feet. He was a large man with two drops of sweat that formed repeatedly over his lip, which he kept wiping with a brown checked handkerchief.

There were also eager parents who had come to see off their children, chatting together at one corner of the quadrangle, telling each other that they had made the right decision in putting their children in this school. My father feared the type of co-mingling with other parents that occurred during such occasions, and been glad of Khan uncle's offer. Chalapati Sir emerged from behind the green curtain that hung over the entrance to the staffroom, his MCC cap at an angle on his head, as though he had just stepped out onto a stage and expected us to applaud. He blew his whistle to bring us to order although it was unnecessary; his presence alone being enough to silence us.

'Move in single file. Shortest first,' he said. Saleem and I proceeded to the front of the queue.

As soon as we stepped onto the bus, we began to fight for the best seats. The photographer had occupied two seats in the front of the bus and everyone wanted the seats adjacent to his. We felt as though we were in the company of a very famous and important person. When he asked one of the girls who had until then been hovering shyly near his seat what her name was, her face immediately rearranged its expression and seemed to say, 'I am special'.

It was a hot morning and the heat knitted us tightly together in the bus. As we turned around the drive, the parents waved to us and we waved back. First, we passed the houses, short and flat, coloured white and pink and yellow, sitting as still as the squares of cake in Prince Bakery's window display. In the distance, however, the sky, unevenly blue, and the noses of hills visible above the fields, appeared to move up and down with the wind or the heat.

The shiny black road soon gave way to a narrow, untarred track. When the bus swerved along the curves, we screamed in unison, and the bus seemed to lift itself slightly as though it was hopping. Tamarind trees, with their waists painted in red, lined either side of the road. We stretched our hands out of the bus to pluck the plump brown tamarind pods from the branches. We scratched our elbows and twigs became entangled in our hair. The tamarind, when we sucked at it between our front teeth, was deliciously sour and made our teeth ache pleasantly.

As soon as we alighted from the bus, even before we had visited any of the animals, Chalapati Sir ordered the photographer to take a group photograph on the lawn. He stood in the centre, while the rest of us swarmed around him, striking various poses, and craning our necks above each other's heads in order to be visible in the photograph.

Once we arrived at the animal enclosures, we dispersed into various little groups, knowing that it would be impossible for Chalapati Sir to keep track of all of us. It was the first time that I had seen a pink pig.

Saleem said, 'What? You never saw a pink pig? My uncle has dozens of pink pigs.'

The only pigs I had seen were grey and, on occasion, brown when they were caked with mud. Mostly, I had seen them loitering around the enormous grey cement dustbins that the town council had constructed in abandoned lots all across the town.

We came to the rabbit enclosure. As I peered into the face of one of the younger creatures, a timid fellow crouching in one corner, he hopped without warning and I screamed. Since the other kids were also shouting and aping the sounds of the animals, I believed my reaction had gone unnoticed. Saleem had sauntered off to see the guinea pigs and I found myself clinging to the iron mesh that separated the animals from us.

I'd had enough of the animals. I decided to return to the bus and wait there. Chalapati Sir, holding in his hand a bottle of Campa Cola that had been brought to him by one of the farm workers, was leading a small group of eager students from one enclosure to another. Here and there, he stopped to describe the animal and to draw attention to its distinguishing features. I noticed the Gopalan twins straggling at the edge of the group, unable to decide whether it would be more worthwhile to win Chalapati Sir's favour, or to jump over the fence and play with the donkeys like the some of the boys were doing.

The bus driver had gotten out to smoke a cigarette or to chat with some other bus driver. The cushion on his seat was deeply indented, and from underneath the cushion, a flimsy magazine stuck out revealing a woman's plump bare legs. Suddenly, at the back of the bus, I glimpsed a pair of feet and a flash of black hair, but when I looked again, they had disappeared. I made my way to the rear of the bus and found Kavita, crouching in one corner with her hand covering her mouth.

'I saw you. You scared the rabbits,' she said, speaking with her mouth full of something.

She was wearing a purple frock held together with safety pins, and which had two large side pockets. One of the pockets was bulging in the shape of a samosa and a dark brown oil stain had started to grow around an embroidered pink rose.

'Why did you scream?' she asked.

'Where did you get the samosa?' I asked, deflecting her question.

She lowered her voice. 'Shh . . .' she said.

She pointed to the aluminium drum wedged under the seat containing the snacks that were to be served later. Carefully, she slid her long arm under the lid and withdrew two samosas. I did the same. We sat on the seat and ate them noisily. Her presence was oddly comforting.

When Chalapati Sir had one of the farm boys distribute the samosas to us, I was no longer hungry and refused. Kavita accepted two, but they went into her pocket. He blew his whistle for us to reassemble on the lawn. He read out the roll call and we made our way back onto the bus, this time in alphabetical order.

For those of us on the bus, the accident happened slowly. The way I saw it, sitting beside the aisle in one of the front seats of the bus, first there was the empty stretch of road visible through the windscreen running a long way ahead of us, the tar on its surface glistening from the heat. A crop of mud huts lay immediately to the right, and in the distance, the two lines of tamarind trees running on either side of the road appeared to converge, forming an overhead arc of foliage, parts of which were almost parrot green where the light caught it. Then, it seemed to me that the length of the road, and not the bus, was moving in a sweeping motion, causing both a plunging and uplifting feeling, a mixture of delight and nausea, in the pit of my stomach, as though I might have been coming down in a Ferris wheel. As the bus crashed into a tamarind tree, our heads were flung forward at first, and then as it jolted to a stop, our bodies were thrown backwards, hurling me and a few others out of our seats. In the commotion that followed, the only thing I could recollect clearly was the blowing of Chalapati Sir's whistle, which despite the din we were making, was loud and crisp, although failing in its mission to bring us to order.

Later, in his interview in the *Rayalaseema Times*, Chalapati Sir stated that he'd had a premonition of the accident and that he had specifically instructed the bus driver to drive slowly on the return journey. When questioned, the bus driver responded that he had no recollection of Chalapati Sir's warning, but his lapse in memory was attributed to the fact that he had knocked his head on the steering wheel when the accident happened, though in a later paragraph, there was mention of his foul-smelling breath, which the writer implied could have been redolent of arrack.

Within minutes of the crash, the villagers from the surrounding settlements arrived and were lifting us out of the bus. An old man with a pointed white beard, who identified himself as the village head, stationed himself at the entrance of the bus and shouted out orders which the others obeyed without questions. Buckets of water materialized. The women began cleaning our wounds with practised fingers, bandaging them with strips of cloth torn from lungis. The nearest phone was six kilometres away, so two young men were dispatched on their bicycles to inform Mr Jacob Esau of the accident and ask him to arrange a bus to transport us back. Chalapati Sir ceded to the older man's authority and looked about the rescue efforts in a state of mute shock.

Several of us had endured similar injuries. In the thrust forward, we had jammed our faces into the metal handlebar attached to the seats in front of us, and found that we had teeth missing, and that our lips were bleeding because we had bitten them without our knowledge. No matter how many times we rinsed our mouths, the metallic taste of blood remained. I had broken one tooth, which I had been lucky enough to find, and my left knee was sore from landing on the floor when I fell. From within the bus came the shrieking sounds of the bus driver as he was being wrested free from the seat his legs had become wedged beneath. Along with the bus driver, two girls, who had incurred deep cuts on their faces, were in need of the most attention. A part of the photographer's camera had been damaged during the accident. Unmindful of the chaos around him, he planted himself under the shade of a tree, spread his checked handkerchief onto the ground and set about dismantling it.

The village head stopped a black Ambassador car that was passing by. It was carrying a family of six. The father, the grandfather, and the oldest boy stepped out willingly to accommodate the injured girls who needed to be rushed to a hospital. The mother immediately enveloped the girls in her arms while the younger son looked peeved at not being allowed to stay behind at the scene of the accident. Jokingly, the father told the driver of his car to drive slowly, and not to cause another crash.

A second car was stopped to transport the bus driver, who had finally been extricated from the bus. The driver of the second car was less enthusiastic to drive his blood-soaked passenger, but realizing that he was outnumbered and wary of the collective fury of a mob, relented. He threw a towel over the back seat as precaution nevertheless. By the time the new bus arrived with the headmaster in it, news of the accident had spread throughout the town, causing panic amongst the parents.

Mr Esau arrived clutching his snakeskin wallet tightly in his hand and wearing a startled expression on his face. Chalapati Sir, looking nervous, explained to him how the accident had occurred. He himself had not suffered any injuries, and he seemed to be embarrassed for it.

'I told him specifically to drive slowly,' Chalapati Sir began, but Mr Esau cut him off.

'All the children are okay?'

'Yes, Sir.'

'Good. Now, how did this happen?'

A young child had strayed onto the main road from one of the huts, Chalapati Sir informed him. The driver had swerved, lost control of the bus and slammed it into the tree.

'All the children are safe,' he kept repeating, almost in an effort to convince himself as much as Mr Esau, who was no longer listening. His eyes were assessing the damage to the school and its reputation. He moved on to the village head. They exchanged a few words and after a moment's hesitation, Mr Esau began fumbling with his wallet. The old man shook his head, but Mr Esau pulled out a ten rupee note and pressed it into the old man's hands. The old man held up the note as though it were an item of curiosity, then spat the tobacco he had been chewing onto the ground with marked contempt before returning the note and turning away.

We were ushered into the new bus. This time, there was no roll call from Chalapati Sir. The women kissed us and waved to us till they disappeared from our sight. Saleem found his way to the seat next to mine. His chin was blue. He laughed when he saw my swollen lip and the gap between my teeth.

'Do you have it?' he asked. I opened my palm to show him the tooth I held in it.

The Gopalan twins had incurred identical wounds on their foreheads. Kavita had somehow evaded being injured, and sat staring out of the window looking bored.

We were driven straight to the hospital so we could be examined before being sent home. From the bus, we could make out groups of anxious parents waiting in the parking lot within the hospital grounds. I leaned out the window and scanned the crowds for my father, but he was nowhere to be seen.

But hiding behind a flower pot behind the tall fronds of a fern, a little distance from all the commotion, was my mother, Parvati.

As I stepped off the bus my mother came up to me, held my hand in a cold wet grip, and led me away from the crowd. She helped me onto an upturned flower pot, stooped to the ground, and began smothering my cheeks with kisses. Her eyes were wet, and she flicked the tears before they fell to her cheek with the back of her palm. She was small, and slight, and the ends of her hair loosely worn in a long plait grazed the ground. I didn't protest. There was someone there to meet everyone else. Neither my father nor Jayamma had shown up to claim me. And to have the attention of a kindly lady, whoever she may be, was not unwelcome.

My mother scrutinized my body for injuries, ignoring the scowling head nurse who had been appointed to manage the parents and maintain decorum amongst them. Noticing my bleeding lip, my mother bade me to open my mouth. She held my chin in her palm and turned my face to the light so she could have a better look. Fresh tears, which she no longer attempted to conceal, fell in big drops from her eyes, barely even grazing her cheeks. The nurse reappeared and persuaded my mother to join the queue that was forming, and gently, my mother took my hand and ushered me to the line. The photographer's wife burst into loud sobs when she saw her husband's broken camera. Khan uncle arrived and immediately made his presence known. He, along with a group of other irate fathers, had surrounded Mr Esau and Chalapati Sir. They were shelling the two of them with questions and shooting down their every attempt at an answer with more questions.

I was about to ask the kind lady where my father was when I caught sight of him pushing through the crowds. When he spotted us, he broke into a run, losing his balance momentarily as he stumbled on a stone on his way.

'What are you doing here?' he said, snatching my hand away from hers. He opened his mouth to speak and then closed it again.

'Where did you come from?' he said, finally.

At first my mother simply looked at him, her face, which had been as tremulous as a ripple in a pond, becoming completely still, as though the pebble that had caused the ripple had now sunk completely. The expression on her face disarmed my father. Just as unexpectedly, my father's face mirrored hers, his indignation visibly subsiding. Releasing his grasp on my hand, he said unexpectedly, 'If you can, forgive me, Parvati.'

He was about to say something else when she lunged at him,

her closed fists beating against his chest with more vehemence than strength. My father tried to grab her by the wrists but she eluded his grasp and struck him on the face. Taken aback, my father instinctively put the palm of his hand against his cheek, as if to ensure the blow had indeed occurred.

Khan uncle appeared at our side, dragging Saleem forcefully by his arm with him.

'What's all this?' he said. He looked from my mother to my father. My father averted his eyes and turned his gaze to me. 'What does this woman want with you, Vasan?'

'Nothing,' my father said. 'It's just a big mistake. Let the poor woman go and let's forget this matter.'

'Arrey! What kind of mistake?'

My father fumbled for words. 'This woman has mistaken my son for hers.'

'What kind of a mother will mistake someone else's son for her own?' Khan uncle turned to face my mother.

My mother wiped her chin, wet with tears, with the back of her hand. She returned Khan uncle's gaze. Now that she was claiming to be my mother, she didn't seem kindly anymore. I knew that she was not my mother because I had seen a photo of my mother. I'd heard my father call this lady Parvati. My mother's name was Devaki.

A small crowd was starting to collect around us. My father, observing the gathering of eyes in our direction, and feeling self-conscious, lowered his voice.

'This is not the time to talk about this, Parvati,' he said, his tone urging.

'I am his mother, don't tell me what to do,' she said, raising her voice.

'Mother? What nonsense is this?' Khan uncle said, looking back and forth at them.

'He is right,' my mother said suddenly, not hearing him and looking at me. 'The most important thing is Hari.

My mother placed a hand on my arm. I pushed it aside. 'I don't want you,' I said, screaming. My mother took a far step back, as if she had been pushed hard. I clung to my father's legs. My father looked down at me. He put his thumb on my swollen lip and wiped a little blood off.

'What the hell is this Vasan?' Khan uncle said in a low disbelieving voice.

'Where are you staying?' My father asked my mother, ignoring Khan uncle.

'Vijay Guest House, on the west side,' she said. 'I'll be there for a little while. My husband is joining me soon.'

'Your husband . . .' my father said.

'Well whatever this is,' Khan uncle said, 'it needs to wait. Could we get out of the hospital first? The boys are a little shaken.' My mother registered the look on my face and seemed to make a decision.

My father was about to speak, but Khan uncle laid a hand on his arm, silencing him. 'Go, Vasan,' he said. 'Get back in the queue. First things first.'

My father was hesitant to leave, but mindful of Khan uncle's impatience, he nudged Saleem and me towards the line. We could not hear what Khan uncle said to my mother but we saw them walk towards the rickshaw stand, and Khan uncle pay the rickshaw driver in advance. My mother turned around to look at me. She waved. I did not wave back. I wished that she would never return.

To appease the disgruntled parents who were tired of waiting and resentful of the children who had incurred fewer injuries than their own, the doctors decided to examine two or three children simultaneously. So long as they were in one of the doctor's rooms, and not in the corridor, the parents seemed contented, the mere illusion of being tended to sufficing for the moment. Soon, there was the sound of packets of potato chips opening, food particles fell to the floor, bottles and bandages discarded along the wall, and the chatter became more convivial.

The doctor that attended to us wasted no time. He seemed to be elsewhere as he examined us, Khan uncle's questions fell on deaf ears and there was none of the usual chit chat. No questions about favourite sports or movie stars. He was quick and thorough as he made me stick my tongue out, and peered into my ear and checked my reflexes. Khan uncle asked him about my bleeding lip. 'It's just a little blood,' he said. He seemed tired. 'Sorry. All you over-concerned parents don't realize . . . there are so many real patients in here. Your sons are fine,' he said, tearing out a note from his prescription pad, and handing it to Khan uncle. 'Here is a clean chit,' he said, smiling for the first time.

'If you are not careful, Hari,' Khan uncle joked, 'you might be leaving home with a brand new set of parents.'

My father did not laugh.

Back at home, my father let Jayamma fuss over Saleem and me, and went to talk to Khan uncle on the veranda. The sun set behind them. They never once sat down or moved during their conversation. Eventually, Saleem's mother telephoned, and requested Jayamma to send her husband and child home.

The next day, my father stationed himself by the phone, moving the planter's chair close to it, so that he could reach the receiver with his right arm. He didn't go to work, and although I was well enough to attend school, there was no mention of it and Jayamma didn't even wake me up in the morning. My father was quiet and ignored Jayamma when she suggested he pick up his rosary, although eventually, he did.

I tripped over my father's abandoned coffee cup, and spilt the remnants onto the floor. I was surprised when my father, who appeared too preoccupied to notice anything around him, said, 'Something is wrong with the boy, Jayamma.'

The concern she heard in his voice made Jayamma laugh.

'What is so funny?'

'You think everyone is like you.'

'You have no notion of when to be serious and when to joke, Jayamma. Can you not see that the boy is not himself?'

If only to humour him, Jayamma contained herself.

'Hari, come here!' he said.

I approached him apprehensively. He moved in his seat to make room for me.

'Look, Jayamma. How thin the boy is looking. Have you seen how his knees stick out like cricket balls? People will think we are not feeding him or looking after him properly. Jayamma, get him some glucose biscuits.'

She went in search of the tin. He drew me close to him and put his arm around me. Unaccustomed to such physical affection from him, I stiffened.

Jayamma returned with the tin of biscuits and handed me

two. They'd gone soft and spongy. I didn't feel like eating them and held them in my hand.

'Hari?' he said. 'What? What is it?'

'You are not going to get anything out of him. In all my life I have never seen a quieter six-year-old,' Jayamma said, piping in. 'Or is he seven?'

My father counted on his fingertips. 'Six,' he said. The number seemed to fall upon him heavily. He closed his eyes. 'Six years,' he said.

He opened his eyes and tilted his head, as he looked at me.

'Are you angry with me, then?'

I was so startled by this question that I moved back involuntarily, and his arm, resting on my shoulder, slipped and fell. He held me back with both of his arms on my shoulders. He shook me as though this action could cause the answers to tumble out of me.

I stayed silent. Reluctantly, he let me go, and Jayamma, waiting at the entrance to the kitchen, enveloped me in her arms.

Late in the evening, the following day, we heard a knock on the door. Jayamma was putting away the dishes, and I was in the hall with my father, who seemed listless and wanted my company. It was Khan uncle.

'Let us go somewhere we can talk,' he said, addressing my father, with barely a glance thrown in my direction. With an anxious look on his face, my father got up from the chair, letting the magazine he was reading from slip to the floor.

My father ushered Khan uncle into his study. Jayamma made two cups of tea without being asked, and followed them into the room, telling me firmly that I was to remain in the hall. Sensing that something was wrong, she had decided to include herself in their discussion. She shut the door deliberately behind her, but opened it again moments later wide enough to stick her head out. She waved a finger at me, indicating that I was not to disobey her orders.

I began to cry. The door remained shut for a long time. I couldn't make out the words, but I'd known that it had to do with the woman who'd claimed to be my mother. I could identify the reasoning tone that Khan uncle used with Saleem's mother, or one of Saleem's older brothers when they wanted to do something their father forbade them from. It was authoritative, but patient. And I could tell from my father's voice, which rose in defiance and then subsided to a whimper, that he'd lost the argument. Khan uncle was the first to emerge, and behind him were my father and Jayamma.

'What is this Hari? You are crying?' Khan uncle asked.

'Am I going to be sent away?'

Khan uncle appeared surprised by my question. He took a deep breath and readjusted his belt, and turned in the direction of my father.

'Vasan,' he said. 'You will need to take charge from here.'

My father fell to his knees and pulled me to him. 'You don't belong with me,' he said, hugging me for the first time in my memory. 'You belong with your real parents.'

That was the only explanation I was to receive. I alone would be plucked from the spot, and preserved, while the rest of my life would vanish, like the lone survivor of an accident. I never went back to school again. Over the next few days, guests began to stream in bearing gifts. Mr Selvaraj, Saleem's entire family, Miss Prema and her sister, and even the Gopalan twins clutching a new kite, that with some prodding from their mother, they parted with.

Finally, my parents Ram and Parvati arrived at the door. Dad in a yellow button-up coat over grey slacks, his hair and beard blowing askew in the wind, and my mother beside him, clutching his sleeve, wearing the red sari which in later days she would call her good-luck sari, appeared to me as foreign as the green Morris Minor they'd arrived in.

Jayamma packed a single trunk of my belongings. It contained some clothes, my orange-shaped lunch box, my Mowgli pencil case, a few notebooks, a water bottle that I hadn't particularly liked, my marble collection, and the photograph of my mother. Her expression was steadfast as she watched Appa board me in the car. She held Julie in her arms until Julie squirmed out of her reach. There were no tears as I cried out for her. She would cry later, after the car had turned the corner and disappeared from view.

10

As soon as I was ensconced in my new home in Madras, my parents set about extinguishing Vasan from my life. His name disappeared behind doors, evaporated from my parents' lips whenever I approached them, and was carefully avoided when we had company. They had only recently made their home in the small, two-bedroom brick bungalow in Adyar, and had few friends. When someone visited, my new parents circled me; my father a warm presence at my back, a hand over my shoulder, and my mother at my side, holding and then releasing my hand, pausing only to wipe the sweat from her palms on the ends of her sari. They answered my questions for me so that I wouldn't tell their colleague Sam who asked me how I learnt to play chess that Appa had taught me, or declare to Gokul, our next door neighbour's son that my favourite sport was kite flying (when Dad guessed it was carom), or tell my perplexed classmates whom they'd invited to my birthday party that I had a dog back home called Julie.

Inexplicably, they retained Vasan's name as my middle name and I became Hari Vasan Sharma.

My parents seemed at a loss as to what to do with me. They had read books on kidnapping and missing children with names like 'Surviving Adoption' and 'Lost Innocence' and 'Stolen Life' that they had especially flown in from London through an acquaintance of my dad's, an Air India flight attendant who was sympathetic and would not take any money for them. But none of the scenarios described in these books seemed to fit ours. During those early months when I cried out for Appa every night, my father had stood by my door, agonizing, feeling as though it had been they who were my kidnappers.

It was a confusing time for them, and not only because they were getting to know me, their only son, at the age of six, but because they were getting to know each other anew having recently reunited. At the time, I didn't know about the schism between my parents, but looking back, it explains why I always found mine different from any other sets of parents I met through school. There was intangible glue binding them that I could only sense because it excluded me. They locked eyes wherever they went. They were attentive and ceding to each other's requests as though they could no longer take each other for granted. They thanked each other constantly, for everything from a tumbler of coffee to a curtain being drawn or a towel being handed over. Having just come from the house in Sripuri where I'd never once heard a please or a thank you, unless it was sheathed in sarcasm, I thought my parents were crazy and I didn't like them.

My parents may have decided that a fresh start was what we all needed.

They had acquired new jobs in the same school, St Aloysius Boys, where my mother became the assistant at the Science laboratory and my father took up a position as one of many head teachers in the English department.

They set about creating a new life for us purposefully. They painted over me; my hair parting went from left to right, my plain shirts acquired checks, my shorts became pants and plastic cars and lorries appeared in place of marbles and kites. I was required to call my father Dad, not Appa like I'd called Vasan, and learn to speak in English. According to them, they'd decided to create new memories for me instantly. They dragged me with them to watch *Fist of Fury* in Anand Theatre not realizing that Vasan was a Bruce Lee fan himself, packing elaborate picnic lunches to eat on Marina Beach, introducing me to cheese (which I found insipid) and noodles (which I found impossible to eat). They took me to the government museum in Egmore and the Snake Park in Guindy, and after I'd fallen asleep exhausted from the day's activities, they sat around the kitchen table passing a glass of rum and coke back and forth, worrying about me as an adult and the problems I might encounter. They were eager for me to start over, so that when I looked back, as I am doing now, I would remember these painstakingly created scenes.

Over time, we seemed, collectively, to draw a deep red circle over everything that happened. I did my homework and played football after school. My father coached the debate team. My mother's favourite student was diagnosed with cancer, and she began volunteering at a hospice for the terminally ill youth. Reams and reams of days unscrolled where nothing significant happened. And in the course of this time, these strangers that I was forced to live with became my parents; normal, regular parents. And Sripuri became sunken, my very own lost city, and with it, slowly, the man I used to call Appa.

With time, they forgave each other, and life was good again

now that they had each other and they had me. Whatever there was to come, there was the promise that they would face it united. The more they shut Vasan from my life, the less they mentioned him at home, the more he grew in my memories. Despite their best efforts, Vasan remained my father for longer than he had proclaimed to be one. I could recall each day with Vasan with clarity, and would forget whole summers with my parents, even if my memories of him were but the Chinese whispers of earlier memories, worked and reworked in my mind, ever changing, and accurate only to the last version of themselves. I continued to call Vasan Appa a lot longer than my parents had anticipated, and I am not entirely sure when I stopped believing that he was my father.

Parvati

11

1963.

It is on a desultory day in August, when the sky hovering between blue and grey promises nothing, that Parvati meets Ram for the first time.

It is the last class of the day. Bhaskar, the ill-tempered peon delivers the news that Mrs Gopi won't be in—Zoology lectures are cancelled for the week. He stands in the middle of the classroom, his face unflinching, and his tone unreadable. Rumour is that Mrs Gopi was wheeled away in an ambulance after collapsing in the staff room. The word cancer hangs in the air, but Bhaskar gives nothing away. He glances at no one in particular, and ignores their questions so that the class, wanting confirmation of the news, is left feeling disappointed.

Parvati doesn't want to go home yet. Lee, her best friend, seated beside her, unwraps a packet of Poppins and flicks a grape-flavoured one in her direction in a carom-striking motion. It is the only flavour of the candy that Parvati likes; usually there is only one in the pack, and on a lucky day, two. Only one today. They wait until the shuffling of feet has died down.

'What are you going to do?' Parvati says.

'Go home I guess?'

Parvati makes her usual ugly face—contorted lips, scrunched up nose, one eye open in wonder, the other closed in disbelief. As Lee laughs, her ample cheeks rise in her face. Becoming quiet, she says, 'I've got this horrible feeling about Mrs Gopi.'

Parvati's driver Muthu isn't in the parking lot, which for the moment has turned into a cricket pitch. She is relieved. The car embarrasses her—there are only a handful of students who have a driver escort them to and from college. This is her father's idea, and although her father considers himself a reasonable man, it would take a good deal of expostulating before she could change his mind. She must pick her battles with him, although she likes taking the bus with Lee, which she does from time to time when Muthu needs to write an exam, or when his sister has taken a turn for the worse.

Muthu is quiet and young, sixteen or seventeen, but seems older. He attends a night college where he is studying for a diploma in finance. Parvati likes his methodical manner, the way his wipes his glasses with a clean white cloth, the soft gentle motion of his hands, how he folds his handkerchief into a perfect square before placing it in his pocket, and how he arranges his books neatly in a small trunk in the boot of the car. He flips through old *Reader's Digest* magazines that her father has discarded while he waits for her. He drinks water from a child's apple-shaped water bottle which she guesses he has kept intact since his childhood. Out of curiosity once, Parvati had taken a peek into one of his notebooks and admired his handwriting. Later, she had been caught out when she had complimented him on it absentmindedly. It has changed everything between them—though they spoke little before, and they speak little now, their silence has altered. Now when she sits in her father's Fiat 1100, she sees herself through his highly-polished lenses: rich, spoilt and inconsiderate.

In the bus, she and Lee make plans for the future.

'Is the Nobel Prize something that we can actually put on our shelf?' Parvati asks.

'Oh dear, I never thought of that before. Is this what they mean when they say "Don't lose sight of the prize"? I do hope they give us one each!' Lee says. 'If we are to share it, then it comes to my house first!' she shouts from the exit as she's about to get off.

A woman occupies the newly vacated seat beside Parvati. She holds a nylon bag close to her chest. It is full of balls of red yarn and a pair of knitting needles sticks out of them.

Their eyes meet.

'You have beautiful hair,' the woman says.

'Thank you,' Parvati says, both pleased and embarrassed by the compliment. 'You should see my mother's.'

The woman goes on about the restorative properties of various flowers and herbs commonly used in hair oil. Parvati half listens.

'Lemon for dandruff . . .'

Parvati's eyes wander. Her mind is writing in cursive. The bus conductor is yelling at a man who's lost his ticket.

'Amla for baldness . . . hibiscus for thickness . . .' the woman continues.

The man has found his ticket and everyone in the bus shares in his satisfied indignance as he holds it up for all to see.

After the woman gets off, Parvati looks out of the window
and is startled not to recognize the neighbourhood. She makes
her way to the front of the bus and requests the conductor to
stop before the next scheduled stop. He curses unintelligibly
before obliging her by blowing his whistle. Once she gets out,
the conductor leans out of the bus; one leg perched on the step
of the entrance, another dangling in the air, and shouts
something at her. His words are swallowed by the roar of the
bus as it pulls away, but the scowl on his face is sufficiently
eloquent. This is an unfamiliar part of town to Parvati. It is
older and more bruised than the area in which she lives. The
street is crowded and flowing with people. The dogs are still.
On either side of the street, the facades of family-run shops,
colourful and run over with signs, give the briefest glimpse into
the dimly-lit dwellings that exist behind them. Each shop is
indistinguishable from the other to her, yet each appears to
enjoy a selective patronage. Parvati is thirsty and pausing at the
entrance of one shop, she considers buying a lime soda or a
pista milk. There is no one behind the counter. She looks past
the magazines which have been strung together over a cord of
rope like a necklace over the entrance, and sees a man and his
dog lying on a cot together.

'Well, come election time, and the wheat and chaff will soon
be separated,' she hears him say to someone she cannot see. He
sits up when he sees her and makes his way to her. He uses his
bare hands to release the marble in the Goli Soda bottle, and
the effervescent liquid gushes forth from the mouth of the
bottle. Parvati warns him that he could hurt himself, maybe
even lose a finger. The man grins, as he takes money from her.
'If that's the case, I should have lost it already.'

She drinks it without pause, and declines when the shop owner asks if she wants another one. She starts when she feels someone at her side. She turns and finds a bespectacled young man beside her. He has the beginnings of a beard and his hair appears to be due for a cut.

'I am in your class,' the man says. 'Ram Sharma?' He is wearing a lungi and a banian. Parvati doesn't remember him.

'And which class is that?' she says, sounding suspicious. One can't turn up to class in a lungi and a banian.

'In the class that wasn't,' he says.

'Sorry, I just—' she begins but he cuts her off.

'Not to worry,' he says, smiling. 'I have a forgettable face.'

'Do you live around here?'

'No, I like the hustle and bustle so much that I choose to live away from it. That way it always seems more exciting when I come to it, like I am approaching a storm. I just came here to fix my cycle.'

Ram turns to look at his bicycle and her eyes follow his. The old bike shop owner joins his thumb and his index finger together to signal that his bike is good and ready. She waits while Ram walks back to the shop. He examines his bike carefully, running his hands along the spine and squeezing the tires fondly. He appears to pay the old man more than he charges him, pressing coins into his hand. He rings the bicycle bell and smiles when it tinkles.

They fall into step—he walks beside her, and gently he nudges his bicycle with one hand. His khadi shirt is wound around the handlebars. His trousers and books are strapped to the bike rack.

'She is old and battered,' he says patting the worn-out seat, 'but I am finding it hard to give up on her.' He removes a cigarette from a fold in his lungi, blows on it, asks a passerby for a light.

Parvati is nervous to be seen walking beside him. She looks about her for someone who might know or recognize her.

Ram leans towards her. 'I could be your brother,' he whispers, reading her mind. 'No one's going to know.'

'I don't have a brother,' she says. Ram laughs. She softens and laughs with him.

The sky lowers around them. He walks her to the nearest bus stop.

'See you in class,' she says.

She waves goodbye from the bus. He pulls his shirt free from the handlebars and waves it like a flag until the bus turns the corner and he is gone from her sight.

12

They don't exchange words for a week, but he is no longer a blotch in the brick red background of the classroom wall—he is a thriving spot in the corner of her eye. One afternoon, after a long lecture on polymers, Parvati emerges from the classroom to find Ram waiting a short distance along the corridor into which the class opens. He approaches her cautiously, smelling of Hamam soap, clutching his notebook firmly in his hand. His white shirt is clean, his brown trousers are cut unfashionably and his shoes are all wrong, yet the ensemble seems to become him. His hair is combed, though it is still too long. His words are already forming in his mouth.

'Good class?' he asks.

It is not what he is really asking. Parvati extrapolates the meaning of his words from the twitching of his lip, the paleness of his fingers that are pressed against his book too tightly, and the apparent change the days of anticipatory waiting has wrought in him since their first meeting.

'It's nice to see you again,' she says, answering a question he has not asked. She grins. 'You look different. More conventional.'

'Lungis are much maligned against,' he says.

'How are you?' she asks.

'Can't grumble. No cause for complaint,' he says, relaxing, reassured by the fact that she has lingered. Lee, only a moment ago walking beside her, vanishes.

'Did you think it was a good class?' she says.

'What?'

'You asked, earlier—about the class. Did you enjoy it?"

'No,' he says flashing a smile. He shakes his head. 'It was a terrible class.

'It wasn't all that bad. She covered some good points—'

'You are only saying that because she is crippled and you feel sorry for her.'

She scrambles for words, but he is laughing.

'It's okay. I got a chance to speak to her just now and told her exactly what I thought of the class . . .'

'You did? What did you say?'

'I said all the fairness creams in the world couldn't make polymers fair and lovely . . .'

'You are in the wrong class if you think that,' Parvati says bluntly. 'Polymers are beautiful.'

Another class comes pouring out of a classroom and the two of them draw a few stares. Ram nudges her back into their classroom without touching her, his hands grazing the air below her elbow. In the vastness made by the room's emptiness, she is suddenly jolted by the intimacy between them.

'I think you are right,' he says earnestly. 'I worry that I am not cut out for the sciences.'

'You don't have to be good at something to love it,' she says. 'Though people will have you think so.' She cocks her head to read the time on his watch. 'But I am getting late and I have to go home.'

'Can I walk beside you?' He follows her, without waiting for an answer. 'My bike is still unwell.'

'No you can't. What's wrong with your bike?' She steps out of the classroom and into the hallway.

'Leg's still wobbly. Why not?'

'Muthu my driver will be waiting for me.'

'You have a driver? And at such a young age?' His tone is mock mocking.

She stops.

'It's my father. He doesn't like people being idle. The driver has nothing to do. My father likes owning a car, but he doesn't like being in it. It makes him nauseous and puts him in a foul mood. He walks to work and forces me to use the car.'

'Your father isn't going to like me then. I am always idle. Tomorrow, then?' he says. 'If there is any chance that you will prefer my company to your driver's?'

'I don't know that I will,' she says. 'And his name is Muthu.'

'Good answer,' he says, as she breaks into a run.

Parvati puts her book down on the bedside table when she has read the same page twice. She turns off the tube light and lights a candle so that her sister Durga, turning in her bed, doesn't wake. She sits on the ledge by the window and thinks back to the day she met Ram, now colouring in the events of the afternoon with little imagined details. She winds and unwinds this scene, altering minor details. She pictures Ram in her mind a few minutes earlier than when she had met him. He is sitting on his haunches beside the cantankerous shop owner, whose air of surliness is dispelled when Ram offers him a cigarette. He lights the old man's cigarette before he lights his own and listens sympathetically while the man, his mood now softened, complains about the water shortage problems they are having. Ram's eyes, always alert, scan the streets for any excitement they may offer up in the way of a beautiful woman, an altercation, or an accident even as he maintains an idle conversation with the shop owner. She thinks with a smile that he quickened his steps when he saw her.

Parvati's mind knits and plots. How will she find opportunities to be with Ram if Muthu arrives at four o'clock on the dot? What excuses could she make to linger after class hours, or to avoid being driven home? Should she complain of Muthu's driving skills, perhaps insinuate that she finds his presence uncomfortable—she knows that such a complaint would cost Muthu his job, and she is momentarily taken aback at the malice her desire is capable of spawning in her. This line of thinking is dangerous for other reasons too. The slightest rumour in her college grounds could snowball through scurrilous gossiping into a scandal. Only a year ago, one of the B.A. girls, Seetha, was expelled for becoming romantically involved with a member of the canteen staff. The father of the girl, a prominent journalist with one of the national dailies, had retaliated by writing a scathing article in the Sunday supplement chastising the university for failing to take responsibility for the incident and making a scapegoat of the girl. Shortly thereafter, a number of new rules were enforced. All classes were to end by four p.m. More women professors were encouraged to apply and were accepted for teaching positions. Canteen hours were limited. The library was divided into a male and a female section, and women were required to wear saris to classes. Parvati considers her own father's reaction if such a rumour about her should reach him. She kills the train of thought, extinguishes the candle, and goes to sleep.

Muthu sends word the following morning that he is unable to come in—he needs to take his sister to the hospital. Parvati feels a twinge of guilt, as though this turn of events is a result of her own scheming.

'So you got rid of the driver. For me?' Ram says.

Class has ended and he is following her to the bus stop. 'Don't come with me,' she says. 'People will look.'

'I don't mind,' he says. He turns left and then right and waves to everyone in an arc. 'I am always looking at other people. I cannot object when it's my turn. It's just not right.'

'I am not worried about you. My father . . .'

'Has spies all over town?'

'You don't know my father. He just might.'

'So, then what are we going to do?'

He grins.

Her bus is early. She takes her time getting in the queue. She sees the back of Lee's head. She knows that Lee will save a seat for her and ask her nothing about Ram unless she mentions it.

'Bus is early,' Ram says. 'Would you believe my bad luck?'

The bus conductor gets off the bus to allow everyone in.

'I am sorry for your bad luck,' she says climbing in.

'How are you, Boss?' Ram says to the bus conductor as though they had been in school together.

'He likes me,' she says to Lee, taking the seat beside her.

'He likes everyone,' Lee says without turning to look at her and pulling the window shut.

Parvati asks Lee if she will cover for her one afternoon. She will only miss a practical class and she can make up for it easily. She will be back before class finishes. Lee tears the last page of her notebook and writes the words 'Nobel Prize for Chemistry' in bold lettering in the middle of the page. Then she makes a plane and sets it flying across the room.

'Bye bye Nobel Prize,' she says.

Parvati's face falls. Winning the Nobel Prize is their standard joke, but it has come to represent their aspirations, and their collective will to make their college education count, so that years from now, they wouldn't begin a sentence with 'I used to be good at—' the way that they hear their aunts and mothers say wistfully to them.

'Don't let your marks drop,' Lee says, in a motherly voice, pointedly touching the tip of Parvati's nose with the tip of her finger.

Parvati thinks for a moment. 'I won't, I promise,' she says.

'It's not me you have to promise,' Lee says.

They are quiet, each considering how their lives are about to change.

'Where is your conscience?' Lee says in an exaggeratedly serious voice. 'You are leaving me stranded with Dreary Diana for a prac partner.'

13

Ram is making bhelpuri to commemorate the occasion of her first visit to his home. It is modest and unremarkable. He gives her a tour of the three rooms that comprise it, and informs her that the bathroom and toilet are at the back of the house, and that she should be careful to look out for Munna, the pit viper. He makes a hissing sound and pretends to strike her with a cupped palm. 'You don't scare me,' she says.

She had expected Ram to be neat, but he isn't. She laughs at his attempt at tidying up for her—piles of books and magazines are arranged in the shape of the letter P on his well-worn writing desk. 'For Pointless,' he says.

His clothes are in a heap on a chair in his room covered over with a towel. His bed is lumpy with a sheet drawn over it in obvious haste.

The kitchen is tiny and contains only a small stove, and Ram explains to her that though he relies mostly on canteens and carrier meals, he is an expert in making chaats and other short eats. He has no chopping board, so he gives the black stone counter a perfunctory wipe with a scrap of cloth torn from an old towel and shrugs when she makes a face. He brings out a large knife from a plastic bucket from underneath the kitchen counter and to tease her, he pretends to wipe it on the side of his trousers. As he chops the onions and tomatoes, his gaze drawn to the vegetables, he draws his lower lip over his upper lip and twists his mouth forming an expression so childlike that though it distorts his face, it delights her. They sit beside each other on the makeshift divan in the living room, a mattress over which Ram has thrown a block-printed counterpane, and a few bolster cushions. They share the same plate, careful not to touch the other's fingers. 'Tell me a story about you,' he says, suddenly.

'What kind of a story?'

'Your pick,' he says. 'So long as it is a true one.'

She stops eating. 'I can't think of one,' she says.

'Yes, you can,' he says. 'Tell me the kind of story you don't tell often. A secret story.'

'I don't have that many secret stories to tell.'

'Sure you do. Everyone does.'

'A happy story or sad story?'

'You know which one I want to hear.'

'It happened a long time ago,' Parvati says, surprised by how much she wants to tell this story. 'We were living in the old family home then. I may have been ten years old or less. My sister hadn't been born yet, and I was often bored at home. I was the only child in a house full of adults. We lived in a joint family. There was my grandmother, my uncle and his wife, my parents and me. My father and my uncle were always squabbling about their jewellery business in those days and in the end they ended up parting ways, but in those years, there were always fights in the house. My mother would forbid me from entering certain areas of the house for fear that I would take something that I wasn't supposed to or break something that wasn't mine.

'I didn't know it then, but I was lonely. Then a boy came to work for us in the house. He was from my father's village. Village boys were thought to be more trustworthy and my father had known his parents from the time he was a young boy himself. His name was Raja. As soon as he came, my world brightened up. He loved the radio. Whenever he had a moment to spare, he would turn it on. He didn't care what was on. He loved it all. The plays, the advertisement jingles, the songs, the newsreader's voice. When he wasn't listening to the radio, he was singing or pretending to read the news in a newsreader's voice. As soon as I came home from school, I would seek him out and he would stop whatever work he was doing to give me his version of the programmes aired that day. At night, we sat on the stone bench in the courtyard and listened to old Hindi songs. He was so nice. One night, as we were sitting there, I put my head on his shoulder and wound my arm around him. I don't know why I did it. He stiffened but he did not push me away. He was still singing when my father spotted us.

'My father grabbed my grandfather's cane and beat him right there in the courtyard. The radio was still playing. I didn't understand then what had made my father so angry. Raja was sent back to the village. I saw him many years later when I went back to the village for a holiday. He had become an ice cream vendor. He called me "Madam" and did not let me pay for the ice cream. I wanted to say something—but I couldn't. I have always wished that I had.'

When she finishes, she cries and cries. She covers her face with a cushion. They sit in silence. They listen to the crowing of crows. A coconut from the tree in the compound falls with a thud. Ram puts the plates away and they wash their hands.

'Tell me your story,' she says, reminding him that he started it. They are sitting on the divan now, closer to each other.

'Okay. Which story?' he says. 'How and why I spent the night in jail? How I ran away from home at fifteen or how I met a beautiful girl at college and got her to leave her driver for me?'

'I want to hear all of those stories.'

'Someday,' he says reaching for her hand. 'You are one secret short now, and you need to create a new one to make up for the shortage.'

There were things that one noticed about people that they, living all their lives within their bodies, would never know about themselves, as though living made one immune to the distinctive elements of one's own composition.

Ram has about him the look of a man who always has time at his disposal. His movements are slow, deliberate and languorous, hinting at latent fluidity, as of an indolent cat. When he orders a cup of tea at the tea stall or buys cigarettes from a shop, he always strikes up a conversation with the vendor. He makes trivial comments about the weather—'It's too humid today, so humid for a minute I thought my grandmother was breathing down my neck,' he says to elicit a smile. He makes these comments with unexpected enthusiasm, and people are compelled into responding to him. He makes jokes that need repeating, which he does patiently, and takes it lightly when no one laughs. She also knows that as garrulous as Ram strives to be, he is happiest when he is quiet and feels no need to talk.

He begins leaving his bicycle at home. They skip out of class, and sit at different ends of the bus, trying not to laugh when they catch each other's eyes. They meet up at the tamarind tree, a block away from his house and then walk the short length together. She tries not to worry when the coconut seller begins to recognize her and gives her a smile when he spots her.

They make afternoons into midnights. Things that had once seemed impossible in her imagination, the touch of a hand, the removal of a piece of clothing, become ordinary commonplace things. They kiss and fall asleep. They move the location of the clock so they can keep track of the hour and make it back to college in time for Muthu.

They trade family secrets.

She tells him that her parents had married young. Her mother, Charu, was only fifteen, and her father, Manickam, merely twenty years old himself. They were distant cousins and although the original proposal had come for his older brother, that engagement had fallen through when the brother had lost his eyesight in a fire in the family factory. Parvati had heard that her father had liked the sight of the girl with the thick eyebrows and a solemn expression, dressed as she was when he first saw her, in a long checked skirt and holding a skipping rope in her hands. She thought her parents might have been too quick to picture the people they had wanted to see in each other during that encounter. Manickam may have thought Charu was sensible and thoughtful, and she that he was sure-footed, and charming, but their disillusionment began almost immediately after their wedding. Manickam realized that Charu was uneducated, only fifth standard pass, and that she wasn't solemn or serious. Charu liked the cinema, her friends, and giving away her things, a clock here, a bangle there to members of her family. She forgot to pay the milk lady and sang out of tune in the bathroom. She in turn learned that Manickam was a bed-wetter and an insomniac, secretive about his movements, and superstitious about small things, the alarm ringing before the cock's crowing, sitting on the stairs, and losing his footwear on the beach.

Ram's family were originally from Delhi, but had settled in Dubai when his father, a civil engineer, had found a lucrative position in a petroleum company. The four children had taken to their new life with ease. Their mother, on the other hand, had developed a depressive disorder when the ailing mother she'd been forced to leave behind had committed suicide, leaving a note that read: You live for your children, then you die alone.

His grandmother had always been cruel and vindictive, Ram said. After that, it was as though a leak had sprung in his mother and her life was slowly let out of her.

'When I think about my mother,' he says, 'I cannot explain it, but my old wounds . . .' He rubs the foot that was fractured in a motorcycle accident. 'They begin to hurt again.'

Ram had arrived in India only a year earlier to join Madras College on the heels of his brother, Kamal, who had already graduated with a law degree from the institution. His two sisters were still at school.

At first, the two brothers had boarded at one of the bachelors' quarters in Triplicane in a building with six tiers of dizzyingly similar rooms overlooking a central courtyard which had become a parking lot for bicycles. When their father, donning his safari suit and polished shoes, had visited them, he had been revolted by the sight of the building with its cracked floors, the walls splattered with bird droppings and betel nut spit, and the rows of white banians and underwear hung haphazardly on clotheslines stretching from window to window. He ordered them to find lodgings elsewhere and berated his younger brother for not keeping an eye on his boys. That was how they had found themselves in their bright and beautiful new house in Nungambakkam. A few months ago, Kamal had married a girl of his parents' choice and returned to Dubai. Now Ram was on the lookout for a housemate.

Parvati laughs. Only Ram would think that the humble home he lived in was bright and beautiful.

14

Lee comes home for lunch on Vinayaka Chaturthi. Their house, into which they moved two years earlier, still wears a new and uninhabited look. It is constructed in a style that seems to reflect Manickam's character—the structure itself is conventional though the veneer, with its mosaic flooring and its shiny white paint on the walls, is modern, and the house too is full of dark nooks and corners.

Charu has laid out the table with the best silver, the plates and bowls which have been handed down to her from her mother-in-law. A gold idol of Ganesha on the sideboard is bedecked with jewellery from Manickam's shop, and sits gleaming amidst the boughs of jasmine, roses and turmeric leaves. Durga trails Lee about the house, admiring her drop pearl earrings, imitating her lilting voice, and pestering her for beauty tips. The three girls pick at appalams and vadas in the kitchen while they wait for Manickam, who is never late to a business engagement and always late to any at home.

Manickam is a thin and wiry man, with carefully parted hair. He dresses only in white and never wears footwear. His business is thriving though one wouldn't know it from looking at his shop front which is nondescript and has Manickam

Jewellers written on its facade in simple black lettering. It stands in sharp contrast to the other jewellery shops for which the area is famous. There are no signboards with beautiful models, not even any jewels in the window display. Instead, through the glass, one has only a glimpse of red velvety curtains, the kind that adorn cinema screens and by which Manickam was inspired. Even inside, only the choicest gems are displayed in the glass-cased tables, and in the gentle light of oil-lit brass lamps they are resplendent. Manickam plies his customers with coffee or soft drinks, a plate of bajjis appears from the canteen down the road while he asks after their sons and daughters and daughters-in-law. He discreetly learns what they are after. He disappears into a dark room behind a heavy wooden door and emerges with a selection of cases as though he has been saving the jewels solely for them. He never forgets a face and has a knack for matching the right jewels with the right women. While he clasps a necklace or slides a ring onto a finger, he asks in a low, hushed voice he has cultivated, after family members who were casually mentioned on a previous visit—children with chicken pox, ageing relatives confined to their cots after a stroke, a newly purchased Pomeranian. If someone mentions a backache, he knows of a great orthopaedic doctor. If talk is of a wedding, then he is well acquainted with the proprietor of the marriage hall, and no, it's no trouble at all to place a call to book it for the date they desire.

Occasionally, Parvati remembers her father as the man who held her hand in a dry warm grip all the way from the house to the shop. He would point at treetops where there were monkeys, for which she had a particular fondness in those days, and buy her bottles of pista milk from the same stall each week. The milk coated her tongue green and left her teeth feeling numb. Those days have long fallen away now, no evidence remaining in their relationship that they had ever held hands.

By the time he arrives home these days, he has exhausted himself of all compassion.

They are hungry, and impatient.

'When is he coming?' Durga tugs at her mother's sari pallu.

'Shoo,' her mother says and waves a spoon at her.

'The words "go on without me" have never passed your dad's lips.' She eats a vada. 'You have to get by in other ways.'

Only Lee's expression of surprise reminds Parvati that she has become inured to the war of words between her parents, never uttered directly to each other, but through her and Durga.

It is past two when Manickam arrives. The mood collapses like the puris have. He washes his hands with soap at the sink, wipes them clean with the thin cotton towel he wears over his shoulder.

He draws a chair for Lee. Lee squeezes Parvati's hand under the table. She is petrified of him.

'How's Mrs Gopi?' he asks Parvati as Charu begins to serve them. Parvati is surprised that he's heard the news.

'We haven't heard any news yet, Uncle,' Lee says. 'I sent her a card.'

'That's very thoughtful of you,' he says to Lee, then turns to Parvati. 'Why is it so hard for your mother to measure out the salt?'

The room falls quiet. They listen to the sound of a ladle scraping a pan in the kitchen. Someone rings the doorbell—it is a boy asking if he can come in and look for his shuttlecock in their back garden. He is just visiting the house next door he explains. 'I'll come back later,' he says, sensing their mood.

'What about you?' Manickam says turning to Parvati. 'Have you sent her a card?'

'No, not yet.'

'Why not? Is ink in short supply around here, unlike the salt?'

'I meant to write,' she says. 'I've just . . .'

'Had your head in the clouds? Leave it there for a little longer . . .' he says, helping himself to some mango pickle. 'She will probably reach heaven faster than the post reaches her house.'

'How is Jayanti?' Parvati asks defiantly. 'Did you send the car to take her to the hospital like Muthu requested?'

Durga gets up and goes into the kitchen where Charu is eating on her own.

'As a matter of fact, I did,' he says, proudly.

'No stipulations? Be home by six o' clock? Don't take the bridge?'

'The only thing I asked, is that he throw a sheet over the back seat. He couldn't thank me enough for my generosity.'

'She has kidney disease, not leprosy!' Parvati says. Lee lays a hand on Parvati's arm.

'I don't mind you talking back to me,' Manickam says calmly, helping himself to more payasam. 'That is how I raised you.'

Lee stands up and excuses herself. 'I will miss my bus,' she says. 'I better be going.'

'I would have had Muthu drop you off if he was here,' Manickam says.

'That's okay, Uncle—'

Manickam cuts her off. 'But he isn't here, and he may never be here. He's passed all his exams. He doesn't need us anymore.'

Parvati's heart lurches, a selfish reflex spasm that occurs before she can control it with her mind. No more car journeys. No one to watch her. Bus rides with Ram every day.

'I'll miss him,' she says, rising. 'I'll see Lee to the bus stop.'

Everyone is assembled in the college auditorium; even the many students who would normally run off to tea shops whenever there is a break in their regular class schedule. Lee appears to be in tears, her eyes and nose are red and she wraps her shawl tightly about her. She reassures Parvati that it is only her cold. She doesn't cry easily. There are chairs, but no one is seated. Parvati links an arm through Lee's.

The principal arrives and steps up to the podium.

'Mrs Gopi,' she begins. There is a collective gasp, even though the news is expected. 'Mrs Gopi passed away this morning. She wasn't much older than most of you.' Her voice breaks, and she dabs at her eyes with a handkerchief, then adjusts the microphone. 'She went to this very college; she sat in the very same classes as you. This university was her home, her passion, and her life. Today, we recognize the achievements of this very brave young woman, who made a difference to so many lives. Her legacy will live on in those of you who were fortunate to attend her classes. Let us take a moment, please, to remember her. If you will join me in a moment of silence . . .'

Someone strokes Lee's arm as they shuffle out of the auditorium.

'I am not crying,' she says.

'Did you know that?' Lee says to Parvati. 'That she was from this college? That she was so young?'

Parvati is silent. Then, 'I am so glad that my father goaded me into sending her a card,' she says. 'When he said it, it seemed like such a small thing. Now it feels so important that I did it.'

Outside, the day is bright, and Lee is back to her pragmatic self. 'This may be the wrong time to tell you this,' she says. 'They handed back the exam papers yesterday when you weren't in class. You got fifty-six per cent. Shukla Sir has written on the front page of yours to pay a visit to his office to discuss some "issues". You better watch your attendance.'

15

Ram is waiting for her in the library landing as she emerges from the reading room and walks down the flight of steps. He looks up from the book he is reading, *A Clockwork Orange*. He places a peacock feather to mark the page, and nudges her in the direction of the secluded alcove under the stairs where for the moment, they are alone. He tells her that he has a new housemate, the son of a friend of his uncle's. He didn't have much of a choice in the matter, he says. He shrugs. 'Doesn't seem like a bad sort.'

His name is Vasan and he is from some small and obscure town in Andhra Pradesh. Ram tells her how terrified Vasan had appeared when he'd gone to the station to receive him. 'He was probably the sort of child who chewed his pencil to the bone. You know?' he says, placing his own pen in the corner of his mouth.

Parvati attempts to keep a straight face.

'He would have been that kid that had to stop a bus in the middle of the journey, his poor mother would have had to explain to all the other passengers how he had diarrhoea, and the whole bus would have watched him go behind the bushes . . . or something . . .'

'You are cruel,' she says, bursting into laughter.

'Actually, I really like him. There is something innocent about him.'

'Well, you'll work quickly to correct that won't you?'

Ram looks around. They hear the thumping of feet on the stairs and wait until they've died down. He leans over and gives her the tiniest of kisses on her lips. She is surprised at how the kiss reverberates through the rest of her body. Heat rushes up her ears. Her palms grow cold.

'How did you get inside my mind?' he says.

The first time Parvati meets Vasan, he comes in wet with bare feet trailing mud across the floor of their house. His shirt is clinging to him. The edges of his rolled up trousers are crusted with mud. Ram gets up from the divan where he was sitting beside Parvati to greet Vasan at the door.

'Are you all right?' he asks concerned, looking around for a towel, and handing Vasan his lungi. 'It's not raining, is it?'

'I've been in the ocean,' Vasan says.

Ram studies Vasan's face and decides not to press the matter. He puts an arm around Vasan, and gives him a shake. Sand grains slide to the floor. Parvati is surprised to find that Vasan is handsome, more so than Ram, with smooth brown skin and large widely-spaced eyes framed by thick long lashes. Yet, he does not seem to possess the confidence of a handsome person. His gait is slouchy, his shoulders turned inward, and when he notices her, he looks embarrassed and turns away almost immediately. 'Parvati?' he says to Ram, barely audibly.

'Who else?' Ram says.

Vasan apologizes to her for his appearance and disappears into his room to dry himself and change into something suitable. He returns in a pressed blue shirt with a pair of brown slacks that seem too good to be worn at home. There are streaks of white over his neck where he's neglected to smooth the talcum powder into his skin. His hair is neatly combed though he's made only a half-hearted attempt to dry it, causing wet rivulets to run down the side of his cheeks.

Vasan seems ill at ease and his arms hang uncomfortably. His eyes scan the room for a place to sit. Ram drags the chair from under his desk and positions it so that it is at a slight angle to where Parvati is sitting on the divan. Vasan tugs at the end of his shirt as though he's finally found something do with his hands.

'Now these are some of the best butter biscuits you are ever going to taste,' Ram says, grabbing a plate of biscuits from the desk and offering it to Vasan in an attempt to get him to relax.

'Sit down first, Guru,' Ram says pushing Vasan down into the chair. 'You know this is your home too, right? I am not the proprietor of a restaurant. This isn't hotel Ram Vilas.'

Vasan takes a biscuit. It crumbles in his hand, and he brushes away the crumbs from his lap, irritably. Ram treats Vasan as though he were a younger brother; this is a new side to him that Parvati finds endearing. He teases Vasan about the mess he has made on the floor and having to wipe up after him, then tells him he will make his special cup of ginger tea because it's cold, and encourages him to talk.

Ram stands behind Vasan's chair and gives his shoulders a squeeze. 'He is such a good singer. You have got to make him sing for you, Paru.'

'I am not that good,' Vasan says to Parvati.

Ram seems both annoyed and moved by Vasan's diffidence. 'What was that song you sang that time? That one that nearly made me weep?'

'I am not sure,' Vasan takes a bite of the biscuit and chews carefully, cupping his palm underneath his chin.

'You know the one, *Chod gaye* something . . .?'

'*Chod gaye balam*?' Parvati asks. 'I love that song.'

Vasan shakes his head. 'Another time, I will sing it for you,' he says. Ram lets out a huge exaggerated sigh. He disappears into the kitchen, leaving them alone.

Parvati takes on from where Ram left off, attempting to make Vasan feel comfortable in his own home. Inside the kitchen, she imagines Ram grinning.

'How do you like Madras, Mr Vasan?'

'Vasan. Just Vasan,' he says. 'Please.'

Vasan seems more at ease with her, though he is still stiffly seated in his chair.

'It is the most beautiful city I have ever seen,' he says. His voice is louder and more assured now.

'You think so?'

'There is no doubt about that. You don't think so?'

'I have never asked myself that question. You don't usually have to look at your own city like that.'

'Like what?' Ram asks, shouting from the kitchen.

'Whether it is beautiful or not,' Parvati says, raising her voice to be heard.

Ram re-enters the room and hands them each a glass of tea. He leans against the desk and crosses one leg over another. He raises his eyebrows in Parvati's direction. 'Well?' his look says.

'Too sweet,' Parvati complains with a smile before turning her attention again to Vasan.

'When you go to another city, you have to decide whether you like it or not. So you begin looking at it from different angles—whether the people are friendly, whether the climate is too hot or cold, are the buildings interesting and so on—but when it is your own city, it is somehow different.'

'What do you mean?' Vasan says. He has stretched out his legs.

'Well, I think that what you consider beautiful changes when you are looking at your own city.'

'That's interesting . . .'

'I mean that-sometimes we love ugly things. We love things for the memories they bring back—we love certain places simply because they have become familiar to us.'

'What do you find beautiful about your native town?'

He has to think about it.

'It's small,' he says. 'When you go somewhere, you always meet someone you know. There is a river that runs through it, and although it's brown and dirty, and the bed is stone dry in the summer, when it runs, you can hear it gurgling. It sounds beautiful.'

'Who'd see beauty in a dirty brown river that gurgles?' Ram asks amused.

'Precisely!' Parvati says, triumphantly.

'Have you been to many cities?' Vasan asks Parvati.

'You have caught me out, Mr Vasan,' she says, grinning. 'I have only been to Bangalore and Delhi. Both times for weddings.'

'Did you like them?'

'I wanted to like Bangalore. Everyone was always saying how

it had the best weather in the world. Lalbagh was so pretty. It was the only place we got around to visiting. But we couldn't stay there long because it started raining. It rained and rained that day. At first it was wonderful. My parents wanted to go back to the marriage hall, but I made them stay. My sister ran into the rain and made me go after her. We got soaked. My mother was yelling at us and my father gave us one of his famous smiles. So tiny, like one of those flowers in Lalbagh that bloom once a year. If you are not looking, it's gone. Everything was great and then suddenly, for no reason, the rain became oppressive. I thought I was going to burst into tears. Just like that. For no reason other than it had turned dark in this awful way. Almost dark, but not quite dark enough. The trees were grotesque in that light. I wanted to run out of that place and I almost did. So now, I cannot decide whether I like Bangalore or not. It's unfair, I know. But that's how I am.'

'She talks a lot when she gets going,' Ram says.

'I find it interesting. I've never had these kinds of conversations . . .'

'Have you been to many cities, Vasan?' Parvati asks, sensing his loneliness.

'This is the first city I have been to,' he says, smiling for the first time.'

They laugh. 'Now Ram is the real traveller here. He's never still for a moment.'

Hearing this, Ram sits down beside Parvati and pinches her cheek. She takes the bristly end of her plait and brushes the hair onto his face playfully.

Vasan looks away. 'There are too many street dogs here,' he says, changing the subject of the conversation. Parvati and Ram exchange glances. What an odd thing to say, Parvati thinks.

'Are you both engaged?' Vasan asks, again out of the blue.

'We haven't told our parents yet,' Ram says, casting a sideways glance at Parvati.

'I am sure you will get a good job, and your future will be bright, both of you . . .' Vasan says, as though he were an older uncle to whom they've come for their blessing, looking uncomfortable, but with assurance in his voice.

Ram throws his head back against a bolster cushion and laughs. He closes his eyes and shakes his head. Then all of a sudden, he opens his eyes and his face is at once serious.

'I don't want my future to be bright,' he says. 'Not right away, anyway. I need it to be dark so I can find my own way out.'

Parvati turns her face to his but he is looking straight ahead, as though he is already gazing at that future that isn't bright and which he cannot see out of.

Vasan is always attentive when Parvati visits. He takes her umbrella at the door to shake it free of its excess moisture, and rushes to hand her a cushion before she takes a seat on the divan. On hot days, when she wipes her forehead with a handkerchief, he points the standing fan at her direction and asks her if she will have a cold glass of buttermilk, though she invariably refuses it. Parvati notices little changes about Vasan during each visit; on one occasion, he is wearing a lungi like Ram, on another, he suggests that they play antakshari. Vasan has a strong singing voice. He starts off shaky, but only from the nerves, and when it unlocks, it takes her by surprise.

'He's got eyes only for you,' Ram teases her.

It is Vasan's birthday and Ram is throwing a surprise party for him. Parvati helps in preparing a menu and a list of essentials.

'My friends don't need much,' Ram says. 'Luckily, Hemant's managed to procure some liquor, he's got Navy friends in high places, so the essentials are covered.'

She gives him an I-don't-know-what-to-do-with-you look. 'This doesn't seem like the sort of party that Vasan would enjoy,' she says.

'It's exactly the kind of party he needs.'

They head to the bazaar together. There is a long queue at the general stores. A tea boy is busy handing out cups of tea while the customers are being served. Ram slips him a rupee note and tells him it's for slippers and slippers only.

'If I come here again, and find that you are walking barefoot, I am taking that note back.'

The boy nods. 'Yes, Sir!' he says, pocketing the money. 'Now will you buy some tea? I've lingered here so long, I probably lost some customers.'

Ram slaps his cheek gently, as though he were rebuking him, but he is smiling. He buys two glasses of tea, but is forced to drink both glasses when Parvati notices the strands of cream from the milk floating about on the surface.

'Are you really going to take him to task if he doesn't buy slippers?' she asks when the boy bounds away in the direction of another customer.

'Of course not,' he says. 'Just providing him with some incentive.'

When it's their turn, they buy phenol and a coconut broom, candles for when the electricity goes.

'You want balloons, cards, matches?' the owner asks blankly, when he hears them mention a party. They buy all three.

At the grocer's, she hands the shop owner a list. 'Wish everyone was this organized,' he says. He reads aloud the ingredients. 'Biryani is it?' he asks. 'You don't need ginger?'

She holds the bunch of mint close to her face to inhale its scent. When she begins to haggle with the price of the carrots which are thin and wan, Ram stops her.

'Don't,' Ram says.

She cannot read his mind, but the look on his face tells her that he's just seen her in a new light. He becomes withdrawn. She attempts conversation on the way back but the streets are full and noisy, and they cannot walk side by side without being parted by passersby or cycle rickshaws. Back home, Ram puts on an Elvis Presley record. *Don't Be Cruel* comes on, and Ram pauses, and she knows in that instant that he had meant to play the A side. The song plays on as Ram goes out to the backyard to grab a bucket. She cannot make out the lyrics, but the music brings her to tears.

Something has altered Ram's vision of her. Parvati recognizes this phenomenon. She's noticed it herself, how people's personalities are fickle, disposable things. People changed their opinions of other people day after day, year after year. Last week's best friend was this week's nemesis, your uncle was an annoying old fogey one year at a wedding, and had 'always been kind' the next. People changed over the course of a lunch, as they sat revealing things about themselves that you'd never known they'd ever possessed. All these images of people were floating about, being trampled upon, eroded, reshaped, glossy one day, and dirty and grimy the next. There was nothing you could do. Every day, you had to navigate a world that was full of potential false moves and pitfalls, and without knowing what it was, she'd just fallen into one.

They scrub the floors quietly, only addressing each other when they need anything, the pail of water, the soap, the towel. They make up the divan with clean sheets. They are forced to cook the biryani in two batches since Ram's pot isn't large enough. She provides him with instructions. He follows them without question. The sun is bright and every crease in Ram's face is lined with sweat.

When everything is ready, Parvati excuses herself. She has a left a small bag of her belongings at his home—a towel, some soap, a tin of talcum powder, and a small container of kohl. She makes her way across the backyard through the growing bramble to the bathroom. She washes her face with soap, and reapplies the kohl. She daubs her face with Ram's towel and the overpowering scent of him untethers her, causing tears to well up in her eyes, but she shakes her head. She doesn't linger in front of her reflection in the mirror—this gesture helps in gathering her composure.

'I'll go now,' she tells him, walking back into the house.

'I cannot imagine that you would go to all this trouble, and not stay for the party,' Ram says, reaching for her hand. She draws her hand away.

She puts on her sandals.

'I am sorry for this afternoon,' he says. 'The grocery guy, he was looking at you as though you were my wife—and it made me look at the two of us like I was up on a plane, and we were cars on the ground.'

'Wish Vasan a happy birthday for me,' she says.

16

Returning home, Parvati notices that the construction workers are working past their scheduled time. She picks up the *Financial Expert* and sits on the wicker chair in her room firmly putting thoughts of Ram out of her mind. Within minutes, she has fallen asleep.

The book has slid to the floor. Durga picks it up and places it under Parvati's pillow, where she's seen her sister store it. She wakes Parvati gently by touching her fingertips with her own.

Parvati wakes with difficulty, the impression of some un-recollected dream still pressing its dark weight in one part of her mind. She has trouble adjusting to the room, the light, the metallic drone from the drilling next door, and her sister's face which is caught in shadow. Suddenly, Durga's features are of a person much older than her nine years. Parvati leans forward and kisses her sister's cheek. In their room, they are often affectionate, expressing a solidarity that embarrasses them in front of their parents.

'Shashi Perima is here,' Durga tells her. Parvati sighs. 'She's been asking for you.'

Whenever her sister visits, Charu is self-conscious and strained, seeking to impress her while simultaneously disdainful of her opinion. Over the years, Parvati has watched them squabble over and over about the same things, enacting the same play, varying nothing more than the props. Their memories of slights and injustices have not softened or been smoothed down with time; instead, they have grown protuberances, renewed by the bitterness with which they are pulled up time and again.

As Parvati anticipates, her mother is full of instructions for Durga and her when they emerge into the hall. The blouse has run colour, and needs to be soaked in soda water. The clothes haven't come back from the iron man, and would Durga run up to his cart? Where is the tea strainer? Can someone locate it please?

She feels sorry for her mother when she makes these small futile attempts to demonstrate that she holds the reins of her household, when she is fooling no one, not even Durga, who has ignored her request and has sat down beside her aunt on the sofa.

'What are you doing sleeping at this hour?' Shashi says with her mouth full. A plate of idlis is nestled on her lap in the folds of her sari. She is a messy eater, and the sight of the green coconut chutney mingled with shreds of the idlis in the cave of her mouth fills Parvati with distaste.

'Come and tell me all the gossip!' Shashi moves closer to Durga, making room for Parvati to sit on her other side. 'What's happening?' She loops an arm through Parvati's conspiratorially.

Parvati leans her head away from her.

'I don't know,' she says. 'I am not even sure what gossip constitutes anymore. They have a new menu at the canteen. Does that count?'

'What's wrong with you?' Shashi says in a mock angry voice, but sounding genuinely annoyed. 'How can you be this tired after such a long sleep?'

'I'm sorry,' Parvati says. 'It's the weather or something.'

'I cannot imagine the luxuries that girls these days are afforded,' Shashi says when Charu comes in with a fresh batch of idlis. 'It certainly wasn't that easy for us. The last time that I slept during the day was when I was pregnant with Sudha.'

As soon as she hears her aunt utter the word 'pregnant', Parvati knows what the matter with her is. The icy cold knowledge gushes through her.

'Maybe you are not well,' Shashi says, taking in Parvati's face, mistaking her fear for illness.

'I am sick,' she says her to mother later that night when she is in the kitchen ordering about the maid. There is a full moon outside the kitchen window. She leans over the counter to take a better look.

'Pournami today,' her mother says. 'No meat today. Are you hungry?'

She shakes her head. 'I might have to stay home a couple of days from college. I am feeling awful.'

Parvati fears the night, of lying in bed alone with her secret. She is afraid she will speak it out loud, that this news will tumble out of her when she is not looking. In the morning, she turns on the radio, and listens to the news while lying in her bed. She tries to focus on the world outside, on the boatmen who are lost at sea, in order to fill herself with another's despair, and not her own. She imagines their wives waiting for them at home, having to light the stoves and cook their children dinner, all the time imagining the water filling up in their husbands' lungs, their desperate unheard cries. Durga flits in and out of their room, to bring her news of the rest of the house. Manickam is furious as he is late for work. He stepped on a cow patty going out and had to hobble on one foot to the tap in the garden to scrape it off with his other foot. 'He's not really late though,' Durga says, climbing into the bed with her. 'You know how he always leaves half an hour early.'

'School bus!' her mother yells and Durga gets up reluctantly.

'I wish I was sick,' she says before brushing down her school uniform and heading out the door.

Outside, the sun, partially obscured by clouds, shines without being invasive. In the little patch of garden that the builders had seen fit to keep, and of which she has an unimpeded view from her window, delicately shaped young mangoes are dangling from the tree. Tiny birds of a kind that she doesn't recognize are flying close to the ground before disappearing from her sight. Wedding music starts abruptly from some part of their street, drowning out the radio. The strains of the nadaswaram, high-pitched and occasionally off-key, are enjoyable for the flaws that she is able to discern in it. The day is deceptively normal and she is fooled by it.

'There has got to be a way,' she says out loud. She gets dressed quickly.

'I am feeling better,' she tells her mother who is surprised when she asks for change from her purse. 'Today's class is important.'

'Don't forget your umbrella,' her mother says. 'Looks like rain.'

She will need to tell Ram.

'I have something very important I need to tell you,' Parvati says when the first class of the day has ended. They linger automatically until they are the only ones left in the room.

Ram clears his throat. 'Where have you been?

'About the other day,' he begins, without waiting for an answer. 'I didn't mean to . . .'

She has forgotten all about the other day. It seems of little importance now. Her mind has been consumed by a thousand thoughts. She wafts her hand in a 'don't worry about it' gesture.

'Usual spot,' she says. 'Now.'

He looks at his watch. 'Now?'

She hurries out of the room and in the direction of Lee, who is in the hallway leaning against the grandfather clock and waiting for her.

For the first time since their trysts began, Ram and Parvati run into an acquaintance of his. It is Ram's neighbour, Mr Suri, a big man with stooping shoulders and a lopsided smile that he is quick to flash. He is recently retired and his days are dotted with minor engagements: a flute concert at the Narada Gana Sabha, a viewing at the film society of which he is a member, a return trip to the market because he's forgotten the mustard oil that his wife needs for her lime pickle. He turns off the scooter, because he is cautious about his petrol usage, and he is in no hurry. On another day, Parvati might have looked for cover. Today, it doesn't seem to matter what anyone thinks. Since learning that she is pregnant, her singular focus on the tiny heart beating inside her has blurred her other senses.

Mr Suri waits for an introduction from Ram, but the coconut seller who's been watching Ram and Parvati for months calls out to her. 'Amma,' he says, though he is older than she is, extending an arm with a coconut balanced on his palm. 'This one's sweet.' He lifts his stool and sets it on the ground with the other hand instructing her to sit.

'What is this Ram?' Mr Suri says. 'You won't show your face at my home anymore? Seems that you've got some new friends and no time for old ones?'

'I've been meaning to ask you, Uncle,' Ram says. 'How was that film you were so excited to see the other day?'

It is enough to set Mr Suri off. The wind is hurling about; it picks up the packet of straws resting on the pile of coconuts, and scatters them, and the coconut seller chases after them. The raindrops fall noisily, and Parvati turns to see Mr Suri slap his shoulder in annoyance as though the raindrops were bird droppings. Past him, in the distance, a telephone line has collapsed.

'No more excuses,' Mr Suri says as he starts his scooter. 'I will accept no excuses from you whatsoever.'

They break into a run to escape the rain. Inside, Ram rushes to find her a towel. He throws it around her neck, and tugs at the ends with both hands to draw her closer. She pushes him away.

'I will not accept any excuses from you whatsoever,' Ram says in Mr Suri's voice.

They are still wet from the rain when Parvati delivers the news. A shriek erupts from the next door compound of a chicken flying from the hands of its slaughterer. Ram does not speak, nor does he look at her. He stoops to pick up a crinkled postcard of the Grand Canyon from the floor and sticks it in the pages of a textbook. He pushes aside a pile of books on his desk and scrapes a stub of candle wax with his thumb. Finally, he looks at her.

'I will come for you,' he says. 'We need to lie low for a little while. I am going to disappear for a few days. I will need to inform my parents. I might go talk to my uncle, sort out the details. And then we can make a formal proposal.'

The room grows long between them. 'You will need to be strong and patient. I will come for you.' As he speaks, the light goes out of his eyes, and she imagines somewhere inside him, all the doors are shutting.

The tears that she's held in check now come streaming as she walks back to the bus stop. No one is looking at her. The roads are flooding and the drainage canals are flowing over. She joins the crowd huddling under the awning of a shop nearby. She is surprised when she hears her name and looks up to find Vasan. He approaches her with haste and animated eyes. A smile is forming on his lips as he crosses the street, oblivious of the cars honking at him as he does so. His expression changes, however, when he draws closer to her and his scanning eyes take in her face. His excitement is replaced with anxiety. He mumbles something about the rain and his office closing, but Parvati is unable to focus on his words, as though he were talking to her from a great distance and she can catch but a few of his words. She is startled when her purse drops to the floor and coins spill out onto the ground. Vasan is instantly on his knees, gathering them up. For a moment, their faces come close before she draws back. Fortunately for Parvati, her bus arrives and she shuffles along with the other waiting passengers forming a queue, barely remembering to thank Vasan for holding his briefcase over her head to protect her from the rain. It is only a short walk from where the bus drops her to her house, but just then there is another short burst of rain and Parvati is soaked. On arriving home, she scans the entrance for her father's umbrella, and is relieved at not finding it in its usual place. She climbs up the front steps in a hurry.

In order to slip into her room, Parvati has to tiptoe past the kitchen. 'Parvati?' her mother calls, even though Parvati has been careful to walk lightly. 'It's me,' she says, slipping into her room. Parvati undoes her ribbon and shakes her plait loose. Her face is cold from the rain. She peels off her wet clothes and changes into an old skirt and blouse. From the music room, she hears the strained notes of her sister's voice, her music master making her repeat the same refrain over and over again. She lies down in her bed and draws a sheet over her body. She hears her mother calling her name again, then falls asleep.

'You're burning up!' Her mother is at her side. She feels the cool touch of her mother's palm against her neck. Parvati struggles to open her eyes, and her mother leaning down to look at her reminds her of Durga, and she is filled with the love she has for her sister. She sleeps fitfully though the night and stays in bed the following day, unable to muster the energy to face the cloudy day, and much less, to face Ram.

17

The phone rings late in the evening. 'It's Lee,' her mother yells.

Parvati is surprised. Neither is comfortable speaking on the phone in front of their families, and the phone is located in a special stand beside her father's chair in the living room. The phone is reserved for emergencies only.

'Hello?'

'Hello, it's me, are you able to talk?'

'What is it?' Parvati asks softly, out of earshot of her mother who is busy instructing the maid. 'Has something happened?' Her father is upstairs, as he usually is at this time, first counting the cash, then cleaning the safe, then checking the ledger, and finally locking up. Durga is already asleep.

'I heard about Ram's dad . . .'

'What about *her*?' Parvati says, using the female pronoun to keep her mother's curiosity in check.

'You haven't heard? I don't understand . . . weren't you with Ram this afternoon?'

'What has happened?'

'Ram's dad had a heart attack; he's going back to Dubai.'

'What?' Her voice shoots up, causing her mother's eyes to dart in her direction.

None of this is making sense to Parvati. 'I had this horrid feeling you didn't know about it,' Lee says at the other end.

'Is *she* okay?'

'He is in the hospital. I don't know much more than that.'

'When did you hear about this?'

'I saw Ram today coming out of the principal's office. He told me himself.'

'How can this be true?' Parvati is incredulous.

'He looked devastated,' Lee says. 'The news was all over the campus.'

Charu attempts and fails to stop Parvati from going to college the next day. Ram is absent from class. Classmates, who have barely acknowledged her presence all semester, stop by her desk and ask after Ram's father. Any news yet, they want to know. Where did all these people come from and how had they known Ram? And they all seemed to know about the two of them. All those elaborately constructed lies, the sneaking away when no one was looking, pretending in class that they meant nothing to each other, making no eye contact, the ducking into the library landing, the bus rides, it had all been a waste. Everyone knew.

The more she thinks about it, the more Parvati is convinced that Ram's lie about his father is a deliberate ploy on his part to detract from conjecture about his leaving. Anyone more superstitious was likely to hesitate while claiming their parent had a heart attack when untrue, or at least suffer the consequences of the guilt of the lie, but not Ram. He always claimed that artifice was an integral part of life, and believed in exploiting it. And yet, she had expected him to seek her out before leaving, to hold her hand once more, to look earnestly into her eyes. She tries to recollect his parting words. He would come for her, he had said. She needed to be patient.

It pleases Parvati that Ram has gone to such lengths to protect their privacy. It comes as a surprise to her that carrying such a weighty secret could be so pleasurable. It has given way to a new place inside her mind; a place raw and terrifying, and yet somehow alluring for the possibilities it holds. As the days go by, she seeks out the solitary corner desk in the campus library where she rests her head on a hardback book that remains unopened while she stares out of the window where a crow pecks at a worm, and a band of dogs doze in the sun. The hours blur, her memories become entangled with her visions of the future, until she can no longer tell whether the white shirt which she sees Ram in when she closes her eyes, is one that he actually owned or one that she's conjured up. She is caught in a haze that prevents her from hearing the class bell when it rings and glazes her eyes during lectures.

Lee follows her through the halls and across the lawns without saying a word. She brings her cups of tea from the canteen and steadies her when she is momentarily dizzy. Eventually, Parvati gives in and leads Lee into the ladies toilet, the walls of which are full of such confidences, and whispers her news to her. Lee's eyes grow wide, then narrow. She clenches her hands, and bites her lip as she does before writing an exam. She is close to tears. They lock themselves in the teachers' toilet which is wider and cleaner than the others.

'How could you?' Lee says. Parvati doesn't answer. There is

no way in which she could gather together the words that would describe to her friend the world in which this act had not only seemed possible but natural. She pushes her sari below her waist for Lee to examine her body for changes.

'Nothing,' Lee says. 'If anything, you look like you've lost weight.'

'Let's go,' Parvati says, readjusting her sari. 'I can't stand this smell.'

But Lee doesn't move.

'What will you do?' she asks.

'Get married,' Parvati says looking at her feet. 'Or elope.'

'What about your studies?' Lee says. 'Have you thought about that?'

'More than I can say.'

There is a tall mirror in Parvati's room that her sister, Durga, uses to measure her height. It is propped up against the wall by the bedroom door and is so heavy that the maid protests when Manickam complains that she has not swept behind it. In the evenings, after Durga has fallen asleep, Parvati slips out of her bed carefully so as to not stir her sister and makes her way to the mirror. She lifts up her nightie above her waist and examines herself in the light of the street lamp. With one hand hoisting up the nightie, she lets the other feel around her waist, slide across her hip and run down the length of her thighs before finally cupping the burgeoning flesh on her stomach. One night, Durga wakes up suddenly and screams at the sight of her sister standing by the mirror. She slides herself next to her sister and as she throws her arm around her to comfort her, she tries to memorize the warmth of her sister's neck on her shoulder. She may not feel it again.

When three weeks pass, one day no different from the next, and the passage of time is discernible to her only in the changes taking place in her own body, Parvati becomes worried. No word has yet come from Ram. At night, thoughts of a life together with him have difficulty forming and snap off in mid-reverie. His silence causes new thoughts to take shape, and fearful of following these to their ends, she sits upright against the bed post, as though her posture might aid her in composing her mind. She leaves the window open and even though Durga, lying beside her, trembles with the slightest gust of wind, Parvati, feeling hot and sweaty, finds that the air is never enough for her. She sleeps fitfully and on several occasions wakes up with a juddering heart. She recognizes that these are the symptoms of fear but she doesn't probe their source. To pinpoint the source of that fear is to shake her faith in Ram, and she needs to cling to every scrap of faith she can.

One night, when sleep eludes her, Parvati lights a candle and picks up a notebook and begins to scribble a letter to Ram. She writes without pause and when she finally stops, finds it to be bitter and angry and tears it up at once. In her classes, instead of taking notes, she makes other attempts. Parvati is inexperienced at writing letters and is disappointed with the results. She tries conjuring Ram up in her mind so she will know what to say to him but that too proves difficult. Already the memories have begun to be eroded here and there and the harder she concentrates on summoning up his image, the more distorted it becomes. When she catches Lee looking askance at her book, she gives up the exercise of writing and composes the letter in her mind, all during the day while she bathes and while she gets ready for college, while she takes her bus, and all through classes, occasionally speaking out aloud and shuddering a little at the realization. In the end, it is a letter addressed as much to herself as to him. A letter that contains just enough hope so that the days that lay before her would be made bearable; but not so much hope that disappointment would be an utter surprise. When she knows every word by heart, and she cannot think of a single word more to add or detract, she writes the letter out in a page from her Chemistry practical notebook seated at her usual corner desk in the library and seals it in an envelope that she has long stolen from her father's files in forethought of this moment.

They'd had no reason to exchange addresses. They had met every weekday in college, and they snuck away to Ram's house whenever they could. They had two whole years of campus life to look forward to, and now, not only did she not know where Ram was, she could not be sure that he would return.

Parvati is certain that Vasan would have Ram's latest address. It occurs to her suddenly that Ram may have expected her to contact Vasan. She brightens at the idea. Vasan is the only friend of Ram's that she's met on a regular basis, and she guesses the only one Ram would entrust with important information. Perhaps he had a letter for her. She shakes her head, discarding the thought—it would be unlike Ram to write a letter, but he may have left word for her with Vasan. The librarian, who is passing by wheeling a trolley of books, stops to ask her if she is okay. Parvati smiles and nods.

'I've just realized something,' she says. 'Thank you.'

The next morning, Parvati tells her mother that she has to stay after her last class to clarify some questions with Mr Shukla. She retrieves her old exam paper with his writing and points it out to her mother. She is listless all day, and forgets to eat her lunch. Then she is filled with a churning hunger so intense that she is forced to eat the coconut rice her mother packed for her in class stealthily behind a propped up textbook. Parvati has never been to Ram's house unaccompanied. As she climbs into the now familiar bus, a sense of loss gushes through her body. She clutches her throat which is all at once dry. The windows of the bus are fogged up from the weather and Parvati rubs at hers with a handkerchief in a panic as though the window was altering the world for her, and it would remain that way, forever blurry. She is relieved to get off the bus. It is nearly five o'clock but the street wears an inexplicably desolate look. As she passes the coconut seller and then Murugan's Canteen, whose manager is a friend of Ram's, Parvati shields herself with the pallu of her sari drawn over her head. It is little protection from their eyes that follow her as she makes her way to Ram's home. She slips off her footwear as she is wont to doing, then slips back into her sandals again, realizing that this action is no longer necessary as she will not be entering the house. After her last awkward encounter with Vasan at the bus stop, Parvati has no desire to prolong conversation with him. She knocks on the door with a painful anticipation. She knocks again. The door opens. Vasan stands wearing Ram's lungi. He opens his mouth wide at the sight of her, then slackens his jaw and straightens his shirt.

'Parvati!' he says, stepping aside, making room for her to enter. Parvati takes a step back.

'I am sorry to appear at your doorstep—'

'Please, don't apologize.'

'Have you heard from Ram? Do you know where he is?'

'His father,' Vasan begins and trails off. 'He is in Dubai.'

So she had been wrong. Ram had not trusted Vasan either to tell him the truth.

'Do you have an address for him?'

'I will ask Mr Sharma, my employer, he is Ram's—'

'Uncle, I know.' The sight of Ram's clothes on Vasan makes her irritable with him.

'I can get his address for you tomorrow. If you can tell me how to contact you—'

Parvati reaches inside her bag and retrieves her envelope.

'Could you please make sure this letter reaches Ram? My address details are here if he contacts you for them before.'

Vasan takes the letter from her with both hands, as though he were receiving an offering from the temple priest.

'Please,' Parvati says. 'Will you get it to him?'

'I promise,' Vasan says.

Vasan

18

1964.

On a hot evening in May, Vasan's father, Sarangan, rapped his knuckles on the dining table in the midst of dinner to draw his son's attention. With a forced indifference in his voice, he informed Vasan that his long-time friend Mr Sadanand Sharma, of whom Vasan had only heard and seen photographs of, had consented to take on Vasan as a junior accountant in the firm of Sharma Associates, Chartered Accountants. Vasan was expected to report for duty on the 1st of June at 9:00 a.m. sharp.

Hearing this news over dinner, the lump of puliyogare rice that Vasan had been chewing lodged itself into the side of his mouth. Later, it occurred to Vasan that his mother had made his favourite dish as a small compensation for the news he was about to receive or to make it more palatable.

Ever since Vasan's first failed attempt at his Bachelor of Commerce final examination, his father had been pursuing what he called his 'Madras Plan'. It was a black day in Vasan's memory when the results had come in. Not finding his son's name in the Pass List, Sarangan had slammed the newspaper down on the table causing some loose change on the table to clang to the floor. 'Not a shred of evidence to suggest that we share the same genes,' he said.

Feeling contrite, Vasan receded to the far corner of the hall, where he stood stiffly against the wall, his palms wet against the cold white concrete. The disappointment in his father's voice was thick and made the room dark.

'He could have taken after any of the illustrious members in my family,' he heard his father say to his mother, Malati. 'But no, alas, he has to take after your brother!' Malati's father had paid 500 rupees to the school in exchange for a Pass Certificate for his son.

'Why are you dragging my poor brother into this?' Malati said irritably. 'What has this to do with him? He has enough problems of his own.'

'Well, don't expect me to cough up money for our useless principal to pocket. No son of mine is going to earn his degree in such a fashion. If he has to sit his exam a dozen times, then so be it. A dozen times it is. I am a teacher! If my own son does not recognize the value of a good education, then what right have I to teach? It ought to be in his blood. Have I not drilled it into his head? Should he not know by rote that "Ignorance is the curse of God; knowledge is the wing wherewith we fly to heaven"?'

To make matters worse, Sarangan added, 'At times like this, I wonder what may have happened had you borne another child. At least, all this—' he sighed as he made a sweep of the books on the shelves with his hands, 'may not have gone to waste.'

'Again, that topic?' Malati said.

'Sorry, Malu,' Sarangan said, thawing. 'Don't be angry.'

'You tell me, how many brothers and sisters do you have?'

Resigning himself to the conversation, Sarangan said, 'I don't have any brothers and sisters.'

'How many siblings do I have?'

'Twelve.'

'And how many of them have fewer than three children?'

'None.'

'So whose fault is it that I have only one child?'

'Mine.'

'Then, again and again, why do you forget it?'

There was a short silence. Malati sat down on the floor and, spreading a handful of jasmine blooms in front of her, began threading them into a garland. Her hands were not nimble and the flowers escaped from her knots. Normally, this task was relegated to Jayamma, but she needed to do something to keep herself busy. Talk of Vasan's future distressed her.

'Father a professor, son, thirty-nine per cent fail! Have you heard the way he speaks English?' Sarangan went on. 'Who would guess that his father is an English professor?'

'Speaking English isn't a bigger virtue than speaking politely.'

'He should go to Madras. He might actually learn something there.'

Malati was not in favour of sending her only son away.

'Over my dead body,' she said.

For all the authority Sarangan appeared to wield in the house, there was no decision that in the end was not subject to Malati's approval. A house in which Malati was displeased was not one in which Sarangan wished to reside. Malati had a volatile temper and Sarangan had never been able to predict how she would react in a given situation. Her anger manifested in innumerable ways. At times, she was given to screaming, her voice hurling itself at him, the words barely intelligible. Other times it became slick and venomous. One day, her lips were quivering while she wept interminably. On another, she sat on the easy chair on the veranda, immobile, with no expression on her face that he could read. Even after twenty-five years of marriage, he could see no pattern to her behaviour. Once, Vasan had overheard Sarangan tell a colleague that he was married to a beautiful marvel. A marvel that even as he wished to preserve, he wished to unravel and destroy.

So, Vasan had written the exam again the following year, and on that attempt, passed with a second class. There were not enough jobs in Sripuri for even those who had passed with a first class. For two years he had applied for jobs in vain. He'd watched his father step away from him when they met acquaintances, forgetting to introduce him, and sending him off on unnecessary errands whenever they met someone Sarangan truly sought to impress.

Now it appeared that his mother too had changed her mind. To Vasan, it was a sign that they had discarded all hope of his ever standing on his own feet. Vasan reached for his glass of water and drank it in one gulp as though he was literally swallowing the news.

Already, his accommodation had been arranged with Mr Sharma's nephew, Ram, who had a vacant room in his house left unfilled since his brother had married and relocated with his new bride to Dubai. Ram had also agreed to meet Vasan at the station when he arrived on the GT Express, a ticket for which had been purchased three weeks in advance and was slotted into the groove of the hanging photo frame of Lord Vinayaka in the hall. He was to arrive in Madras one week ahead of his joining date which would give him sufficient time to settle into his new surroundings. Two new sets of clothes were awaited from the tailor. A pair of black leather shoes from Bata, along with the free Cherry Red polish that came with them, was lying in a box under his bed. It was too late for Vasan to object even if he had been the sort of son who challenged his father's decisions.

Vasan accepted his fate. He had excelled in no particular subject or sport. He saw himself as that boy one found straggling at the edge of a group of children on the playground. He seemed to be there only to make up the numbers. When he went to university, it was no different. He found for himself a comfortable place on the periphery of his class. If his classmates forgot to invite him to go to the cinema or to the cricket match with them, as they often did, he tried not to resent them.

'Why didn't you go along?' his mother would urge him. 'Didn't they call you?'

'It's a stupid film. I am not interested,' he said, defensively, before locking himself in his room where he sat with one of his father's books that also held no interest for him, but which he forced himself to pay attention to. Had he been invited, he would have gone along and then wondered if he had made a mistake when he realized that he wasn't having as much fun as the others.

During lectures, he took notes diligently, making sure that every scribble on the blackboard found a place in his notebook, paying more attention to the act of note-taking than to the subject being taught. He didn't hesitate to lend his notes to someone else who had been goofing around at the time, and if

the notes were not returned in time for an exam, he was
reluctant to ask for them, and ended up studying in the library
with whatever material he could find there. Becoming furious,
Malati would insist that he demand his notes back. The
embarrassment of seeing his mother angry on his behalf would
impel him to lie to her.

'What do you know? Manu's mother is sick all the time. He
needs my notes. Poor fellow was in hospital more than in class.'

He never professed an opinion on an issue unless he was
provoked. Rarely was his opinion sought by anyone except
Malati and they were both surprised by the alternating irritation
and affection in his voice when he spoke to her. In the presence
of his father or his coterie of friends, Vasan was infallibly polite,
preferring always to hold his tongue.

Vasan's life had been complicated by the fact that Sarangan
was the Head of the English Department Faculty at Vivekananda
College. While on campus, neither father nor son acknowledged
the other's presence. It had been a conscious decision for both.
With time, this gap between father and son had only widened.
For Vasan, Sarangan's lofty demeanour and what Vasan thought
were his 'filmy' affectations had created an insurmountable
divide between him and his father. He didn't understand the
bawdy jokes his father told friends at gatherings. He cringed
when he saw Sarangan flirt with women twice or half his age.
He failed to comprehend how these women laughed or why his
own mother only shook her head and joined them.

Vasan found himself identifying with the people his father
considered his subordinates. Thus, he felt the bemusement of
the tea shop owner to whom Sarangan tried to teach English,
the humiliation of the bank manager when Sarangan corrected

his pronunciation in front of his colleagues, the unspoken bitterness of a poorly-paid colleague as he watched Sarangan drive past him through the college gates and wave to him carelessly every morning. Vasan himself preferred to walk to the campus but did not find the courage to protest if his father told him to get in the car with him. He agreed with the driver of the Fiat who had once told him conspiratorially that literature was a waste of time, although after chancing upon a poem by Rabindranath Tagore, Vasan had temporarily changed his mind.

'Such is the friendship I have with Sadanand,' Sarangan said, as Vasan boarded the train to Madras. 'You know what he said when I asked him about you?' His father gave him a prolonged look. 'Treat people as if they were what they ought to be and you help them to become what they are capable of being.

'That was Goethe,' Sarangan added for their benefit, although neither Malati nor Vasan had heard of Goethe.

'You cannot keep tiptoeing through life,' his mother said. 'You have to take some big long strides.'

The train departed from the station two hours behind schedule. Vasan's seat was situated by the window, but a family that had boarded the train at a previous station had occupied his seat. 'You sit here,' a portly old woman with a mouthful of betel nut leaves ordered him when he showed her his ticket. 'Let the child have the window.'

She patted the seat beside her to indicate where he should sit. Vasan wedged himself beside her and a man who had fallen asleep with a handkerchief thrown over his face. Having never travelled on his own before, Vasan checked continually in his breast pocket for his wallet, folded into which was a sheet of paper with Ram's address as well as Mr Sharma's telephone number (to be used in an emergency alone, his father had warned him). He carried only ten rupees in his wallet; the remaining money he had tucked into the folds of a brand new pair of grey trousers within his suitcase. He felt unsteady and a little nauseous.

Every time the train halted at a station, the compartment was filled with the distinctive smell of the train itself: a pungent metallic odour settling like an unwelcome guest and only being hurled out by the train's lurching movement as it left each station, and a breeze came in. With every successive stop, more and more people crowded into his compartment, although it was a second class compartment meant to seat only passengers with prior reservations. He had left home after having eaten a light breakfast of idlis and although he was hungry, he found himself unable to muster up the energy to stop any of the vendors who whizzed by him at a frenetic pace. He cleared his voice and attempted to raise it over the insistent cries of the other passengers who fought for the vendors' attention. No sooner than he would decide to buy something than the effort of having to do it would push him back into his seat. The vendors went in one station and out the other, their hands nimble, and their feet quick. Guavas, masala vadas, shundal, and papayas, all passed him by in cane baskets, their fragrances arriving before the voices that were selling them, and lingering long after the sellers had disembarked.

Disappointed with himself, Vasan closed his eyes to shut out the sight of the food. What chance had he of succeeding at a job at the prestigious firm of Sharma Associates when he did not have the courage to stop a shundal seller? He imagined Mr Sharma's embarrassment at having to dismiss him after having only hired him as a favour owed to his father. Remembering his father's mantra that it was a bad omen to think negative thoughts when embarking on a new venture, he looked out of the window and attempted to shake them off.

Through the grilled bars of the window, houses were steadily increasing in size, the painted advertisements on their walls peeling off like the gold shavings on barfis. The scent of leaves changed to the putrid smell of sewers, and at railway crossings, throngs of people waited on cycles and rickshaws, the children amongst them invariably waving to the passengers on the train. Soon, the jostling movement of the train caused him to fall asleep. When he awoke, he found that people were beginning to gather together their luggage. In following suit, he inadvertently knocked a man on his thigh with his suitcase. The man growled. 'Where do you think the train is going after it reaches Central Station? Sit down. We are all getting off.'

Vasan apologized before sitting down in his seat again, chastened.

Unaccustomed to the humidity and from nervous anticipation, he was drenched in sweat. He considered what he should do if Ram did not turn up at the station to receive him. He promised himself that in that event, he would first buy himself something to eat from the station canteen before taking a taxi to Ram's address. He felt for his wallet again in his pocket. Having decided this course of action, he felt a little better. He struggled to remain patient while people started to push their way past him to the exit. He made his way to the access and experienced a moment of panic when he saw that there were two arches above it. He had only been told to wait at *the* arch. He was relieved when he spotted a man in a white shirt holding a placard with his own name written on it. On approaching him, Vasan realized that the man was younger than he had seemed from a distance. He had a broad face and an untrimmed beard which provided an angularity to his face. His pupils were radiant against the white of his eyes despite the ill-fitting glasses he wore which gave him a bookish appearance. His lips were turned into a large smile. The man tucked the placard under his arm and held out a hand. 'Welcome to Madras, Vasan. I'm Ram.'

'Thank you. I hope you weren't waiting long?'

'I've got time,' Ram said. 'And it was a pleasant wait. A trainload of college girls got off the Bombay Express earlier.' He paused to wink. 'You just missed them. From Bombay. Bombay beauties.'

Vasan smiled. Despite himself, he relaxed. Ram took his suitcase without asking and led the way past the eager coolies and taxi drivers that were assailing them outside the station. At the taxi stand, a man was arguing with a taxi driver for charging him excess fare. His wife and three children sat on the pavement with their luggage strewn about them. The wife had an exasperated look on her face. A beggar who had been watching the altercation was placating her. 'Don't worry,' he told her. 'You have plenty of time. The Brindavan Express is always late.'

It was late afternoon but the sun was still high in the sky. Vasan was thirsty and hungry. He wiped his face with his handkerchief. His feet felt cramped within his new shoes and he longed to take them off and soak them in cold water. They crossed the main road, Ram weaving through the oncoming traffic effortlessly while Vasan tried to stay close to him. Ram waved down a taxi, explaining that they were cheaper from the farther end of the road. During the taxi ride, Ram sat in the front seat and chatted with the driver, occasionally pointing to some landmark, while Vasan looked out of the window. When the taxi turned into a vast road that ran beside the sea, Vasan felt his mood lifting. He welcomed the breeze that came skimming off the surface of the sea and ran through his hair. Suddenly, Ram asked the driver to slow down so that he could point out the college where he was finishing his Science degree. 'Beautiful, isn't it?'

Vasan nodded. He could hardly believe that the splendid rose-coloured colonial-style building was nothing more than a college.

'Hungry?' Ram turned around in his seat to ask him.

'Not very,' Vasan lied. 'I ate some shundal on the train. I am okay.'

'Forget shundal. I'll show you where you get the best fried fish in all of India.'

'I am sorry but—'

'Vegetarian?' Ram guessed. 'Looks like your father forgot to tell me. I think you'll change your mind when you try this fish.'

He laughed when he saw the worried look on Vasan's face.

'Don't look so frightened. I am not going to force you into eating it. I am just going to tempt you with everything I've got.'

'I am not worried,' Vasan said with a laugh, but the expression on his face was one of relief.

'I will tell you this much for free, you are missing out.'

The taxi halted in the middle of a forsaken street. None of the houses on it resembled each other in shape or size.

'Now this street,' Ram said. 'The houses don't look like members of the same family—they may not possess the same genes, you know? Their faces are all too distinctive, but inside them, I tell you, the people are identical. They've all attended the same schools, the same universities and belong to the same clubs. You meet one, you've met them all.' He grinned. 'You've met me,' he said as he unlatched the door.

Ram's house was small and inviting. The living room was filled with light from an enormous window that looked out onto the main street. Against this sat a large writing desk, unevenly brown, its legs a paler shade than its surface which had seemingly absorbed all the sun. A chair, simple in design, square and squat with a leather seat showing the concave scoop of frequent habitation, fit snugly under the table. Two Science textbooks, some bound notebooks and a ream of carbon paper were thrown across it. Some ink had spilled onto one of the books and left a stain on the table. There was no other furniture except for a mattress on the floor, which was covered by a kalamkari-printed counterpane and was made to appear like a divan with the use of bolsters and cushions covered in a similar print. Vasan's bedroom contained a single metal bed, but the mattress was opulent and hung over the sides of the bed frame. There was a window that looked out onto a large vacant plot of land run over with ferns and bushes, and pushed against the window-sill was a green metal table with a matching folding chair. On top of the table stood a black gilded incense holder in the shape of a lotus. There was a Godrej almirah in one corner which creaked when Vasan opened it and emanated a faint scent of talcum powder. They stood side by side by the door and surveyed the room. 'Like it?' Ram asked.

'It's excellent,' Vasan said, eager to please Ram.

'My brother was a lot tidier than I am. My girlfriend is a lot less tidy. She makes a mess every time she's around here.'

'Oh, you have a—' Vasan started and finished after a pause, 'girlfriend?' The word had come out of his mouth with difficulty but had a pleasant ring to it afterwards.

'Yes, Parvati. You'll meet her.'

'She is your girlfriend,' Vasan repeated as if to confirm what he had heard.

'Yes, *girlfriend*. Have you never heard of love?' Ram's tone was teasing.

'Not so much,' Vasan confessed. Ram looked at him with an expression of mock disbelief, lowering his eyes and pushing down his glasses.

'You think people in your little town don't fall in love and run off together?'

'They must,' Vasan conceded. 'I just haven't met any of those sorts of people.'

Ram laughed. 'You're funny,' he said. '*Those sorts of people*— you think we are another species or something?'

'No, not at all,' Vasan said too quickly, fearing he had offended Ram. 'I didn't mean that. I just—I come from a different place. I am sorry.'

Ram touched Vasan's shoulder lightly. 'I am an oaf—the way I talk sometimes. What will Uncle think if I scare his son away in one day? You are nothing like him, you know.'

'You have met my father?'

Ram shuddered dramatically, eliciting a smile from Vasan. 'He frightens the hell out of me.'

They moved back into the living room and Ram seemed to

forget what he was saying. He swung himself on top his desk. 'So you have met my father?' Vasan said, prompting Ram and settling down on the divan.

'Many times.'

Ram paused to consider Vasan's face. 'You are nothing like him. It's incredible.'

'No,' Vasan said, in a voice that suggested he had been complimented.

'Are you both planning to marry?' Vasan asked suddenly.

'What? Me and your father?'

'No. You and . . . your girlfriend?'

'What's the hurry? Are you trying to chase me out of my house already?'

'Nothing like that. I was merely enquiring.'

'One day, maybe. But not right now. Right now, I am starving.'

By the time they set out for Murugan's Canteen, the only eatery within walking distance of the house, the sun had lowered itself and left a ring of varicoloured light on the horizon. Despite its shabby appearance, Ram reassured him that the food at the canteen was always superb. A sign had been planted into the ground outside it which read: Murugan's Canteen Hotel. Added underneath the painted lettering in an unsteady hand were the words: 'Curd 25 paisa extra'. The manager of the hotel sat at a high desk at the entrance of the canteen. In the middle of a yawn, he smiled at Ram.

'New friend?' he asked Ram, whilst looking Vasan up and down.

'New and best friend,' Ram said, putting an arm around

Vasan and giving his shoulder a shake. Despite the melodramatic tone of his voice, Vasan was moved by the genuine warmth in the gesture.

'Vasan, Rajuanna is the reason anybody can stand this hotel.'

'That's right, Guru,' Rajuanna said, chuckling, and revealing a set of stained and uneven teeth, 'I am the only reason I can stand this hotel myself.'

'Vasan is going to be staying with me, Anna. He also gets family privileges, okay?'

Rajuanna contorted his face into an expression of exaggerated anger, his bulbous lower lip sliding to the left. 'You have to tell me who is family and who is not in my own house? Go, go! Sit down before I decide to throw you out.'

Ram nudged Vasan towards a table at the far end of the room. It was a long room crammed with tables which left little aisle space between them. Vasan nearly knocked a bowl of rasam onto the floor from an unclean table which still had mounds of food sitting atop plates and stainless steel dishes, as though the diners had been recalled suddenly with some unexpected news. Vasan wondered if the food was likely to be as good as Ram had mentioned if so much of it had been wasted. Reading his mind, Ram explained. 'People who come for the first time always order too much. How many idlis do you get in a plate normally?'

'Two?'

'Here, you get four. And you should see the size of the idlis!'

Vasan raised his eyebrows, as was expected of him.

'Yes, really. Brings in more customers.'

Rajuanna raised his arm without any urgency and waved a waiter in their direction. Vasan looked around the canteen. Many of the tables were occupied by other young men, students by the look of them, with the same thin faces wrought from being away from home for too long. At the adjacent table, two sated elderly men, having finished their food and in no hurry to return to their homes, were reclining heavily on the unstable benches upon which they sat. Their plates were empty but encircling their plates were rings of scattered rice grains. To the other side were three young men sitting in a row which, despite their physical resemblance, ate with the intensity of strangers. The other tables had been haphazardly cleaned and their Formica tops reflected the smears the cleaning cloth had left on them.

'When that door opens,' Ram said, nodding in the direction of the kitchen, 'don't look. If you look, you may not feel like eating.'

A waiter entered through the door bearing two plates piled with food. The puris atop them were glistening, golden and still puffed up with steam. Just as his appetite returned, Vasan caught a glimpse of the kitchen through the door, past the waiter's rawboned frame. It evoked in him the same revulsion as looking into an unclean tumbler congealed with the remains of coffee.

'I told you not to look,' Ram admonished him. 'You'll get used to it.'

Vasan approached his food cautiously, but the first taste of the vegetable korma was enough to overcome his distaste. 'What did I tell you? Good, isn't it?' Ram said, pleased with the change in Vasan's countenance.

'Two years ago, when I first came here, I had the same problem. All this filth and flies and shit everywhere . . . I was queasy for one whole week. But all the tasty things in the world aren't where you expect they'll be. You have to seek them and find them.'

Ram told Vasan about his family.

'After Kamal got married, it was so boring. We are not like brothers. We are friends,' Ram said, twisting his index and middle fingers together to indicate the strength of the bond that they shared. 'I missed him at first but then I met Parvati, and there are advantages to living on your own.'

Whenever Ram mentioned Parvati, Vasan found the train of his thought derailing. A moment of silence ensued as he steadied himself by thrusting a fistful of rice into his mouth. He chewed deliberately to afford him room to think. How was he to act normal when he was faced with a situation so new and intriguing to him?

A puri fell over the edge of the plate and skimmed the table and Vasan pushed it to one side of his plate. 'Next time, it won't bother you,' Ram said, laughing. Just then Rajuanna, deciding to stretch his legs, ambled over to their table. 'What is this, Guru? You are going to insult me on your first visit here?' He was looking down at a forsaken puri on Vasan's plate. Caught off guard, Vasan moved his fingers to the offending puri, but Ram stalled him with a touch on his arm.

'What, Boss? Next, you'll be asking us to eat food off your floor? That puri is pristine no longer, having fallen onto the table.'

Finally, Rajuanna said, 'Today, you don't pay,' speaking pointedly to Vasan. 'Tell your *best* friend, if he wants to eat here again, he had better learn to talk to his elders with respect.'

Laughing, they left the hotel in a pleasant mood. Ram listed the places Vasan should visit during the day when he would be at his college. The sky was large and Vasan's head was filled with possibilities.

19

The bountiful mattress was not as comfortable to sleep on as its appearance had promised. It was lumpy and the cotton had not settled uniformly, sinking near the small of his back, while in other parts of his body, tight fists of cotton prodded him. The night was darker than the nights he had experienced in Sripuri. Involuntarily, he began chanting the prayer his mother had taught him as a child to ward off fear.

Buddhirbalamyashodhairyamnirbhayatmarogataajaatyam-
vaakpatutvam cha Hanumatsmaranatbhavet.

He repeated the chant over and over again, drawing courage from the words until they broke apart, and sleep finally came to him in the early hours of the morning. He awoke suddenly when he heard a sharp piercing sound outside his window. He thought at first that it was a woman crying out for help. His room was already filled to capacity with light. He glanced at his watch and was taken aback to discover that it was past ten in the morning. Wrapping his veshti around him, he went outside in the direction of the sound. Ram had already left for his college. His bicycle was not parked in the front yard. The road was deserted but for a small mongrel dog that was limping towards the gutter. He looked ill fashioned, his head too large and nosy for his lean body, the skin stretching tightly over his frame. His hind leg was bleeding. Perhaps, Vasan thought, someone had thrown a stone at him or he had gotten into a fight with another dog. He tried to approach the dog, but sensing danger, the dog began to limp away faster. Returning indoors, Vasan rummaged in the kitchen and found a tin of rusk biscuits. He ate one and grabbed a handful for the dog. The dog had moved to the other end of the street. Clutching the biscuits in his hand, he approached it with exaggerated stealth. From one of the houses, a man came rushing out to the gate.

'He is scared. Put it down there. He will come for it later.' Vasan did as he was instructed. In his loose-fitting white banian and veshti, the man looked both comfortable and hot. He had one of those unusual faces which one, even whilst looking at it, was aware that it appeared younger than it was. He stood behind his gate, resting his elbow in a groove that the lattice work provided and flicked his nose with his index finger.

'You are new, isn't it?'

'Yes, Sir. I just arrived yesterday.'

'Which house?'

'108.'

'Ah, you are Ram's friend. I am Suri. Number 66. I know all about how you bachelors live. You had better come in and have some tea. My Mrs will want to meet you.'

There was a table on the hooded veranda upon which rested a chess set clearly in the midst of a game. It was an alluring sight. But Vasan needed to go to the toilet.

'I will come another time, Sir,' he said, thanking him for his hospitality and was forced to repeat his promise a few more times before he was excused.

Pumping water from the bore well into the bucket, he made his way through the thorny path in the overgrown garden leading to the tin-doored toilet and bathroom at the far corner. The latrine cleaner had already come and gone. The back wall, which adjoined a vacant plot, was embedded with shards of amber glass as a deterrent to agile thieves. The bathroom was dark and its floor slippery. He kept knocking his arm against the copper boiler, now disused because it was summer. He emerged from the bathroom smelling of Lifebuoy soap. He unpacked his suitcase, folded his clothes neatly into the almirah and placed his few remaining possessions on the table: a framed picture of Lord Srinivasa, his diary, a fountain pen, a bottle of unopened ink with an extra refill, a tube of Odomos and a packet of incense. He rearranged the incense burner so that it faced the picture. Having unpacked, suddenly he too felt empty. Convincing himself that he was unwell, he lay on his bed with a pillow over his head, leaving the house only to have a meal at Murugan's Canteen, but in the absence of Ram, Rajuanna failed to recognize him, and there ensued an awkward moment when he failed to acknowledge the enthusiastic smile with which Vasan greeted him. By the time Ram arrived home, there was genuine weariness on Vasan's face. Misinterpreting the reason for it, Ram asked him if he had gone to the Mylapore temple, which Vasan had placed at the top of the list of places to visit the previous night. But Vasan, in a weak and sickly voice that surprised even him, explained that he had a slight fever, lingering on the word 'slight'. Ram gave him two Anacin tablets to swallow.

The next day, Vasan felt worse. He would not admit to himself that he was homesick, but with nothing to do in the way of a distraction except to wander from the divan to the bed, his thoughts kept returning home. Absurdly, he missed his father's books which had given him no pleasure while he had had access to them. His home had already faded in his vision. He knew the rooms were not as big or as small, as cluttered, as spacious, as bright or as dark as they were in his mind now. They had gone through the transition of all memories. They no longer sought to represent actual times, places or things; they were as malleable as Plastecine, tucking into crevices that needed to be filled.

It was Wednesday before Vasan left the house again. He awoke with a gnawing hunger. Ram had brought him a packet of upma from the canteen the night before and insisted that he eat it, and Vasan ate it from the packet with relish. Today, he wore a new shirt and combed his hair for the first time in days. The image in the mirror pleased him. In his new clothes, he felt transformed and filled with hope. With purpose and determination, he set out of the house towards the canteen but to his disappointment, it was closed. The owner of the bakery next door was pulling down the metal shutter of his shop furiously. He had his back turned to Vasan and did not hear Vasan's approaching steps even though he had deliberately dragged his feet over the ground to draw attention. The man seemed to be in some hurry, so Vasan waited while he swiftly double-locked the shutter. The man started when he saw Vasan. 'What time does it open?' Vasan asked, pointing to the canteen.

'You haven't heard?'

'Heard what?'

'Panditji is dead.'

'What? Which Panditji?'

'Which other Panditji? Pandit Nehru!' the man said, annoyed at having to explain.

'Oh my God, Pandit Nehru! How? When?'

This reaction seemed to please the man.

'Just now only I heard on the radio,' he said. He made a fist and thumped his chest with it. 'Heart,' he said, theatrically. 'He had a delicate heart.'

Vasan sat down on the steps to the shop and placed his hands on his forehead. All the optimism he had felt in the morning slowly drained from him, and once again, his mind was filled with worry. It was his bad luck that Nehru had died just as he was about to join his first job. It seemed to him portentous that his new life should be prefixed with death. Was there not enough chaos in his life already?

'No canteen wanteen today,' the man said, climbing onto his bicycle. 'If you want, you can come doubles with me. I'll take you to the main road,' he said, but Vasan declined. He walked all the way to Mount Road, where everyone else was heading in small groups. He passed a line of old men in their crisp white jubbahs arguing vociferously at a bus stop about whether Indira Gandhi was a deserving successor.

Returning home, he was surprised to find a party in full swing.

Like Ram, his friends were of wealthy lineage. Their parents owned petrol bunks, cinema halls and confectionary factories. They wore jeans that had been sent to them by their aunts and uncles settled in New Jersey or Connecticut, and which were enveloped in a sheath of foreign scent that never seemed to wear off. The sleeves of their plaid shirts were turned back, the ends only half tucked in determined nonchalance. Sitting atop

Ram's desk, they swivelled packets of Charminar cigarettes and flicked matches with deft kicks of their fingers. They changed records, and sang aloud with the chorus. They had procured a bottle of Old Monk rum with great difficulty and they drank it straight from the bottle.

As the night wore on, they lapsed from spouting political theories, why and how Operation Leghorn had gone disastrously wrong, to telling dirty jokes. They recalled their favourite women from the brothels in the area, comparing their legs and thighs and breasts and disagreeing on each other's descriptions. And when they had exhausted these, they complained about the desultoriness of their lives, recounting in mock disparaging tones the unreasonable demands of their girlfriends, and in graver tones the characteristics of the brides that they would one day inevitably take home. The house became heady with the smoke from the cigarettes they exhaled, the dank smell of the rum they drank.

Ram had not pressed him to join them, perhaps knowing that Vasan would feel out of place. Citing a headache, he went to bed before the party broke up. It occurred to him that no matter what happened to the country, the lives of these men would quaver only a little. Unlike the men he had seen lining up on Mount Road on whose faces he had seen the fear of what tomorrow would bring. For these men, a little adjustment, and life would go on as before.

Mr Sharma left a message with Ram that Vasan was only needed to report to the office the following Monday. Vasan took to walking around the city.

Everywhere he went people's voices were filled with emotion and their hands filled with newspapers. Wherever he looked, in trains, buses, roadside ledges, teashops, and verandas, he saw people pleating and unpleating newspapers. And the papers were full of testaments to Nehru's glorious achievements, at once burying his flaws in line upon line of thick eulogizing. Something was happening to the country.

From a stall outside a bus stand, he bought a copy of *The Hindu*. Tucking the newspaper under his arm, he walked to the beach. Hot and feeling self-conscious, he walked hurriedly, counting his steps absentmindedly in his mind, a habit he resorted to when he was troubled. There, beneath the shade of an abandoned fishing boat, he sat, his newspaper spread out in front of him on the sand. He was now in Madras; he would have to learn to think like a modern man like Ram. The world was full of signals, and he would have to learn to read them. It was not enough to want so little, a small home, a little family of his own, a woman and a child to look after and to love. How was it, he thought, that the world could exist all around him and yet he himself was nowhere in it?

He recalled a friend of Ram's taking a jibe at the shirt he had been wearing on one occasion. 'Town tailors like to make bolder statements than city tailors,' he had said, laughing and tugging at one of the collar ends. 'You'll never have to worry about drowning with that shirt on.'

What happened to people like him? If you weren't talented, then you needed the belief that you could succeed, if you didn't have the belief, then you needed luck on your side, and if you didn't have luck, you needed a helping hand. And a helping hand would only stretch so far. Would he survive the endless trampling world? Would he drown or learn to swim amongst the ocean of men? As if to put this question to the test, he rolled up his trousers, discarded his footwear with two swift kicks, peeled his socks off impatiently and strode towards the water's edge. The water was colder than he expected, but as if to taunt him, he heard his mother's voice in his mind.

'You can't always tiptoe through life,' the voice urged him on.

His forehead was hot and flushed, but a cold current travelled up his legs as he waded into the water. Defiantly, he plodded on, the water now reaching his thighs, pressing against him with a force that seemed entirely deliberate to Vasan. He pushed back at it, awkwardly lifting his knees high above the water. Soon the water was up to his chest. For one cold moment, he thought his breath had ceased. He exhaled with effort. He slipped out of his shirt and wound it around his neck. A breeze came at him, stinging his nipples and scratching at his skin. A wave which had seemed innocuous at first struck him hard on his face, forcing bubbles of water through his nose, and splaying his legs before he was able to find ground again. When the water receded, he felt the tingling tug of the sand escaping from underneath his feet, straining his hamstrings and causing his knees to shake. Then he was caught in a cross current between waves that came at him together, but they were soft, frothy and grazed him lovingly. Every thought in his head died with their touch and he closed his eyes instinctively.

His shirt wrangled free from him. Without opening his eyes, he reached for it, attuned to the current, sensing the direction in which it would have drifted. He laughed when he caught it. When he opened his eyes, he saw the frames of two bare-chested fishermen as lean and brown as incense sticks, signalling to him frantically with wild arm movements. He had drifted a long way in. As he made his way back to the shore, he thought the water was pleading with him to stay, holding his shins, as a child might beseech a parent to stay longer in the playground, but he kept on marching, right past the fishermen with the bemused look on their faces. His slippers were missing, but in his elated mood, he did not concern himself with searching for them. It was in these high spirits that he returned home. It did not worry him that Ram's friends might be home. He was ready to face an army of them. Neither their drunken talk nor their crude jokes could bring him down today. What he was not prepared for was the beautiful woman he found sitting on the divan when he entered the house.

20

She was smiling at him, a warm but tentative smile, which seemed to contain some questions as well as some answers. She sat with her legs pulled together so that her long braid, which hung over her left shoulder, fell to her feet. Her eyes were unusual, the upper lids heavy, making her seem as though she had slept too long, while the irises under her thick flickering lashes were sharp. There was a sense of unsettling authority about her eyes as though they saw more than his did. Ram was seated beside her at the edge of the divan. He rose to greet Vasan.

'Parvati?' Vasan asked Ram.

'Who else? What's this? You left your slippers behind and brought the beach with you?' Ram said, examining in amusement Vasan's bare feet, the trail of sand on the floor, as well as the grains that were sticking to Vasan's arms.

'Please, give me one moment,' Vasan requested, feeling foolish and at a loss for an explanation. In his room, he calmed himself while he shook the sand off his body and changed into fresh clothes. He sprinkled some talcum powder onto his hands and rubbed some of it on his face. When he emerged, Parvati smiled. This time, it was a more definite smile, warm and effusive. There was no other place to sit except beside her. Feeling embarrassed to sit in such close proximity Vasan waited until Ram drew a chair for him. It unsettled him, the height at which he was looking down on her. Ram disappeared into the kitchen to make tea.

'Are you liking it in Madras, Mr Vasan?' she asked, raising her chin to him.

'It is the most beautiful city I have ever seen,' he said, meaning it. Vasan felt a peculiar excitement in speaking to her. As Parvati went on about what she thought was beautiful and ugly about cities, Vasan had trouble staying focused. Not only was he unfamiliar with discussing matters of aesthetics, never before had he spoken this familiarly with an attractive woman. He tried to stay calm, but the effort caused him to miss hearing the last of her words.

'Tell me, do you find your town beautiful?' Parvati asked him.

'In its own way, yes.'

'What exactly do you find beautiful?'

He had to think about it.

'It's small,' he said. 'When you go somewhere, you always meet someone you know. There is a river that runs through it, and although it's brown and dirty, and the bed is stone dry in the summer, when it runs, you can hear it gurgling. It sounds beautiful.' As he spoke, Vasan was moved by his own words. He noticed that there was a small gap between her two front teeth. Ram returned with cups of tea. The two of them were playful with each other, which indicated to him that they'd been closer to one another than he could imagine. The intimacy of their gestures made Vasan look away. Never before had he been in the presence of lovers. Vasan had not been the sort of man to whom his college mates had made confessions of this kind. And here he was in a room with two lovers, carelessly entrusting him with the knowledge of their love, as though love was a commonplace thing. 'There are too many street dogs,' he said, changing the subject of the conversation, not knowing himself where the words had come from.

He was aware when Ram and Parvati exchanged glances. It had been a silly thing to say.

'Are you both engaged?' Vasan said.

'We haven't told our parents yet,' Ram said.

'I am sure you will get a good job,' Vasan said, feeling certain that he would. It was plain for him to see. Ram had a bright future ahead of him whether or not he wanted one.

21

The office of Sharma Associates was located off an alley on Mount Road. Vasan had to endure two bus journeys during which his pressed clothes became crumpled, and the smell of jasmine or coconut oil came undone from somebody else's hair and clung to his own skin. Fortunately, the bus dropped him off ten yards from his office beside a tea shop where he drank a cup of rejuvenating, sugary tea before heading to his new office. A young man identifying himself as the office peon ushered Vasan into a cabin.

'Your name?' Vasan enquired.

'Peon,' the man said, without any humour.

The office was empty. On a table, an open book tossed its leaves restlessly from a sudden breeze through the window.

'All these days holidays, no? They will come late today. Only Sir is always on time,' Peon informed him, sounding disappointed.

Mr Sharma was seated at his desk, twiddling the cap of his fountain pen and listening to the radio. He nodded sympathetically as he listened to it, as though he was listening to a client's complaints. He was a large man with a face that appeared to be embedded in his chin. He rose from his chair with some difficulty, and greeted Vasan warmly in a soft, lilting voice.

'Is everything well with you, my boy?' he said. 'Is my nephew taking good care of you?'

Before Vasan could speak, Mr Sharma bade him sit down at the opposite end of the desk. A tourism poster for Himachal Pradesh was pasted on the wall behind Mr Sharma. It was a photograph of a young girl biting into a red apple standing against the backdrop of an apple orchard; the apples became little red dots in the distance. Beside the poster, there hung a newly-framed portrait of Jawaharlal Nehru pictured in profile, his aquiline nose occupying centre stage in the photograph. A plastic garland of red and white flowers was draped over his neck. Mr Sharma lowered the volume on the radio. 'Difficult time for you to come, I know. But everything must go on, no?' he said.

'You are very kind to give me this job, Sir,' Vasan began, but Mr Sharma interrupted him.

'Sir? No Sir business. With me, no formalities. I am your uncle. When you were young, you used to call me Mango Uncle. You know why? I brought mangoes to your house one mango season and you never forgot. From then on, you always called me Mango Uncle.'

Vasan sat awkwardly at the edge of his seat, his hands clasped in his lap. He had no recollection that connected him with the man who sat before him.

'I am worried I have not worked anywhere before. I hope I will be worthy of this opportunity—'

Mr Sharma waited, but Vasan was unable to finish his sentence.

'Why, Vasu, are you thinking about all these things?' Answering his own question, Mr Sharma said, 'I know your father well, so I can imagine that he must have filled your head with a lot of this and that.'

'It is not my father, Sir. He was the one who insisted on my coming here. Actually, I was not so keen, but now—' He hesitated, feeling abashed, 'Only, you see, I thought you should know that I am not very good at Maths. I did not pass my exam.'

'You failed your exam, I know. But you passed on the second attempt, no? Sometimes you fail. People fail. It is very common. And it is not always a bad thing.'

'But I only got second class.'

'Forget all that. Forget marks and exams.'

He turned over a book that was lying on the table. 'Sometimes, the less you begin with, the more likely you are to learn. The better for you. I am here. People are here. If you make a mistake, we will solve it together. But your father would not understand such things, would he?'

'No, Sir.'

He laughed. 'No, he wouldn't. Marks were always very important to him. For some people it is easy—the marks are just heaped upon their plate, without their having to try. No need to study. No need to pay attention. Their minds work differently. Your father could go straight from the cinema hall to the exam, and he would still top the class. I was not so lucky. I have dents in my head from where my mother prodded me with her fist for every question I got wrong in an exam. I failed at my first attempt at SSLC also and was made to sit the final year of it again. That is how I ended up in your father's class. He didn't want to hang out with me. It was shameful for him to be seen with a failure. I sat next to him in one exam and successfully copied his answers. I passed! I even got more marks than him. Suddenly, your father was very interested in getting to know me.'

'Did you tell him?'

'Of course, I had to gloat. But by then, it was too late. We had already become friends. We were like Laurel and Hardy. Now, what about Ram? Are you adjusting well?'

'Yes, Sir.'

'He is a rascal. Don't let him bully you. I don't know what he gets up to. Just like his father. No care or thought about tomorrow. All the time—fun, fun, fun. So many times, I have told him to come and join me here, but he has some grand plans. One day, he is going to catch crocodiles and the next day, he is going to climb mountains! Every time I see him, I tell him that I want to see him do something useful. Get a job in a good company. But if everybody does only useful things, then what will the world become? Boring, no?'

Mr Sharma assigned another junior accountant by the name of Sainath the task of finding Vasan a desk and something to do. Sainath came from a small town like his in Andhra Pradesh, and was delighted to learn that his new partner spoke Telugu. He was a movie buff who went to the cinema three or four times a week, sometimes watching the same film twice in a row. His favourite actor was Nageswara Rao and he was a prominent member of the Madras chapter of the actor's fan club.

Vasan felt listless on the first day of work despite Sainath's friendliness because he was not given any work to do. He felt as stiffly starched as the white cotton shirt he was wearing. The ceiling fan was loud in its whirring, but the corner where he sat at his desk was not included in its sweep.

Unable to sit still and feeling guilty to be seen idle, he spent all morning rifling through some publications issued by the Chartered Institute of India. At lunch time, because he had not packed anything, the other staff donated a portion of their own food. The result of their generosity made an unattractive combination on his plate. The beetroot porial was bleeding colour and a portion of the coconut rice had turned purple and soggy. Half a dosa, torn in haste, was lying on top of the rice, and a piece of mango pickle at the top of the pile. When he protested, a large middle-aged woman, Renuka, told him to, 'Just sit down.'

'I know you are feeling shy,' she said, passing him the plate. 'We all know what it's like on the first day.'

Although he could not imagine Renuka having ever been shy, he was thankful for her decisiveness which put an end to the matter.

Noticing that he had little work on his hands, some of the other accountants began giving him bits and pieces of their own work to do. Within a week, he decided he was busy. The work itself was easy and consisted primarily of typing up handwritten copies of documents, pointing to clients the locations on the paperwork where their signatures were required, answering those questions that Mr Sharma had been too busy to respond to, rubber-stamping documents, sending out the mail and ensuring that the stock of bond and carbon paper, ink-pads and other stationery items was abundant in supply.

Under the overcast sky, Vasan thought Madras was the most beautiful city in the world. In this light, the city appeared softer and was infused with a wet and salty smell. On a brighter day, the edges of the buildings were sharper, the colours more radiant, and the buildings appeared too defiant. He preferred the dull glow that came to the city under a grey sky, when it appeared as though it was cooling off after a heated argument.

It was a city that awoke before it slept. It was always rising. No matter what time of day or night, there was always tea brewing in tea shops. Vasan had to be at his office at eight o' clock each morning but by the time he stepped out of the house at seven, it seemed to him that already the city had gone on without him and he had arrived in it too late. Initially, in the vastness of the city, Vasan felt lost. The crisscrossing of roads, their bends, their tendency to narrow suddenly, and then to open up unexpectedly, rattled him. There were long wide endless roads in one part of the city, from where you could see the steeples of churches a long way away and then there were the narrow gullies in another part running through craning multi-storey buildings. He had known every little street in Sripuri, but here any mental maps that he made of the city proved useless, becoming confused with all the other maps that he was continually storing in his mind. However, with each passing day, and with every road that became familiar to him, every signboard, temple or hotel that he recognized, Vasan felt the increasing joy of feeling at home in Madras.

Sometimes, after a day's work, Vasan would go with Sainath to one of the cinemas on Mount Road. But he preferred to go to the beach, which offered up a remarkable array of people, luminous in the evening light as the shells that the sea had coughed up along its shore, if only one chose to examine them. There he sat by himself on a mound of sand, or by a forsaken fishing boat, his feet bare and tingling with the cool touch of the wet sand. There were all sorts of combinations of people: a policeman was chatting with a fisherman, a group of young girls walked with their younger siblings on their hips, an adolescent was urging his blind grandfather to get his feet wet. Men in suits with rolled-up trousers lined the ice-cream stall, a briefcase in one hand and an ice-cream cone in the other. Several newly married couples or lovers strode along the shore holding hands and leaning towards each other in whispered intimacy. Then there were the loners like him, other men perched on dunes, wonderstruck by the seeming glitter in other people's lives.

Every once in a while, he sensed that a plane was flying by overhead because of a thud he felt in his heart. He had never before seen a plane before arriving in Madras, and each time he caught a glimpse of one, it was a reminder to him that his world had changed, that the sky he had known all his life had been forever altered by the sight of this sky, and that the former would always lay beneath the latter, submerged by it.

Afterwards, he ate a vegetarian thali meal at Murugan's Canteen and walked slowly back to his house. Often, when he arrived home, Ram was just heading out on his bicycle to meet his friends.

If Vasan learnt beforehand that Parvati would be home the following day, then he skipped his lunch break and worked diligently until three o'clock and then rushed home from work.

Whenever he found Parvati at home, Vasan's spirit lifted and it was these evenings spent in their united company that he enjoyed the most. They played Antakshari, sitting together on the floor in the hall, with Parvati insisting each time that it was Vasan's turn to sing and that he sing the song in its entirety. She shushed Ram while Vasan sang, though she would later concede that he could join him during the chorus of a song, which Ram did loudly and deliberately off-key, except when he became drunk and sang in tune and outshone Vasan.

Vasan could not stop looking at her all through the afternoon, feeling on each occasion that he had never really looked at her before. He noticed new things about her each time, the deep dimple that formed in her chin when she smiled, how she inhaled before she spoke and that her laughter always ended abruptly, as though the air had just sliced it.

The monsoon broke one afternoon in early October. First the wind came wheeling in, cloaked in the pale orange hue of the sand that it had roused up off the ground. It knocked the windows about in the office and brought in leaves shaking like half-alive insects before depositing them on the floor. It sent sheaves of papers from their desks into a flurry. People left their seats to wait for the rain by the windows.

The sky, clotted with clouds, sagged. The room darkened suddenly. Below on the road, street vendors were covering up their wares with gunny sacks, knotting them with string and leaving in a hurry. Someone stretched their hand out of the window to feel for the rain, and just then it came.

'Like a slap,' he said, laughing. The first drops were large. One fell on the envelope Vasan was holding in his hand, smudging a large portion of the address. Within moments, there was not a spot of tar left on the road below that was not glistening as black as though it had only just been laid. From downstairs, the voices of two girls shrieking as they pushed each other into the rain brought laughter to the office. Water that collected on the skirting of the window slid off the wall and fell to the floor where it became brown on contact with the dirt. The windows had to be shut and the sound of the rain outside was as inviting as the applause in a cricket match that you only heard from a distance. No one was in a mood to work.

Sensing the listlessness of his staff, Mr Sharma ordered Peon to bring them packets of bajjis from the teashop across the road and told them they could leave early if they wished. As soon as there was a break in the weather, one by one, cautiously, so as to not seem too eager, everyone except Peon and Mr Sharma shuffled out in the direction of bus stops or their bicycles. Once outside, they waved to each other enthusiastically, as eager as children disbanding for the summer holidays.

As his bus was nearing his stop, Vasan saw Parvati from the window across the road. She was at the bus stop on the opposite side of the road. She stood underneath the awning of a grocery store where other commuters like her had gathered to shelter from the rain. He felt a sudden coursing of blood from his neck to his head. Without thinking, he pushed himself past the people standing in the aisle to the door, mumbling an apology as he squeezed himself through. The conductor whistled and the bus halted abruptly. Distracted and unmindful of his movements, he stepped into a puddle and slapped his knee in irritation. He crossed the road with long strides, side-stepping bicycles and potholes, his hands poised in the air ready to wave, but Parvati's head was turned in anticipation of her bus.

'Parvati!' he yelled across the road.

He saw her turn and scan the road frantically for the source of the voice. At first, she seemed relieved to see Vasan. She returned his wave with a short swift movement of her hand, but as soon as he approached her, she was distracted and gave him the weakest of smiles without meeting his eyes. Today, dressed in a half-sari and with her hair in two long plaits, she appeared younger. She had hoisted up her skirt a few inches from the ground and tucked the resulting folds into the waistband of her skirt. The fall of her skirt had absorbed the rain water, causing brown stains to climb up along the length of it in the shape of craggy hills on a skyline.

'I saw you from the bus,' he said, feeling that an explanation was required. He had rushed to her side impulsively, but now that he was beside her, he felt flustered and at a loss for words. Eager to disguise his unease, he kept talking.

'So much rain today! Our office closed early you know? No one wanted to do anything useful. Water was coming inside the office. It was like night inside. So dark with the windows closed. How can you work in such weather? Thank God it has stopped now. I was worried how I was going to walk to the house. That's a mud road you know?'

'Yes,' she said, craning her neck to examine the number board on the bus which had halted. It was not hers.

'Where are you coming from?' he asked. 'You must be coming from Ram—our house, am I right?'

Parvati did not answer this question. She was clutching her

coin purse in her hand and let it fall to the floor. They stooped in unison to locate it. Their faces came close for an instant, but Parvati straightened herself and allowed Vasan to retrieve the coins for her.

'It is such a surprise to meet you,' he said, wiping a coin against the fabric of his trousers and handing it to her. 'Very long time since I last saw you. Busy exam time?'

Parvati did not respond.

'You are not feeling well?' he asked, searching her face for an explanation for the marked contrast in her behaviour from that of their previous meeting three weeks earlier, when he had attempted to teach her chess. It may have lasted only a few seconds, but her face was changing shape, and Vasan saw the tiny muscles beneath her skin rowing against the tide to maintain her composure. Momentarily, her eyes welled up with tears before she recalled them with what appeared to Vasan to be pure will.

She tilted her head in an indeterminate manner and looked again in the direction of the bus. As she turned her face, he noticed the faint streak of a tear on her cheek. His first instinct was to wipe the tear stain with his hand, and astounded by this realization, he stepped back from her and tightened his grip on his briefcase. He was exhausted of words and filled with a new sensation. He felt unable to leave her side and incapable of comforting her. So he stood beside her, silent, the hair on his arms prickling in reaction to the cold and her presence. He waited till the bus arrived and held his briefcase over her head to protect her from the rain as she climbed into the bus and was swallowed by the swarm of people already inside it. As he walked home, he grew furious with himself for having been a fool. What had possessed him to run to her in such haste? He chided himself for his ineffectual conduct. He quickened his steps when it began to drizzle again. Clearly, something had transpired between Ram and Parvati that had distressed her. Rather than offering her words to console her, he had gone on about the weather.

When Vasan arrived home, he found Ram lying on the divan with both his head and his feet propped up on an assortment of pillows, bolsters and cushions. In one hand, he held his most recently arrived copy of the *National Geographic* and in the other, a cigarette which made a crackling sound when he pulled at it. The smoke was blue and translucent, quick on its ascent and slow and lingering on its descent. An ashtray that Ram had himself fashioned out of a coconut shell using only a razor blade rested on his chest. He wore a white banian over a pair of khaki cut-off shorts. The banian was speckled with ash and was fraying at the edges. The sheet on the divan had become untangled and lay twisted around his body. Finding Ram reclining in this indolent posture, Vasan was momentarily nonplussed. He had tried to walk slowly despite the rain, hesitant to arrive home because he had expected to find Ram in a frame of mind that mirrored Parvati's. The encounter with her had left him feeling dejected.

'Anything happened?' Vasan asked from the entrance as he removed his shoes.

'Nothing except for the rain,' Ram said, waving the magazine across the window and repositioning himself on the divan. 'Nothing at all,' he repeated in a lilting voice.

Vasan was disarmed by the casual tone of Ram's response. For the first time, it occurred to him that there existed a hidden dimension to Ram. For that moment, however, Vasan decided not to mention his encounter with Parvati.

'No college today?' he asked instead.

'Look at the day,' Ram said, turning to the window. He shook his head at the rain. 'One should be shot for doing anything else but enjoying the rain today.'

Vasan's shoes were caked with mud. Rolling up his trousers had not prevented them from becoming wet or being splattered with muddy drops that had left imprints along the back of his trouser legs. His feet were cold. His hair fell limp and wet on his forehead. He glanced out of the window. The day itself hung wet and heavy. Through the rain-streaked window, the houses along the road were melting shadows of themselves. The street was desolate; in his vision, the rain had white-washed it, obscuring the line of houses and the trees that stood alongside them. And yet, Vasan recognized the truth in Ram's statement.

'Tea?' Ram asked, making a half-hearted attempt to rise.

'I'll get it,' Vasan offered. He fetched the flask containing the tea from the kitchen along with two stainless steel cups. There was a new boy at Murugan's Canteen whom Ram had persuaded into delivering them fresh tea and idlis each morning on his bicycle for a fee of fifty paisa per delivery. Following Ram's lead, other families in the neighbourhood had also begun to request deliveries, a scheme that Murugan now advertised to all his regular customers. The tea was sweet and warm. Ram emptied his tea in one gulp and refilled his cup.

'You know, in parts of the world like South America, sometimes it rains frogs and lizards? Even birds.'

Vasan shook his head.

'I know what you are thinking,' Ram said, refilling his cup. 'You are thinking that Ram's gone crazy, and to tell you the truth, that is exactly what I too thought of the man who first told me of this phenomenon. He was a man I met on a bus journey in Kerala. He was from Switzerland. He had very blond eyebrows and eyelashes. Let us just say that the sun did not agree with him. Red as a freshly-slaughtered goat. But I don't suppose vegetarians are familiar with the colour of freshly-slaughtered goats. You probably turn your heads away when you pass a butcher.'

He grinned and rolled over to grab another cigarette.

'Peter, that was his name—he told me how he had witnessed a village in Chile become inundated with tiny lizards. I thought he had a screw loose in his head, but I kept him talking. He was a good sort and anyway, I had nothing better to do. Conversations make a journey seem shorter, you know?'

It struck Vasan as peculiar that Ram and Parvati had each emerged from their rendezvous in such vastly different moods. While Parvati had been teary and so withdrawn as to appear to him an altogether unfamiliar figure, Ram was even more loquacious than usual.

'You think I am joking?' he was saying now. 'It doesn't happen very often, but it does happen. I read somewhere that it is due to the force of the wind. It scoops up these frogs from one part of the land and deposits them in another. Wouldn't you like to see that kind of rain?'

'No,' Vasan said, trying to put the vision of raining frogs out of his mind.

'But wouldn't it be great to witness something like that?

Frogs from the sky? How many people in this world can say that they saw such a rain? Frogs in their hair, frogs on their shoulder—'

'I am not very fond of frogs,' Vasan said.

'Yes, I remember what happened the last time you saw one. I don't understand it. Snakes, yes I understand. Frogs, no.'

There had been an unfortunate incident involving a frog in the latrine which Vasan had not handled with much grace.

'I just don't understand why you are afraid of frogs. They are harmless.'

Vasan was only half-listening. All this talk of frogs and rain seemed to him strange and absurd. He remembered how his mother had burst into laughter when she had first learnt of the death of her father from a telegram. It was a laugh devoid of any frivolity, and the expression on her face had told him that it was a curious, desperate form of crying. Only then had he realized that there were expressions that were especially created as foils for certain human emotions. To Vasan, Ram's words, deliberately casual, had all the elaborate construction of a lie. But he doubted that Ram himself was aware of his deceit.

From his pocket, Ram produced a small cloth pouch which had been rolled tightly in the shape of a finger and tied together with string. He unwound the string, drew the mouth of the pouch to his nose and inhaled deeply.

'What is that?' Vasan asked. His curiosity was aroused.

'Paradise. Only a small portion of it, I admit. But you've got to take paradise in whatever portion you can get it.' From a drawer in a desk he removed a black terracotta chillum, explaining to Vasan as he packed the substance into it what a chillum was.

'Look at it,' he said, handing the chillum to Vasan after he had filled it. 'I paid a man ten rupees for it. He overcharged me. It was worth only five to him, but it's worth a lot more to me. See the carving?'

Engraved on the face of the chillum was the head of Ganesha, his serpentine trunk merging into the mouth of the chillum. 'Ever tried it?'

'No.'

'Want to?'

Vasan hesitated. To him, it wasn't the ganja that was tempting. It was the invitation. The encompassing nature of the two simple words Ram had spoken, with their promise of drawing him out of his own world and fusing him with another's—the invitation alone was alluring.

'It's not like eating meat,' Ram teased him. 'No animals were killed, I promise you. Only plants. And they were treated very gently. Come on. It will be good for you.'

'I don't know.'

'You'll know a lot more after you try this.'

Vasan was irritated. Why did people always talk to him as though he didn't know himself what was good for him? First, his father, then his mother, and now Ram. While Vasan was making up his mind, Ram lit the chillum. A sweet, unfamiliar scent occupied the space between them. Ram inhaled deeply and pursed his lips deliberately. With his lips still pursed, he tried to smile, eliciting a laugh from Vasan. He tapped the air with his finger to count down the time before he exhaled slowly and with pleasure. He leaned back on a pillow and closed his eyes. When he opened them again, one of his eyes had changed shape.

'My right eye, right? It does that every time. Gives me away every time. My left one behaves beautifully, but my right, the wretched thing, fickle. Wretched and fickle as a . . .'

'Is it bad for you?' Vasan asked, a little concerned.

'Everything is good for you, my friend, if it doesn't kill you.'

He lit the chillum again and repeated the process before passing it to Vasan, who held it awkwardly in his hands.

'You saw how I did it. Don't hold it so tight, you'll break it. It's only clay.' Vasan's hands were trembling.

'Just inhale. You can do that much, can't you? You have to keep the smoke inside or there is no point. We can't afford to throw away paradise.'

With the diligence and enthusiasm characteristic of new learners, Vasan endeavoured to follow Ram's instructions. But he only succeeded in taking a short stiff puff which he then attempted to stretch into a longer drag. He held his breath with exaggerated effort until Ram signalled to him that he could exhale.

'This time, relax. Pull gently but deeply,' Ram said.

On his second attempt, Vasan could feel the warm path the smoke traced through his mouth into his chest. He experienced a mild burning sensation which was not altogether unpleasant.

'Who would have thought it? You are the same. Look at those eyes.'

'Really? My eyes too?' Vasan rose to examine himself in the mirror in his room and returned with a satisfied smile on his face. Ram was engrossed with the chillum again. Once more, the air filled up with the scent of ganja, but like someone who was accustomed to it, Vasan could no longer smell it. They sat beside each other on the divan, throwing their heads back against the wall. The drumming of the rain intensified with their silence. The ganja had a soporific effect on Vasan and he relished the calmness now flowing through him. Although barely an hour had passed, already the events of the morning, the papers flying away from the desks, the excitement of his co-workers at the office, the shrieking of the girls who had run out into the rain, even the encounter with Parvati seemed to him at a distance, and seeing them now in his mind as events that had occurred a long time ago, he was able to view them with compassion. In this state of mind, he was even able to forgive himself for the inane remarks he had made about the rain to Parvati. Momentarily, an image of her floated in his mind. Ram and Vasan each savoured their individual silences.

'I met Parvati today,' Vasan said, breaking the silence when the image of her lingered on.

'Oh yeah? You did? Where?'

'At the bus stop. I was coming home. She was waiting for the bus.'

Ram scanned the divan for his packet of cigarettes and found them underneath a bolster. Vasan waited while Ram fumbled about with the matches.

'She had been crying, I think.'

'Crying? As in tears?'

'Yes, there were tears, I am sure. She did not speak much.'

'That's unusual for her.'

'Even I thought so. Did you have a fight?'

'I don't fight. You know what I am like,' he said. He turned to look at Vasan, seeking affirmation in his eyes. 'I am a peace-loving man. You know that, right?'

'Yes, that is for sure, but she seemed very troubled.'

'Parvati likes to cry sometimes.'

'No one likes to cry.'

'No, I beg to differ. Everyone likes to cry. It's like the rain. For a little while, it makes everyone happy. But if it goes on for too long, it becomes unbearable. Tomorrow, she'll be sprightly again. She will be fine in the morning.'

Vasan considered this statement as he glanced at his toes. He lost the trail of his thought. His nails needed cutting. They seemed extraordinarily long. His big toe was bruised and swollen. He had stubbed it against a table at the office. He would no longer be accused of tiptoeing through life, he thought pleasantly. And then he was asleep on the divan.

When he awoke, it was dark, and he could barely make out the shapes in the room. His throat was parched, and as he felt around with his arm to reorient himself, he found the bottle of water that Ram had placed at his arm's length. He drank the full bottle of water without pause. Slowly, the room became familiar again, objects springing to recognition, the light sufficient now that his eyes had adjusted to it. Ram had placed a cushion under his head and flung a sheet over his body. He sat upright on the divan, wrapping the sheet around himself like a shawl. Vasan thought he heard a voice on the radio coming from Ram's room, but then realized that the hour was long past the last radio programme. The night felt deep and dark.

He rose to investigate and found that Ram's door was ajar and that his light was on. Ram appeared to be asleep, front down on the bed with his face buried into a folded arm. He had no shirt on and wore just a pair of pyjama bottoms. Vasan approached the door quietly, intending to switch off the light for Ram, because it occurred to him that he might have fallen asleep in the same manner that he had on the divan. As he proceeded towards his room, something about Ram's frame caught his attention. Ram seemed to be holding his breath. Vasan tiptoed a short distance past Ram's room, and then waited, his mind sharp and his ears alert. There was no sound at first, then he heard the ticking of the clock, and finally he heard it. A loud exhalation followed by a burst of sobbing. In his room, Vasan lay awake unable to sleep. He listened as Ram wept into his pillow, and wished he had something to offer him, an act of kindness, a gesture of friendship, like the cushion that Ram had placed under his head and the sheet over his body. In the end, he decided the kindest gesture was his silence.

The first that Vasan heard of Ram's plans to leave Madras was late the next day. Vasan was already in bed. It was a sultry night. He opened the window cautiously but the mosquitoes were waiting for him and he shut it with a bang. He heard the jingle of Ram's bicycle bell rattling as he rode it on the mud track. Vasan listened for the clicking of the front gate and was surprised when he heard a loud banging on the door. When he opened the door, Ram fell forward slightly but pushed away Vasan's outstretched arm when he attempted to steady him. He slumped onto the divan and closed his eyes. Vasan was about to return to his room when Ram, opening one eye, said, 'You are not going to stay up and talk to me? What with me leaving tomorrow?'

That was when he told an alarmed Vasan that he had to go back to Dubai because his father was seriously ill. He dragged a suitcase from under the bed in his room and placed it on the floor in the living room. He did not know how long he would be required to stay, he said. He would have to take it as it came.

Ram did not mention what had befallen his father so Vasan assumed the worst—a heart attack seemed the more likely cause. Shocked and rendered speechless, Vasan rushed about the house collecting Ram's things, his towel that was drying out on the wire line in the backyard, his three pairs of shoes which had been scattered about the house, offering his assistance in the packing in lieu of words which would not come. Ram himself appeared calm and Vasan admired him for the strength he showed under duress. As he packed, he chatted just as he normally did. Now, Vasan recognized both the mellowing and talkative effect the ganja had on Ram. In the light of what had occurred, it seemed poignant to Vasan that Ram was warning him that the prices at Murugan's Canteen had gone up and insisting that he demand 'family rates'.

Ram entrusted his bicycle to Vasan and begged him to look after it in a voice filled with emotion. 'Take my clothes, my books, whatever you want,' he said. 'I won't miss anything but the people.'

Ram grasped Vasan by the arm. He looked up into his eyes. 'Parvati,' he began, but was unable to continue. 'These wretched mosquitoes!' he said, instead slapping his thigh. 'That's one thing I won't miss.'

'Don't tell my uncle about what's happened. He doesn't know. We've decided not to tell him until we know more . . .' He scrambled around for a cigarette and lit it. 'He has a heart condition, my uncle. I've given him some other reason for why I am going away. If he starts talking to you about my grand schemes, just ignore him . . .'

When Vasan returned home the next evening from work, he was taken aback to find his landlord waiting for him. He appeared to have been waiting a while, for he launched into an outburst as soon as he saw Vasan. He'd heard about Ram's departure, he said. From whom, Vasan could not have guessed, for he himself had told no one.

'Not so much as a goodbye after all that I've done for him,' the landlord said. Every day that the room was uninhabited, he was losing money. He would be sending a boy to clear out Ram's room. He was paying for his kind-heartedness, for his tendency to trust people. Time and again people took advantage of his good-nature and left him feeling disappointed. His face was puffy and when he shook his head from side to side in disbelief and despair, the skin on his cheeks flapped about his face. Never again would he trust students, he said.

Feeling that some conciliatory effort was required on his part, Vasan offered to clean Ram's room. A look of such relief settled on the landlord's face as though at once his faith in humanity had been restored. He told Vasan that he would come to inspect the room in a few days' time. He had implicit faith in Vasan, he reiterated, and shook Vasan's hand with both his to express his gratitude.

The house felt hollowed out without Ram. The house keys were on the desk along with a wad of rupees that Vasan guessed was to cover about two months' rent.

Vasan wandered from the living room to Ram's room, surveying articles of clothing left behind, pieces of furniture and other items that Ram had said now belonged to him. Vasan had never entered Ram's room before. He had only glimpsed at it through a half-opened door. The windows were shut and the room had trapped the smell of smoke, rum and cologne, each indistinguishable from the other by having simply become the scent of Ram. The room was bare. The bed had been stripped of its sheets. One of the pillows had fallen to the floor. Vasan picked it up and placed it on the bed. The walls were bereft of the posters and wall hangings that had hung there, made conspicuous by a series of nails. He opened the wardrobe and found a stack of clothes and a jacket in one of the shelves. Rummaging through them, he found two unopened bottles of whisky, a half-used bottle of cologne, a pair of brown leather shoes and a magazine which made him look left and right involuntarily to check for another's presence. When he flipped the magazine, its pages fell open at the centre-fold. Between a pair of woman's breasts was stuck a note in Ram's almost childish writing. 'For you, Vasan. Enjoy them,' the note read. Vasan knew with conviction that Ram was not coming back.

The house became all his. The bottles of whisky, the magazines, the women in them; they were all his. He came home from work each day and at once pulled the bottle of whisky from its place on Ram's vacated shelf. His movements were furtive—he had not accustomed himself entirely to his newfound freedom. He poured himself a glass, and settled on the divan. Around him, books collected dust. The curtain stayed closed. His appetite diminished with every passing day.

Then, one evening, a knock on the door. Who knew of his existence? The landlord, he thought and looked about the house hurriedly. He smoothed his lungi down quickly, hid the whisky bottle under a cushion, and tucked the edges of the counterpane under the divan. Another knock, this time more insistent.

Parvati stood before him, a stranger once again without Ram's presence. She stood on the doorstep, without a smile. She came straight to the point. Did he know where Ram was, had he heard from him, had he left word?

He could not bring himself to tell her that Ram would not be coming back.

He took the letter she handed him. He made an impression of her face in his mind as she spoke. The hair framing her face, the eyes that were puffy from crying, the dry lips, the dimple in her chin. He would make sure that the letter reached Ram, he promised.

After Parvati left, Vasan clutched the envelope to his chest and took it with him to his room. He sat on the bed and held the envelope to the light. He read aloud the address written on the back of the envelope in her neat cursive hand. He rested his head on the pillow, laid the envelope on his chest and held its edges with the tips of his fingers. He let it rise and fall with his breath. In his inebriated state, he thought he was holding love itself in his hands. He felt aroused and then shame engulfed him. He placed the letter beneath his pillow and fell asleep face down on it.

22

'How are you, my boy? Everything all right with you?' Mr Sharma said in his sing-song voice when Vasan entered his room during the lunch break. It was Monday and Vasan had spent all that weekend wondering how he would obtain Ram's address from him. Ram had warned him not to broach the subject of his leaving with his uncle, and in his haste to do good by both Ram and Parvati, Vasan had made two contradictory promises. How was he to learn Ram's whereabouts without mentioning him?

From Mr Sharma's mood, Vasan conjectured that no bad news regarding his brother had yet filtered down to him. Mr Sharma ate alone at his desk. His three-tiered tiffin carrier was disbanded into its many parts and arranged neatly on a cotton towel. Looking at the ghee floating on top of the halwa in one of the containers, Vasan felt as though he was staring at the root of Mr Sharma's heart trouble.

'Have some gajar halwa. Made by my Mrs. It's one of her specialties.' Mr Sharma said, following Vasan's gaze.

'I couldn't, sir,' Vasan said, patting his belly. 'I've just eaten my lunch. Very full, Sir.'

'I hear you are doing wonderful things in the office. I was very glad to report this to Sarangan when I last spoke to him.'

There it was. No matter how far he had come from Sripuri, or how much he'd worked to earn a name for himself at the company, a report card was still being sent to his father.

'What is the matter?' Mr Sharma said, registering the look of dismay on Vasan's face. 'Is there a problem you wish to talk about?'

'I wanted to find out about Ram.' He let the words hang. 'Have you had any news from him?'

'You miss that scoundrel, don't you?' Mr Sharma said, swivelling in his chair. 'Well I imagine he is running amok in America. He got admission in some good college there, I cannot remember which it was. He found a professor whose work he admires—a writer as well as a geologist or some such thing. Well, Ram always had unusual ideas about things . . . as I am sure you know, having lived with him all this while . . .'

What was Vasan to understand from this? Was Ram in America as Mr Sharma claimed, or was this the scheme of which Ram had spoken when he mentioned that he'd suggested another reason for leaving Madras to his uncle? Would he be getting Ram into trouble for probing him for an address?

'He is not coming back?' Vasan said blandly.

'People who go to America don't come back, my boy.'

'Yes,' Vasan murmured. 'I expect they don't.'

'When I hear from him,' Mr Sharma said, 'I will be sure to tell him how much you miss him.'

And with that, Mr Sharma rose to wash his hands in the sink. He wiped his face and his hands and escorted Vasan to the door.

'Peon!' he said. 'I am ready for my tea.'

Nearly a month passed before Vasan received news of Ram again from Mr Sharma.

'Heard that your best friend is in Canada,' Mr Sharma said, puffing as he grabbed his briefcase on his way to a meeting. Vasan followed him to the gate. 'He is travelling with some friend he met over in America. He can't sit still a single minute . . .'

'He is not joining a college then?'

'Yes, apparently he is, but the American system is different. They follow the seasons over there. He has to wait until spring, so off he's gone traipsing around Canada. You know Ram. Can you start the scooter for me please, my boy?'

The following Saturday morning, Vasan ate a hearty breakfast at Murugan's Canteen. A plate of idlis followed by a plate of upma, which he washed down with a hot cup of coffee. Rajuanna sent over a plate of kesari, and not wanting to displease him, Vasan ate every last crumb. Then he set out in search of Parvati's home. He had not formulated a plan of action. He simply wished to relay to her the unwelcome news that Ram was in Canada, and that he would likely not be returning to her.

He carried the letter with him in the pages of one of Ram's *National Geographic* magazines. On the bus, someone asked to borrow it, and Vasan was forced to shake his head, as though to remove the letter from its pages in public was tantamount to revealing its contents.

Once he reached Alwarpet, Parvati's house was not hard to find. Vasan remembered that she was the daughter of the proprietor of Manickam Jewels. The tea shop owner, who he stopped to ask, pointed the house out to him. 'You can't miss it for a mile,' he said, chewing tobacco.

As he approached the large white brick house with the green gate, Vasan's hands began to sweat. He wiped them against the sides of his trousers. He looked around for an inconspicuous spot to gather his thoughts, and decided on one in the adjacent construction plot, beside a scooter that was parked on the road. He checked himself in the mirror quickly. From there, he watched the door of the house. Twenty minutes passed with no activity.

'Who are you waiting for?' he heard a voice shout behind him. Startled, he turned around quickly, and a man emerged from within the partially-constructed house. Vasan had no time to come up with a reasonable explanation.

'I was waiting for the daughter . . .'

The man studied Vasan's appearance. 'Have a cigarette?' he asked.

'No, sorry, I don't smoke.'

The man retrieved a packet from his own trouser pocket. 'It's the last one, you see?' he said, grinning. He lit the cigarette and inhaled deeply. He twisted his mouth to blow the smoke away from Vasan.

'Which one?' he said. 'The big sister or the little one?'

Vasan had not known that Parvati had a sister.

'You meant the big one,' the man said, nodding as though he understood Vasan's predicament. 'What do you want with her?'

'I have to deliver a letter to her. From a friend,' he added.

'She's gone,' the man said. 'She left a week ago, maybe. Along with her mother, and two big suitcases. Then the mother came back without the daughter. One of the boys here knows their old driver. He said Muthu had been specially requested for the trip. He dropped her off at her aunt's village. The boys miss her. They were used to seeing her coming in and out. Nothing much here in the way of entertainment. Usually, when a girl gets shipped off like that, you know, there is just one thing . . .'

'What is that?'

The man laughed. He crushed his cigarette stub under his foot.

'Ask the *friend* who sent her that letter,' he said, turning his back on Vasan.

The letter's presence in the house irked Vasan. He shifted it from place to place; one day placing it in front of the picture of Srinivasa on Ram's desk in his room, another day slotting it into a groove in the window sill in the hall. Finally, he decided to insert the letter into the pocket in the inner lining of his briefcase. Thus, he took it with him every day to the office, only glancing at it briefly now and then to ensure that it still existed.

With Ram gone, the days seemed endless to Vasan. A new housemate occupied Ram's room. His name was Ganesh and he was a quiet, secretive chap who was associated with the film industry in some way—he did not specify the details. He kept odd hours and closed the door of his room immediately upon arriving home. When they met each other, he smiled and asked that Vasan take his clothes with him after a bath and not leave them hanging in the bathroom. He cleaned the house thoroughly, and rearranged the furniture. The divan was okay in the living room, but could Vasan please take the desk into his room?

Earlier, the minutiae of his work had not bothered him, it had not even occurred to him as such. Now, as he pointed to a client the twelve places on the document where he was required to sign his name, a brusqueness crept into his voice so that Renuka, sitting across from him, stopped the clicking of the typewriter in mid-sentence to look up at him. He yelled at Peon when he found the cup of tea that he had brought him was cold. He smeared Amrutanjan on his temples to ease his headaches.

He was promoted to senior accountant.

He did not feel companionable, yet he sought Sainath's company to fill the void of his evenings. Often, they went to the cinema, sometimes watching the same film twice. During the film's screening, Vasan's mind would wander and later, when Sainath enthusiastically talked about the intricacies of its plot, Vasan would be distracted and nod absentmindedly. Afterwards, they ate at a roadside café. Sainath, still buoyed by the film, would hum one of its songs pleasantly, while Vasan became increasingly deflated. Still, Sainath's company was preferable to the solitude of his home.

One evening, after they left the cinema, Sainath persuaded Vasan into visiting his home. He assured him that it was not a long distance away from the theatre, which surprised Vasan. The next day was a second Saturday, and office was closed anyway, so Vasan accepted his invitation. The night sky was bright with a moon, and he could taste the salty air on his lips. As they made their way, Sainath told him that he had big news to share, but that Vasan would need to wait until they were home before he could reveal it. Vasan could no longer follow the route they were taking. They turned into gulley upon gulley until they stood in front of a house. Sainath knocked, four times. An old woman opened the door, and led them through a narrow corridor and up a flight of stairs. They stood facing another door. The old woman nodded. When Sainath pushed the door open to reveal a concealed bar, Vasan was astounded. Sainath relished the expression of surprise on his face. 'Here are all the men in Madras who cannot afford to have ideals,' he said. 'And I am proud to be one of them.'

Vasan glanced at the men occupying the tables. They didn't look like men without ideals; they simply looked like regular men. The expressions on their faces were familiar; each time he scrutinized a face, he was reminded of an old school teacher, a shop owner, a bus conductor or a neighbour he had known. Sainath led him to a table at the far end of the room and ordered them two large whiskies. The lighting inside was of low wattage, and the commonplace music which came from a transistor radio secured by a hook on the wall was, as a result of that diaphanous light, transformed into a more meaningful melody.

'I am going to get married next month,' Sainath told him, chinking his glass with Vasan's. 'Who knows if I shall be able to come here anymore?'

'First class news,' Vasan said, shaking his hand and congratulating him. 'Who's the girl?'

'Her name is Roopa. She is also in the fan club.'

'So, it's a love marriage?'

'Love? It's not just love, it is destiny!'

'That is even better,' Vasan said, taking a large gulp of his whisky, and wondering what destiny had in store for him.

'The first film of Nageshwara Rao Sir's I saw was *Pelli Kanuka*. It is also the first film that she ever saw! We both joined the fan club on the exact same day. She was wearing a white sari with a brown border. I was wearing a white shirt and brown trousers. Can you believe it?'

'What a coincidence!' Vasan said, unsure of the response expected from him.

'Coincidence? I tell you, it is destiny. Coincidence has nothing to do with it.'

Some of the customers had begun to make their way to the upstairs section of the bar through a curtained exit, for the nightly cabaret performance. Becoming drunk, Sainath suggested that they visit a brothel. 'But you are getting married!' Vasan said, taken aback.

'I am going to miss the girls,' Sainath admitted, sighing. He swirled his whisky around in his glass and gazed into it longingly as though it contained all of his past. 'What about you? You have no love, nothing, what's stopping you?'

Vasan evaded the question by rising to go to the toilet. When he returned, Sainath was singing along with a popular song that had come on the radio. Other people soon joined him, and Vasan found himself mouthing the words alongside them softly.

Love, to Vasan, was a vaporous concept constructed from second-hand emotions and images garnered from various sources over the years. When he thought about love, he thought about the plump glycerin tears on the face of the heroine on a cinema screen waiting for her lover to return from jail, and the inscrutable expression on the face of the middle-aged woman sitting a few seats from him watching her. He recalled with shame, the parting in the neckline of a woman on a poster stuck to a compound wall, the letter A in red lettering indicating that it was for Adults Only. He remembered the doggedness of the notes that had gone from hand to hand across the classroom to an invisible lover at the other end of the room. All the shuffling and the lingering in the hallways of the college. How Ram had pinched Parvati's cheek on that first meeting. From these recollections, Vasan had spun together an idea of love. He himself was always removed from this idea, as though love was something rare and expensive displayed in a shop window; to pass by, consider, linger over, but never to hold or take home. And yet, Sainath sitting before him had found it.

Once, in his first year in college, a girl, Devaki, had been taken with him enough to trail him around the campus. He'd been flattered, and when she had sought him out at the end of the semester for his address, in the canteen where once more the bearer had taken someone else's order before his, he'd been happy to write it down for her in her diary. In her first letter, Devaki wrote of the boredom of being confined in her house, of a boating expedition she'd undertaken on the lake in her town, and the flower show that her mother was helping to organize. He wrote his response standing at the counter at the post office on an inland letter. He thanked her for her kind regards, all was well with him. He'd become a member of the new library on

Bulbul Street. He was practising chess daily, and lately, he'd been thinking about taking up painting.

Her next letter was a surprise for Vasan. She was looking forward to classes recommencing simply for the sake of seeing him again. She thought about him as she lay in bed. She would telephone him in secret if that was possible. She'd sent a photo of herself. Could he send one too? He was surprised that the girl he recalled as being shy and quiet could write with such passion in her letters.

He sent no response. A few days later, he received a third letter. Had he received the previous letter with the photo? She hoped that he was in good health. She was waiting for his response daily.

When classes resumed, she ignored him. He caught her eye every now and then. He observed how she wore a different flower in her hair every day, and the sight of her stooped over her desk, writing in her notebook, had stirred him more than the words in her letters. But it was too late to make amends. From then on, she avoided all contact with him.

Vasan was intoxicated when he returned home from his evening with Sainath. He fumbled with his keys, and when he entered the house, realized that it was empty. Vaguely, he recalled Ganesh mentioning that he would be away on location, but he'd provided no details as usual. He surveyed the living room. The divan was immaculately constructed, and each cushion arranged symmetrically. On an impulse, he made towards Ganesh's room. Of course, he'd padlocked it.

Vasan lay fully clothed on his bed. Night upon night, there would be nothing to look forward to the following day. He thought about Ram, drinking with his new friends in Canada or America. He thought of Parvati, banished to a village. It was a tyranny, he felt, that he'd been trapped within this immutable personality. He'd been no different as a child, he was no different as an adult, and he would be no different as an old man. Year after year he'd attempted to shake himself free of his personality. He'd made resolutions to change; this year, he would make more friends, this year, he wouldn't let his father talk down to him, this year, he would apply to be on the college board. Every year, he felt alone. He kicked the sheet off his legs. He heard a thud as the briefcase, which in his preoccupied state he'd carried to bed, fell to the floor.

He turned on the light. The briefcase had cracked open. He placed it on the bed and removed its contents one by one. He reached into the pocket in the inner lining and removed Parvati's letter. Holding it now in his hands, though the envelope had been worn thin by the weight of the papers he carried normally, the letter seemed to come back to life and along with it, all the feelings he had sealed and packed away just as efficiently with it. He opened it quickly, aware that if he held it in his hands for one moment too long and paused to considered his action, he would be unable to proceed with it. With trembling hands, he tore open the envelope, causing the ruled notepaper to tear at the edge from the pressure of his thumb.

He read it six times. He did not sleep that night.

My love,

I remember your voice telling me to be patient and to wait for you, even as I am writing this letter. It is my prayer, and you know that I am not the praying kind, that this letter will reach you. Every day, it seems to me that I am being walled inside my room. Although no one else has yet made out any changes in me, when I stand in front of the mirror, I can almost see the skin stretching right in front of me. I feel that underneath that skin so silently cool to my touch, something almost violent is happening—that some fluid is rising and frothing as one might see happen in a mixie.

Every morning when I wake up, I hope that I will receive word from you, and every evening I fear that I will be found out. Although it has only been three weeks since you left, already, whenever I think of you now, you do not come back to me as a whole person. You come to me in little pieces. I might see just your arm on my pillow lying there folded like a towel. Or else I see your face, behind the thick frame of your eyeglasses, the one eye drooping, as it does when you are tired. The deep arch from your ankle to your heel, where I sometimes imagine my face resting.

This is how I spend the time before I fall sleep, stacking all the pieces of you I recollect so well, one on top of another, collecting them as a shop assistant might stack bills and receipts into one of those metals stands on a shop counter. Your smells, your body parts, all the assorted looks on your face, the jingle of your bicycle, even the vast tracts of your life that I haven't known but which I have imagined.

During the evenings, everything in my window shrinks to the same size. I don't know why, but this makes me feel suffocated. At this hour, when dusk is turning to night, I can smell everything. I can smell sand from the construction site next door, and the milk that is boiling in the next house, and the cabbage that is overcooking in my own kitchen, even the distinctively fetid smell of the neighbourhood cat that only visits us once a fortnight, and whose face I cannot recollect at will. All through these thoughts, I keep the hope alive that you will find a job soon, that you will knock on my door dressed in a white shirt and a red tie and will let my father see that, despite what has happened, you are the good man that you are.

Till such time,
Patiently Yours,
Parvati

In the morning, Vasan telephoned Mr Sharma at his home and informed him without a trace of remorse in his voice that he had contracted the flu and would not be coming into work for the remainder of the week. He sat in the train thumbing his ticket to Sripuri in the knowledge that only a few hours stood between him and his father who was not expecting to see him. Since having read the letter, a nebulous fervour had taken hold of him so that he performed the tasks that would normally have aroused anxiety in him with ease, as one might attend to the particulars of arranging a funeral whilst residing simultaneously in a vast continent of grief. He had stood for two hours to purchase a ticket at the railway station behind a man who reeked of urine and he hadn't baulked. He packed his suitcase, arranging his clothes as he had seen his mother arrange them before his departure from Sripuri. He was not sure how long it would be before he returned to Madras, so he swept the house, cleaned the kitchen and bolted the windows. He strode to Mr Suri's house and knocked on his door.

'I am going away for a few days,' he said. 'A personal matter, nothing to worry about. Would you please keep an eye on the house?'

Mrs Suri, rushing to offer Vasan a glass of ginger-flavoured tea, suggested in a teasing tone to her husband that in all likelihood Vasan was returning home to look for a bride. This assumption pleased him unexpectedly and he took it as a good omen.

Since the idea had taken hold of him, he never once questioned it and he felt single-minded in his resolve. At the train station, he ran into an old classmate who was travelling on the same train and all the while that he chatted with him, recounting at his request his working life in Madras, Vasan felt a feverish excitement.

His mother opened the door. Her short burst of joy at seeing Vasan soon turned to panic when she registered the solemn and inscrutable expression on his face. He walked into the house and sat down on the sofa. He asked after his father, but Malati informed him that he was still at the college. He tugged at the stitching on the sofa while his mother pressed him with questions. He did not respond to them and asked instead for a cup of coffee, a tablet of Anacin and something hot to eat.

Perturbed, Malati sent word through the gardener to Sarangan at Vivekananda College to come home immediately. Shortly afterwards, Sarangan arrived, the muscles on his face and neck already taut as though he was bracing himself for disappointment.

Vasan had rehearsed his words. 'I met a girl in Madras,' he said, standing up. 'She is pregnant and I am going to marry her.' It gave him unexpected pleasure to utter those words. Even the mute shock on his father's face was strangely comforting; it was evidence to Vasan that his life was transforming right in front of his eyes. He wanted to tell them that he would no longer watch life, that life had given him an opportunity to participate. He was filled with purpose. The letter had come to him for a reason. He thought about Parvati, banished to the village, raising her child alone. He'd seen the films in which the heroes gave up their lovers to other men or offered themselves to women they did not love. Sacrifices were what the world needed. Vasan decided he would make his sacrifice. His mother let out a wail, but the look of genuine surprise on Sarangan's face slowly turned to one of acceptance, and finally pride. Within minutes, Sarangan had booked a trunk call to Manickam.

Only a week had passed since he had left Madras, but as Vasan sat looking out of the car window on his way to Parvati's home, the landscape appeared anew, as though he may have been looking at an old shirt of his worn by someone else. It was dusk when they entered the city. The sky was wringing out the last of its colour. Houses in the distance lit up. A lake became a sliver.

His heart quickened as they drew closer. Sarangan drove himself, and Malati sitting beside him asked him to stop at a fruit seller's. She bought a dozen apples and bananas, a large bunch of grapes and placed them on the silver tray on which she'd already arranged an assortment of auspicious items: turmeric, coconuts, betel leaves, and nuts. 'They'll laugh at the puny fruit we get in Sripuri,' she'd said earlier.

Sarangan had arranged with Manickam to have a driver bring her back to Madras. Vasan touched his moist forehead and pushed away the strands of hair that clung to it.

An electricity failure had left parts of the city in unexpected darkness. Manickam stood at the gate, holding a lantern in his hand, his customary white shirt and trousers yellowed by the light.

The hall was aglow with the light from the kerosene lanterns which lined the length of the walls. Parvati stood up from the sofa, holding the baby in her arms, when they entered. When she saw Vasan, Parvati started and looked about the room in confusion. She returned her gaze to him. He acknowledged her with a blinking of his eyes. Malati let out a cry of delight when she saw the baby's face and rushed to Parvati's side. Parvati retreated from her with a sharp turning movement. Sarangan did not budge. He was scrutinizing Parvati's face. Everyone was on their feet, though the hall was filled with an assortment of chairs that seemed so plush to Vasan that they resembled thrones.

Parvati scanned the room again, as though Ram was just

behind the doorway in the hall and she expected him to emerge at any moment.

'What is all this?' she asked finally.

'Can I talk to Parvati?' Vasan said, turning to his father. Sarangan looked at Manickam. Manickam nodded.

'May I?' Malati said, taking the baby in her arms. Parvati handed the baby to her with reluctance.

Vasan led Parvati into one of the guest rooms. He closed the door behind them, though leaving it unlatched. In a hushed tone, he said: 'Ram is in America. He is not coming back.'

'I had accepted that a long time ago,' she said, calmly. 'Until I was fetched from Madras and made to believe otherwise.'

'I will marry you,' he said. 'The baby—they think it's mine.'

Vasan waited. The room went still. Parvati looked beyond him at the walls of the room, white-washed and bright and dazzling. She pushed at Vasan with both arms and rushed to the window. His presence in the room seemed to suffocate her, for she flung open the window and stuck her head out. Then, slowly, she pulled her head back inside and turned to him. She hardly seemed to open her mouth, yet he thought he heard her say that he could not have what didn't belong to him. She walked out into the hall where all eyes turned to her. Vasan followed her and stood beside Sarangan. He watched as Parvati grabbed her son from Malati's arms, ignoring her pleas to hold him for a little while longer.

'I am not marrying him,' she said to her father. 'He is not Hari's father.' The room went quiet.

'How many men are going to come forward and claim to be the father?' Manickam said slowly.

In the pit of his stomach, Vasan felt the surging of an

emotion that he did not at once recognize. It manifested as a sharp ringing sound in his ears. He felt faint. He turned to Sarangan. 'Let us go,' he said.

'Please,' Manickam said. 'Wait!'

'You have two choices,' Manickam told Parvati. 'Make a life with these fine people here. Or make your life wherever else, I don't care, but not in this home. But where will you go? You haven't even a degree to your name . . . you can't even get a secretarial job. Even your uneducated mother will have led a better life than you.'

Charu stared at her feet, as if accepting this statement. Parvati glanced at her mother, for once devoid of any compassion for her, and then shook her head. 'No,' she said. 'I don't accept these choices. In fact, they are not choices at all—they are traps. Hari and I will manage.'

'The baby is ours,' Malati said. She approached Sarangan, paying no heed to Parvati. 'He is my grandson. My son's no fool to claim another's child as his own.'

Vasan's tongue felt thick in his mouth, words forming and crumbling. He made a move towards his mother, placing an arm on hers, but he could not speak. He could not swallow. All his life, he'd waited to perform one single act of courage. Now he saw it for what it was: a colossal mistake. He was emptied of courage. He could not admit that he was that very fool.

'These are unusual circumstances,' Malati said. 'We came here with the best intentions. We accepted our responsibility and came with open arms. Though this will be the talk of our town, my husband has always stood up for what is right. We did not expect to be rejected. What your daughter wants to do with her life is her business, but my grandchild is now my business.'

'No!' Parvati shrieked. She began to speak, hurriedly, looking toward her mother for support. 'Please!' she said. 'You have misunderstood!'

She tried to explain. Vasan was not the father. Ram was. No one seemed to be listening to her.

'We cannot separate the child from the mother,' Sarangan said. 'We must consider—'

'You have a younger daughter to think about too,' Malati said to Manickam, cutting her husband off.

Durga, who'd been standing behind her mother, ran to her sister and clutched her hand. She wept for her sister, who was still urging them to listen to her. Though she was young, Durga seemed to know before Parvati that she'd already lost.

'If you are the wise man I think you are, then you will be wise to let the child live with us,' Malati was saying. 'We can provide him with a life you won't be able to, even with all your wealth . . .'

Malati didn't want to leave anything to chance. 'We cannot trust that the mother won't pose problems later,' she explained to Sarangan. 'She seems flighty.' Six days later, Manickam signed the papers, which were brought over by the young lawyer Sarangan had hired, certifying that his daughter, Parvati, was mentally unstable and that full custody of the child was to be given to the father, S. Srinivasan. Two days later, on the auspicious day that was Ram Navami, Malati arrived to take Hari home to Sripuri.

Two months later, Parvati returned to college, a year below her best friend Lee. Her mother only said: 'One day, you'll see that this is for the best.'

Ram

Parvati,

I am not much of a letter writer, Parvati. I got your letter, after all these years, out of the blue and there was no way that I could sit still. I got into my car and drove for miles and then I parked it, and just walked by the lake here in Wisconsin for hours. I thought about the devastation I brought you. Vasan wrote that he was sorry that he held on to the letter, sorry he took Hari from you, sorry he loved him too much to return him earlier. But he couldn't be sorry half as much as I was standing in front of that lake.

I was the one that walked away; no, I ran. I don't know how to explain it. Perhaps you will understand, perhaps you won't. Other men had ambitions. They wanted families and jobs and wanted to do something significant with their lives. I wanted the opposite. I wanted to disappear, to be something of a failure. I wanted to be a fleck. A dot amongst all the other stars. I don't know why that is. Some psychiatrist would have a field day with me. I wanted to be of no significance to anyone and have no one be of any significance to me. I thought that was freedom, being this moving, charged particle—to have no one's expectations of me determine my path. And I figured I was young and owed that. I won't lie to you either—my way of life was fun, until one day it stopped being fun.

I came here, and I let the freedom unravel. I got a useless degree that I have never used. I had a few girlfriends, but no one stuck around. I did some bookkeeping—they think we Indians are Math wizards here. I did this and that. I drank too much. I have a job now tutoring kids at the college. Kids that I want to slap because they remind me of me at that age.

I am average, just like everyone else. And that's the only lesson I learnt here. They tell everyone to keep climbing here. Up and Up and Up. Reach right up there for the stars and strive to be above everyone else. I am here now, and I can tell you that average is good. Don't get me wrong—I am not talking of average as in mediocre. Or poor. Or dumb. I mean having measured wants. These are people who are truly making the world run. Average is the best I've been.

I have a son who's grown up away from me, a woman I left behind, and today, these are the people I cherish the most. I hope to see them again. I hope for more, but I don't, I know—I don't deserve to hope. I will though. I will hope a little.

If you don't ever respond to this letter, I will understand. In fact, I expect no response. I don't know your circumstances. Perhaps you are a great research scientist. Perhaps you are married with five kids. Perhaps you are both. I've thought about you often. I've thought about how it felt being with you, holding you, how it felt when the thick feeling like lead that I always had in my chest just melted and ran out of my body. Sometimes I would hear of a fellow who thought he'd 'knocked up' his girl—that's what they call it here. And then he would come back and say that it was all a false alarm. Many times I told myself that this could have been the case with you. This is the sort of thinking that causes cowards to become brave men.

This right here is the price of that freedom that I once believed in. But I write to you not as the same Ram you once knew, but as the Ram that values love, permanence, trust.

You, me, our son. Could it ever be?

Yours,

Ram

Ram,

Thank you for your letter.

I have to tell you that your explanations, heartfelt though they may be, are no longer of any pertinence to me as far as the events that took place are concerned. The shape of the events were themselves their own explanations, and it is not necessary to engender in me a sentiment to encompass the past so that it looks better than it was.

Forgive me for being so blunt, but your interest in me, and in Hari, might provide me with the hitherto impossible opportunity to reclaim Hari as my son. As I am not legally of sound mind, I have little chance of obtaining him without any backing. My heart is bursting to think that, with your involvement, I could get Hari back.

I don't know how this will work, or what happens to people who were intertwined as we were when they come together again after a divide so great it swallowed up a child. I don't know. Whatever occurs, I am never letting go of my son again.

I am making arrangements to go to Sripuri.

Please meet me there at the earliest.

Parvati

Hari

23

Hari sat down on the lone chair in his apartment and held his phone in both his hands. He'd waited until he was home to check his messages. He had always subscribed to the 'pull the band-aid off slowly' school of thinking, preferring his serving of pain to be spread over time rather than heaped all at once, quickly. He opened the SMS from his mother and his eyes deliberately sought the very last message. 'Condition stable,' it read. There was no need to scroll up to read the complete trail of events that he knew, in her diligence, she would have attempted to communicate. Here was the only piece of information he needed to know.

Hari surveyed his apartment. It was lucky that Sudha, the cleaning lady, hadn't skipped today, he thought, observing the zigzag streaks her mop had left on the floor. On her second day, Sudha had brought in a clay dia and a wad of cotton wicks, and had set about lighting it on each of her visits. Often, when he arrived home, the flame had already petered out, and only a scent of its smoke lingered in the room. Today, however, he found the flame flickering, and its presence was oddly comforting.

His dad had deterred him from forming attachments to

objects throughout his childhood, urging him to donate his favourite cricket bat, his marble collection from Sripuri (he had refused), his Amar Chitra comics, and his Walkman when he no longer had use for them. 'The only things that are worth preserving,' he had said again and again, 'are the things that tell a story. Not their story, but yours.' Without realizing it, Hari had lived by this rule. Already, in his mind, his bookshelves, his CD player, the fridge and the television, the armchair and the standing lamps were flying out of the room and onto Ebay, with nary a protesting thought forming in his head in their defence.

There were a handful of articles that did tell his story, or at least a fragment of it, and Hari had learnt to treasure them. These were already packed up in the most prized of all his possessions, the trunk into which his life had already once been compacted. He went into the bedroom and pulled the trunk from the bottom shelf in his wardrobe. He hadn't had occasion to inspect it in years, not since he first moved into the flat. His hands barely fit into the metal clasps, and the trunk itself felt light, seeming more like a curiosity in an antique shop than an item built for practical use. He placed the trunk on the bed and unclasped the lid, but the hinges held tight, and he had to hold down the bottom and yank the top off with some pressure before it would give.

Here were his Mowgli and Friends pencil case and a book titled 'The Four Noble Truths'. He'd sold three boxes of books to a second-hand bookseller in Shivajinagar years ago, and the vendor, who'd paid fifty rupees for the lot, had sent a boy chasing after him to return a thousand rupee note he'd found within a book's pages. Hari had paid hundred rupees to buy the book back. Within the leaves of this book were two photographs, but Hari would not look at them. The first was of the woman he'd believed was his mother, and the other was a photograph of his dad and Vasan together, taken outside the house they'd once shared. Hari had slid the photo away from his dad's folder of photos when he'd first encountered it, and he had sought this image of Vasan to re-impress his face into his mind, whenever his visual memories of Vasan had frayed. Still, in the very nylon-bag in which the very first marbles he had owned had come, lay his entire marble collection. Finally, there was a pair of binoculars that he'd been given only a few days after his arrival at his parents' house in Madras. He'd whooped and pressed the binoculars to his chest while his parents had exchanged looks and held hands at his obvious pleasure. He ran up the steps to the roof, hobbled over the hot tiles and stood with his toes curled on the parapet wall to get a better view of the streets. In his naivety, Hari had imagined that the binoculars would fetch for him a vision of Jayamma or his father on Coramandel Street. He hadn't known how far he had travelled away from home until that day, when no matter the direction in which he looked, every single street broke up into unfamiliar houses and within them, foreign and peculiar faces. Hari had fallen four feet onto the landing of the first floor, and his parents, who heard the thud from their window, drove him straight to the hospital, though he had sustained no major injury but a burn mark where the strap of the binoculars had cut into his neck.

Hari drew his overnight bag from under the bed, and began packing his clothes. He grabbed his office shirts that had come from the dry cleaners, still crackling with the crisp newspaper that they'd slipped under the fabric, and two pairs of jeans and one pair of smart trousers (just in case). He crammed his toiletries into a packet and tucked it into his bag. He plugged his phone into the charger, then shut down his laptop and gathered all of its accessories and zipped them up into its leather case.

He heard his phone ring in the living room and saw that it was Sunil. He let it ring out as he opened the fridge to check for perishables. He was suddenly hungry and he emptied the remainder of last night's veg chow mein from its box onto a plate and ate it cold, standing up by the kitchen counter. He drank what remained of the orange juice, then emptied and cleaned his fridge. He packed the sauces and the jam jars, the cheese spread, the butter and jam, and the unopened jars of pasta sauce into a cloth bag. He wrote a note—'Please take: all edible'—stuck it into the bag and made a quick dash to the landing where he deposited the bag by the window ledge.

He heard the televisions come on all at once and the familiar jingle of the local singing competition flooded the building. As he locked his door, he heard Mrs Joshi's voice again. 'Taking a trip?' she said, eyeing his belongings. He saw that she was straining with the weight of the bag of groceries he'd left out. He put his luggage down on the doormat, and told her to watch it, while he carried the bag up to her doorstep. 'You are a gentleman, Hari,' she said, upon his return. 'Somebody left perfectly good groceries out. Can you believe it?'

He told her that he was going home for a few days. 'Yes, I know,' she said. 'Everyone is going home for the holidays except me.'

At the bus stand, the queue was long, and the agent told Hari as he approached him that every single bus was full, and that he was damn lucky that he could find him a seat at all during the busy December season. He charged him a hundred rupees more than the regular fare price.

He sent a message to his mother. 'On the bus. Be home around six.'

As he sat in his seat, a cold draught seeping in through a crack in the closed window, Hari became increasingly apprehensive. He had drawn a big circle around the events of his childhood, and placed a PRIVATE–NO TRESPASSING sign on it. At first, he had been given no choice. His parents had been meticulous about not mentioning Vasan's name or alluding to his life in Sripuri. Still, occasionally, his Dad made an innocent remark about something, like the mango tree in the neighbour's yard that was dropping fruit onto their side of the compound wall, or his mother had come home one day with a puppy she had rescued and instantly, inadvertently, Hari had recalled the mango tree on Coramandel Street, and remembered the velvety touch of Julie's skin on his hands. However, such memories were contained, and were only to be dwelt upon in the privacy of his own head. Today, the mere mention of Vasan's name had caused a tear to occur in that carefully constructed circle beyond which he had felt forbidden to venture, and an unexpected entry had formed into the past.

Hari took a prepaid taxi from Central to his parent's home in Adyar. As soon as he opened the gate, a light went on in the living room. A curtain parted and he could make out his dad's tall frame behind it. It was early. When he opened the gate, a couple of the stray dogs sleeping beside it stretched, moved a

few paces, then curled back to sleep. His dad opened the door
and came out to meet him on the front porch.

'Your mother's not joining us,' he said, quickly. He made an
ineffectual gesture to take Hari's overnight bag. His eyes were
tinged with pink. 'It's just better we don't talk about it until we
are on the road.' He wore a loose, heavy coat over his pyjamas
and his hands were bunched up in their pockets.

His mother was at the computer checking her emails. She
got up to say hello and her eyes rested on the trunk that Hari
held in one hand. Their cat, Minu, shuffled past his feet and
jumped onto their coffee table. Hari went to wash up and when
he returned to the room, his father was fixing a breakfast of
upma and coconut chutney. Hari grabbed the plates while his
mother drank coffee and asked him how his journey had been.
His mother provided a bright contrast to his dad in her crisp
green sari and matching cardigan, her hair already coiled into a
bun, and a red bindi on her forehead. She worked early hours
and was often ready to head out to the hospice by seven o'clock.
She told him there had been a change in the weather overnight.
She pointed to the windows that were fogged up. She pulled the
ends of her cardigan closer together and pushed her plate away.
They didn't say much else. The sound of their spoons clattering,
and of the urad dal crushing between Dad's teeth, was
unbearable.

His parents had always held back their opinions. Through
school, his friends had often thought of them as 'cool', though
they had never seemed that way to him. His father always had
music playing in the background, and his mother made them
fresh lemon drink with the lemons from their tree, a pinch of
salt, and a little sugar. Together, the two of them would whip up

some treat or the other. In the summer, translucent slices of cucumber topped with coriander and lemon appeared, or slabs of golden pineapple sprinkled with chilli powder found their way to the table. When it was cold, there would be katoris of rice payasam, with flakes of cashews, and occasionally hot milky tea with ginger and cardamom. Neither uttered a word as his friends flew in and out of their rooms, scavenging for a length of cloth for a makeshift tent, and emerged with one of his mother's saris, or pried open the radio, and left it disassembled on the couch, or broke a vase as they hurtled down the stairs. Furthermore, his parents seemed eager to join in their activities. His mother would drop a bundle of old newspapers on to the veranda and tell them that they were going to learn to make papier-mâché bowls, and his dad would come up with the idea of making cardboard dinosaurs and arrange them in a circle on the living room floor, press tracing paper into their hands and encourage them to draw. Hari had been to his friends' houses and he had seen them walloped for staining their shirts or losing their pencils, and even at times for things they hadn't done.

In other years, he had tested his parents. They hadn't flinched when he came home with a red and infected tattoo of a dog on his arm, hadn't questioned him when they caught him sneaking a girl into his bedroom. They sat by his bed and fed him sweet corn soup when he'd broken his shoulder while attempting a motorbike stunt. Hari got the feeling that his dad fully trusted him to navigate his way, and that any guidance offered would only be in the way of his own experiences shared and the hard lessons he had learnt, but there would be no direct pointing in any direction. His mother made it perfectly clear where she stood in any matter, and what direction she expected Hari to take, but she too refrained from chastising him, using instead the perfectly honed aura of her disappointment to prevent him from going too far astray. It was why Hari had never drifted as far as Sripuri, either in conversation or in reality.

It occurred to Hari now, that perhaps his parents had refused to give him advice because they felt that their own lives had been lived in error, and that those mistakes had in their minds deemed them ineligible to dole out counsel to him.

With their heads so close around the table, it seemed to Hari that their thoughts were train lines crossing. As though his mother had just heard what he'd thought, and his dad, when he moved his head, had nodded in agreement.

The phone rang and his mother went to answer it in the bedroom, closing the door shut behind her.

'Is she ok?' Hari said.

'You know your mother,' Ram said. 'She's a trouper.'

'We should get going soon,' he added. 'The traffic will be hell if we hit rush hour.' They discarded the uneaten food into the bin and gathered up the empty dishes in a bucket for the cleaning lady.

In the bathroom, Hari examined his face in the mirror. His hair had grown long, and he wished he'd had time to get a haircut. He shaved carefully, plucking the hairs from his nostrils, cutting his fingernails. He took a shower and changed into his best office shirt and the grey trousers he normally wore to client meetings.

His mother was standing beside the sofa, watching his dad pack his bag, when he emerged from the bathroom.

'You look nice,' she said. 'Vasan will be so happy at how you turned out.'

They both looked up at Parvati in surprise.

'What?' she said. 'You have to do what you have to do. Doesn't mean it's easy.'

She walked up toward him and gave him a kiss on the cheek. 'Please, please stop smoking,' she whispered in his ear. At that moment, Hari loved her, for not holding back, for saying the exact words he needed to hear.

⁂

'Yesterday, she was telling me about the first time she saw you in Sripuri,' Ram said in the car, once they had merged into the heavy traffic on Sardar Patel Road and were moving in a trickle. 'She'd driven down with Lee . . . there were only a few lady drivers in those days, and the two of them attracted a few stares on their way there. Your mother was irrationally afraid that someone would recognize her and alert Vasan before she could reach you. Your mother got Lee to get out of the car to make a few discreet enquiries while she hid in the back seat. They went to a few different schools and it didn't take them very long at all; in the course of one afternoon, which was much easier than they ever thought possible, they had located you.

'You were sitting on a swing in the playground when your mother found you. You were wearing your white sports uniform. Your mother stood by the swing and watched you. She said she had always had a vision of how you looked lying on her chest the day you were born, with your hair flat and wet against your skull, and there was something of that vision preserved in you still that day. It meant so much to her.'

The traffic broke up for a short while and they turned onto

the highway. 'The plan was to wait for me to arrive. We weren't married, so I'd hoped to get to the registrar's office quickly . . . but before I could get there, she heard about the bus accident that had occurred, and there was no way that she could sit still. She waited with trepidation. You came out of the bus and you were bleeding. She was able to kiss you for the first time since you were taken away. Put her flesh to yours. But then all you wanted was your Appa. You literally pushed her away. I can't get that image out of my mind.' He shook his head.

He had slowed down involuntarily, and a car behind them honked.

'I don't remember any of that,' Hari lied. 'Dad, it was all a long time ago. When did you get married?'

'We didn't. We never have. Common law.'

He let out a big sigh and unrolled the window for some fresh air. The air outside was filled with smoke, and changing his mind, he buzzed the window shut and turned on the AC.

'Driving makes me hot,' he said. 'You are not cold?'

'No,' Hari said. Ram wasn't a natural driver. He wanted him to be as comfortable as possible.

'For a long time, I thought of your mother as having the fortitude of a nurse; someone who had seen it all. That she had become inured to the grime and the pus and the shit of life. The things she sees in her line of work for instance . . . I don't know how she does it.

'But now, I think I was mistaken, that in fact the opposite is true. She is a child. With a child's capacity to accept surprises in her stride. Only a child can accept such turns of fate . . .' He seemed to realize the significance of his own words and turned to catch Hari's eye.

'I guess like you,' he said. 'Look what we did with you. We took you out of your home and everything you knew ... and here you are—'

'—Dad,' Hari cut him off, 'I haven't got anything to complain about. Mine is a perfectly ordinary life.'

Ram went quiet. Hari was hankering for a cigarette but his mother's words had haunted me and he didn't want to smoke.

'I am going to tell you something that is contrary to what everyone on this planet will tell you,' he said.

'I know,' Hari said, smiling at him. 'Ordinary is good.'

Hari suggested a coffee, and they pulled into the parking lot of the next garden restaurant they spotted, where they changed their minds and drank two fresh lime sodas instead.

When they got back in the car, his dad seemed to be in a different mood altogether. He turned on the radio and they listened to three advertisements in succession. 'To be honest, that rascal Vasan was probably the closest friend I ever had,' he said. 'He was just so damn sincere. We lived under the same roof, but I can swear to you that we did not inhabit the same planets.' He smiled at some private memory and tuned the radio to a classical music station. 'This way, I can still think and drive,' he said. 'I get all muddled up trying to figure out the words in the lyrics otherwise. Besides, no one advertises on the classical music station.'

They were gliding along the highway smoothly. A line of hills ran the length of the horizon beyond uneven blocks of paddy fields on either side of the road. The boughs of tamarind trees along the road were swaying in the wind and the overcast sky seemed portentous.

'Dad,' Hari said. 'Are you superstitious?'

Ram turned down the music. 'You need to ask me that question? What did I ever do to deserve that question?'

'No, it's not that. Lately . . .'

'You are not that old,' Ram snapped. 'Not old enough to begin sentences with "Lately".' He laughed a little, and stopped when he noticed that Hari wasn't joining him.

'So, for three years in a row now, there's been a death of someone close to me, in December.'

That got Ram's attention.

'First, there was the old man in 3C, you know that gentleman who lived above me, and whose daughter I was briefly—you know?'

'He was old,' Dad said. 'He had pneumonia, didn't he?'

'Yes, and then there was my colleague Badri who had a heart attack at his desk. He didn't even make it to the hospital.'

'You said he was extremely obese. It wasn't totally unexpected.'

'That's not the point, Dad. They died in December, year after year. It is December . . .'

He seemed to consider what I said.

'And then, of course, Lee last year.'

'Yes, Lee. Well, I for one didn't think she'd go before me. She was such a poster girl . . . for life! She would have been the one they picked to represent us on Mars.'

He wasn't taking Hari seriously.

'Dad,' Hari pleaded with him. 'I can't shake this horrible feeling that . . .'

'One can connect the dots however one wants to,' Ram said. 'That is what we do, what everyone does. That's how life stories form. By connecting all these little dots. But they are just dots, gaining strength and significance when you link them together. It's up to you how you join them up. It will make no difference to what happens in the world. The world will remain an indecipherable, pretty mess.'

Ram took his phone out of his pocket and fiddled with it.

'Dad!' Hari exclaimed, and Ram threw the phone on top of the dashboard.

'Well, I just checked,' Ram said. 'The outlook for today is not dark and gloomy. It's in fact bright and sunny.'

It was a surprise how quickly they arrived at Sripuri; a place that was so far away in Hari's mind was only a three-hour journey in actuality. Fairy lights had been poured over the trees and buildings lining the river to spruce up the town. They'd been left on, and in the daylight they seemed to have the opposite effect, taking the sheen off whatever gloss the town may have had. As soon as they went over the bridge, the water gurgling beneath them, plentiful after the monsoon season, Hari's heart lurched with recognition. As they entered East Side, he began scanning the landscape for familiar places. The car halted at the same old railway crossing that had once been on his school bus route, and looking to his left, Hari saw that the Lakshmi Theatre was still standing, but that it had been upgraded to a multiplex. At the mouth of Bazaar Street, the same Gandhi statue greeted him, and there was still the same row of jewellery shops, indistinguishable from one another, although they too had been given facelifts. The shops had made a stab at Christmas decorations. Cut-outs of stars hung outside their entrances.

There were skinny red Santa Clauses, red and green streamers, and white cotton snow scattered over sale signs in their display windows. They passed the temple tank and finally Hari caught sight of the gopuram of the Lakshmi temple. Everything else appeared to have shifted or risen up around these landmarks. Only a few freestanding houses remained on Small Coramandel Street, which had been widened, and the drainage canals along the roads were all closed. Hari was heartened to see that Saleem's home still remained in its place, though there had been additions to the house, and it was now two stories higher than it had been.

Ram slowed down to let a buffalo cross the road and then they finally arrived at the gate of 12 Coramandel Street. A yellow apartment building stood in place of the old house, with the words 'Coramandel Apartments' engraved on a granite slab embedded into its front compound wall. A guard sat in a booth and watched cricket on a mini TV monitor.

Ram turned off the ignition and unloaded Hari's things from the car.

Hari's phone rang. It was Sunil.

'What's up, dude? No news from you?' He heard Sunil say at the other end. Feigned concern crept into his voice when he added, 'Is everything cool, is there anything I can do for you? Just let me know, take as much time as you need . . .'

'Well, as a matter of fact, I'm going to need a lot of time.'

'How much time are we talking?' A little of the warmth faded from his voice.

'I thought you just said I could take as much time as I needed.'

'I'm all for flexibility . . . but there's time off and there's time off . . .'

'I'm quitting,' Hari said. 'I'm done.'

'You can't do that, dude!'

Yes, he could, Hari thought as he hung up the phone and Ram gave him an affirming nod before returning to the car.

Hari closed his eyes then opened them again to take in the expanse of the new building, with its immaculate lawns and the car park where once the mango tree had stood. Slowly, he inched forward to the gate. There was no room for conjecture as to what other changes time may have wrought. His brow was creased with sweat, and the white shirt he had chosen with care was already crumpled. His tightened his grasp on the trunk.

All manner of things would come and go. But he only had two fathers.

ACKNOWLEDGEMENTS

My family—Foremost, my sister Nithya Dorairaj, for her infinite love and for being the first to provide me with the joy of seeing my work in print, and T. Pradeep, Sunder Madabushi and Valli Seshan for being my anchors.

My editor—Deepthi Talwar, for her patience and her light, yet sharp, editing.

My friends—Rajni Shrestha, Charles Miller, Varsha Rangarajan, Vaishali Pathak, Jillian Anderson, Stacey and Dudley Levell, Fiona Guyan, and Dominika Ferenz, for their unwavering support and encouragement.

My fellow writers and readers—Chetan Raj Shrestha, Kate McKee, Amy Prodromou, Sue Woolfe, and Derek Keogh, for their wisdom and perspective, which helped shape this book.

My boys—Krishna, Kanha and Taal, for being joyous obstacles.

My husband—Jason Bernal, for being all of the above, as well as the source of the love that fuels my work and life.